THE VESTAL VANISHES

THE VESTAL VANISHES

A Libertus Roman Mystery

Rosemary Rowe

This first world edition published 2011
in Great Britain and the USA by
SEVERN HOUSE PUBLISHERS LTD of
9–15 High Street, Sutton, Surrey, England, SM1 1DF.
Trade paperback edition first published
in Great Britain and the USA 2011 by
SEVERN HOUSE PUBLISHERS LTD.

British Library Cataloguing in Publication Data

Rowe, Rosemary, 1942-
  The vestal vanishes. – (A Libertus mystery of Roman
  Britain)
  1. Libertus (Fictitious character : Rowe)–Fiction.
  2. Romans–Great Britain–Fiction. 3. Slaves–Fiction.
  4. Vestal virgins–Fiction. 5. Great Britain–History–
  Roman period, 55 B.C.-449 A.D.–Fiction. 6. Detective and
  mystery stories.
  I. Title II. Series
  823.9'2-dc22

ISBN-13: 978-0-7278-8029-1 (cased)
ISBN-13: 978-1-84751-348-9 (trade paper)

All Severn House titles are printed on acid-free paper.

Severn House Publishers support The Forest Stewardship Council [FSC],
the leading international forest certification organisation. All our titles that
are printed on Greenpeace-approved FSC-certified paper carry the FSC logo.

Typeset by Palimpsest Book Production Ltd.,
Falkirk, Stirlingshire, Scotland.
Printed and bound in Great Britain by the
MPG Books Group, Bodmin, Cornwall.

FOREWORD

The story begins in Glevum (Roman Gloucester, a prosperous 'republic' and a colonia for retired soldiery) during late August 191 AD, at the birthday feast of the Emperor. Attendance at this feast and appropriate sacrifice – Commodus had pronounced himself to be a living deity and the reincarnation of the god Hercules – was compulsory for every citizen, though it is doubtful that many seriously believed he was a god. (The compulsion was real enough: St Peregrine was arrested, tortured and finally martyred in Rome, not for being a Christian – that was not, of itself, at this period a crime – but for publicly opposing this birthday sacrifice.)

The Emperor was by this time increasingly deranged, and his lascivious lifestyle, capricious cruelties and erratic acts were infamous. He had renamed all the months, for instance, with names derived from his own honorific titles (which he had in any case given to himself) and, after rebuilding a portion of the city following a fire, announced that Rome itself was henceforth to be retitled 'Commodiana'. Stories about him barbecuing dwarves and having a bald man pecked to death by sticking birdseed to his head are (probably) exaggerated, but the existence of such rumours gives some indication of the man. However, he clung tenaciously to power and, fearing (justifiably) that there were plots against his life, he maintained a network of spies throughout the Roman Empire.

Britannia had been part of that Empire for two hundred years by now; the most far-flung and northerly of all its provinces, but still occupied by Roman legions, criss-crossed by Roman roads, subject to Roman laws, and administered by a provincial governor answerable directly to Rome (most probably Clodius Albinus at this period, although the date of his appointment is open to debate). Latin was the language of the educated, people were adopting Roman dress and habits, and citizenship, with the precious social and legal rights which it conferred, was the aspiration of almost everyone. But then, as now, there were small groups of dissidents who refused to yield. Although most of the quarrelsome local tribes had long since settled into peace, there were still sporadic raids (mostly against military targets) by small bands of Silurians and Ordovices from the west, who had never forgotten their defeated leader, Caractacus, and his heroic two-year resistance to Roman rule. The army had taken steps to suppress this discontent (creating special 'marching camps', where legionary and auxiliary forces were kept in tented camps ready to move quickly against insurgent groups), but there were still occasional forays, although at this date there is no record of any occurring as far east as the action in this story suggests.

However, it is well-attested that these rebellious Celtic bands were often associated with Druid practices – perhaps as an act of additional defiance against Rome, since the religion was officially proscribed. (Unlike Christianity, Druidism had been outlawed for some time, because of the cult of the severed human head, and adherence to the sect was technically a capital offence.) Stories were circulated of its gruesome practices: the sacred groves adorned with severed heads of enemies, the wicker man-shapes filled with human forms and torched, and the use of living human entrails as a divination tool. This suppression of the cult served to drive it underground and secrecy soon added myth to mystery. In the popular imagination the old nature-worshipping religion quickly became a fearsome thing, associated with witchcraft and sorcery – as the text suggests.

This is the background of religious and civil discontent against which the action of the book takes place. Glevum (modern Gloucester) was an important town: its historic status as a 'colonia' for retired legionaries gave it special privileges and all freemen born within its walls were citizens by right.

Most inhabitants of Glevum, however, were not citizens at all. Many were freemen, born outside the walls, scratching a more or less precarious living from a trade. Hundreds more were slaves – what Aristotle once described as 'vocal tools' – mere chattels of their masters, to be bought and sold, with no more rights or status than any other domestic animal. Some slaves led pitiable lives, but others were highly regarded by their owners, and might be treated well. A slave in a kindly household, with a comfortable home, might have a more enviable lot than many a poor freeman struggling to eke out an existence in a squalid hut.

Of course, the worst fate of all was to be born with some disability. There was no provision for a person who could not compete. Deformed or weakly children were exposed at birth, but some problems (such as deafness, as in this story) were not immediately manifest and therefore law permitted a father to dispose of a 'defective' child, perfectly legally, until it was three years old. If for some reason (like Paulina in the story) such a child continued to survive past this age it was regarded as a 'moral lunatic' with no rights at all in law, not even to inherit when a parent died.

Power, of course, was vested almost entirely in men. Although individual women might inherit large estates, and many wielded considerable influence within the house, daughters were not much valued, except as potential wives and mothers, whereas sons were the source of pride. Indeed, a wife of a rich man who produced no surviving male might well be divorced, although – as suggested in the tale – something resembling haemophilia, (which exclusively affects the males) was clearly present in the population at this time, making the afflicted mothers' lives doubly tragic. Marriage and motherhood were the only realistic goals for well-bred women, although trademen's wives and daughters often worked beside their men and in the poorest households everybody toiled. But females were rarely educated, except in household skills, they were excluded from public office, and a woman (of any age) was deemed a child in law.

There was, however, one notable exception to this rule. The Vestal Virgins were a class apart, and this forms the basis for the story in this book. Chosen exclusively from patrician families and subject to the most stringent requirements for entry, prospective Vestals were taken from their homes very young (from six to ten years old) and were bound to the temple for a span of thirty years: ten years in training, ten years of active duty at the hearth and the final ten years training the new novitiates and – it appears – sometimes dealing with suppliants. During the thirty years of service at the shrine she must remain a virgin on pain of dreadful death, but on retirement she might marry while still enjoying a pension which – uniquely – was provided by the state. (The old saying that 'life begins at forty' is said to have its origins in the Vestal life.)

Duties at the shrine included keeping alight the sacred Vestal flame, on which the fate of Rome itself was rumoured to depend, as well as making the special 'mola salsa' which was used at public sacrifices. So important was their role perceived to be that the priestesses of the hearth had special rights: a Vestal Virgin could testify in court, sign documents and make legal contracts like a man. Her life in the temple was a luxurious one, but the punishment for failure to observe her vows was horrible (being ritually walled up with a day's supply of food and drink – so that no one could be directly guilty of her death). She was considered to be legally 'married' to the shrine: she wore a costume and distinctive hairstyle very like a bride's, entered the temple with a dowry and although the Vestal House enjoyed the usufruct of that (just as a husband would) it appears she was permitted to take it with her when she retired (rather like a woman who might have been divorced).

If she chose to marry afterwards (as many did) these privileges automatically ceased and she passed under the aegis of her husband, like any other wife, but since a retiring Vestal was likely to be both wealthy and well-connected, it is perhaps not surprising that such a bride – as the book suggests – was regarded a considerable catch.

Moreover, there were very few Vestals overall – the original Vestal House in Rome housed a maximum of eighteen at one time: six in training, six in service and six to teach the newcomers. It has been argued that this is the only proper shrine, and that therefore there were only ever six serving Vestals at once in the entire Empire.

There is, however, some counter-evidence: there are remains of what was, almost certainly, a Vestal temple in Pompeii, and relics of the cult – or something very like it – are found in all corners of the eastern empire. It is therefore reasonable to postulate an equivalent daughter-house in Britannia, although there is no indisputable archaeological evidence for where this might have been. There have long been rumours of a Vestal hearth in Waltham St Lawrence, and that location has been accepted in this story as the likely site.

The rest of the Romano-British background to this book has been derived from a variety of (sometimes contradictory) pictorial and written sources, as well as artefacts. However, although I have done my best to create an accurate picture, this remains a work of fiction, and there is no claim to total academic authenticity. Commodus and Pertinax are historically attested, as is the existence and basic geography of Glevum. The rest is the product of my imagination.

Relata refero. Ne Iupiter quidem omnibus placet. I only tell you what I heard. Jove himself can't please everybody.

ONE

I t was the Emperor's birthday, so – like every citizen in Glevum who valued life and limb – I was at the temple for the public sacrifice. Not that I actually inwardly believed that Commodus was a deity at all, let alone the living reincarnation of Hercules, as he claimed, but it was not wise to say so. Our Imperial ruler might not really be a god, but he is certainly the most powerful man on earth and he has ears and eyes in every part of town. Casting doubt on his presumed divinity was likely to prove fatal in most unpleasant ways.

So I was there, with all the rest of my fellow citizens, dressed in my best toga and cheering right on cue. I had proffered the obligatory little flask of perfumed oil – bought for the purpose at a special booth – and had it accepted by the attendant priest to be poured out on the altar at the proper time. I drew the line at paying a whole denarius to buy a withered branch of palm, though the streets around the temple were crammed with stalls of them.

I had learnt my lesson at last year's sacrifice. Palms did not grow in this most northerly of provinces, and the ones that were imported in honour of the day were not only expensive, but so dry and fragile they had a tendency to crack if they were waved too hard. Moreover, some of them looked suspiciously like plants I recognized, carefully slashed to resemble the traditional frond – though I could be wrong, of course, I have never seen a proper palm tree in my life. So I'd ignored the traders this time and contented myself with finding a safe spot at the back of the temple court beside the colonnade where any lack of waving was inconspicuous. (We were in the Capitoline temple for the spectacle – the Imperial shrine was in a smaller building in a grove within the grounds, but there was not room for everybody on a day like this.)

However, I was quite prepared to cheer. The birthday ceremony gave us a real excuse for that. After the sacrificial animal was killed, its blood was offered up as an oblation to the gods, but when the immortals had imbibed their fill and the priests had made a ritual meal of the proffered entrails, the rest was generally taken off and cooked and shared out among the congregation as a feast. And judging by the animals lined up for sacrifice this year, there was going to be a generous distribution later on.

Of course there was always a competition on a day like this, with wealthy men attempting to impress the populace and trying to out-do their counterparts by offering the most perfect and expensive specimens. Quite a tradition had grown up locally – not one birthday offering, but a whole string of them: pure white calves and spotless goats and sheep, as well as the more humble pigeons, larks and doves. No doubt the donors hoped that news of their devotion and generosity would (given the fact that spies were everywhere) reach the Imperial ears.

Today, however, there was an even more impressive sight than usual. Someone had provided an enormous bull with gilded horns – a splendid creature, white from head to tail. One of the attendants had just appeared with it, and was leading it by a scarlet halter around its neck, at the head of a procession of civic dignitaries followed by a choir singing loyal hymns of praise and a young minstrel strumming on a lute. They moved towards the altar where the chief Imperial priest, the *sevir Augustalis*, stood awaiting them: a hooded figure in a reddish-purple robe, with the bronze diadem of his office barely visible beneath the hood. The sevir raised his knife. There was a sudden hush.

The temple was so crowded that it was hard to move, but a man on the step beside me – a citizen-trader whom I slightly knew – caught my eye and nudged me sharply in the ribs.

'Just look at that, Libertus. A perfect sacrifice. That must have cost somebody an enormous sum!' he whispered gleefully.

'Almost as gigantic as the animal itself!' I murmured in reply. 'Someone hoping to impress the Emperor no doubt, and hoping for preferment at the Imperial court.'

'Then I hope his prayers are answered,' he retorted with a grin. 'I shall feel he deserves it, if we get a piece of that.'

A stout man in a woollen toga, in the row in front, turned

round and frowned warningly at us. 'Don't be so disrespectful. Don't you know who gave the bull? It was Publius Atronius Martinus – that visitor from Rome. So just be grateful and keep your inauspicious comments to yourself. Suppose the priest had heard you, and all this had gone to waste!' He snapped his head away and went back to watching the ongoing spectacle.

He had a point, of course. Any inappropriate noise or sight which reached the priest – or even a trivial error in the rite, like putting the wrong foot forward – would stop the sacrifice and the whole of the ceremony would have to start again, most likely with a different animal, since this one would be ill-omened by that time. But it seemed that all was well. The celebrant was pouring wine between the horns, and scattering the *salsa mola* – the sacred bread that only Vestal Virgins make – onto the creature's head. Obviously the singing of the choir, which was designed to drown out inauspicious noise, had drowned us out as well. That was fortunate. Interrupting the sacred ritual today, and causing the Emperor's birthday rite to stop, was likely to prove ill-omened in more ways than one.

My trader-friend, though, was undeterred by this. He made an unrepentant little face and mouthed silently at me, 'Who is Publius Martinus?'

I was so startled that I almost answered him aloud, but I controlled myself and only muttered from the corner of my mouth, 'You must have heard of him! He's come to Britannia to collect a wife – the very Vestal Virgin who made the sacred cake. Though of course she's now retired.'

He pulled his face down in a goggling mask. 'A Vestal? Then he must be seriously rich.'

'One of the richest men in Rome, apparently. So you're wrong in one respect. Publius Martinus might have bought the bull, but not because he's seeking patronage.' I was still speaking in an undertone. 'More likely a celebration that his bride agreed the match, especially since the girl has money of her own.'

He arched an eyebrow. 'Well, of course she would have. Vestals all come from patrician families.'

Perhaps it had been an unnecessary remark, but I whispered stubbornly, 'I meant that she wouldn't have to marry just because she has retired. And it must have been her choice. Vestals are not like other women – they can make contracts and manage their affairs without the consent of any relative.'

He made a little face. 'That's true. Yet she can't have met this Publius, if he comes from Rome. I wonder what made her decide to give up her special status and all the privileges that go with it? Perhaps she simply longed to have a family life – they say some women do.' He sniggered mockingly.

I thought of my own wife, Gwellia, who would have loved to have a child. It made me answer rather acidly. 'Is that so very strange? The bride has done her thirty years of service to the flame. She reached the anniversary only recently and now she's free to do as she thinks fit. This Publius is a widower with three daughters and son – maybe she thought he looked a likely match.'

My neighbour nodded. 'No doubt you are right. But if he is merely a visitor from Rome, why should he come here to Glevum and donate this sacrifice? There isn't a Vestal temple anywhere near here.'

'Her family lives nearby, apparently. I understand that she is on her way, herself.'

He looked impressed, then puzzled. 'How do you know all this?' he whispered. His expression cleared. 'Oh, from your wealthy patron, I suppose. I'd forgotten that His Excellence Marcus Aurelius Septimus told you everything. I suppose as the most important man in the colonia, he's likely to hear the gossip about everyone who comes. And . . . here he is in person.' He nodded towards the group of celebrants.

My patron had joined them on the temple steps, together with the High Priest of Jupiter. They had emerged dramatically from inside the building, to the general amazement of the crowd, though there was really nothing remarkable in this: there was a hidden passage from the priest's house to the shrine, especially to facilitate appearances like this. However, they were greeted with an approving roar and certainly they made an impressive sight. The priest of Jupiter was all in spotless white, while Marcus was resplendent in a toga with a broad patrician stripe, with a wreath of gilded laurel round his head and a heavy gold torque around his neck. These two were joined a moment later by a stout, bald, red-faced man who was clearly out of breath and had his wreath askew – presumably from unaccustomed scrambling through the passageway. He looked quite unimportant in comparison, but his toga's purple edge announced him as a patrician of some consequence. Obviously this was Publius Martinus himself.

My neighbour nudged me sharply in the ribs. 'Hardly a Greek statue, is he – if that's the bridegroom, as I suppose it is? I hope the Vestal isn't disappointed in her choice. When she sees him, perhaps she'll change her mind.'

I shook my head. 'From what I hear from Marcus Septimus, she's formally agreed, and since she is a Vestal . . .' I broke off and glanced around. I was half-expecting to be 'shushed' again, but I realized that other people were listening in to this. I was being indiscreet! So I said no more, except, 'But shh! Let's watch the ritual.'

The sevir was already plunging the knife into the bull and had seized a chalice in which to catch the blood. The beast began to stagger and was soon sagging at the knees and as it fell the crowd gave out a cheer. The trained attendants, the *victimarii*, fell upon it to disembowel it and hack it into pieces for the public feast.

'I hear they give the creatures poppy juice to keep them quiet,' my neighbour muttered as the noise died down again. 'That would make sense, I suppose. Terrible bad omen if that ran amok and gored a priest or something.' He nudged my ribs again. 'Can you see it all from there, or is that pillar in the way? The *hirospex* is reading the entrails, by the look of it. Oh great gods, he's hesitating! Is there something wrong?'

I stood on tiptoe to get a better view. 'It doesn't look like it. He's put them on the altar fire, so they must have been all right, and he has decided that the omens spell good luck.'

My neighbour grinned. 'Except for the poor animal, that is. Still, I won't be complaining, if I get a decent slice.'

He was getting disapproving looks again, so I looked away and tried to pretend that he was not with me. In fact he wasn't really. I had come here with Junio, my adopted son, but the pressure of the crowd had separated us as soon as we came in and he had been borne down nearer to the front, though he was still in sight. He was crammed up against a pillar not very far away.

He turned his head and saw me and flashed a smile. It was obvious he was enjoying this. It was only the second Emperor's birthday festival that he had ever seen – last year had been the first; up to that time he had merely been my slave, and slaves were not generally brought into the temple court at feasts, but left outside waiting for their masters to come back. But now that I had freed him and adopted him he was a citizen and therefore entitled – and expected – to attend the rite.

I looked at him with pride. He wore the awkward toga effortlessly, as if he'd done so all his life, and looked more like a proper citizen than I did myself. Of course it was likely he did have Roman blood. He was born in a Roman household, before he was sold on to the trader that I got him from, so – though it is certain that his mother was a slave – his father was probably the master of the house. (The owner of a slave girl has exclusive rights to her – she is not permitted to consort with other slaves – and if a resultant offspring is not required by the house it will either be exposed and left to die, or passed on to a slave trader prepared to keep it till it is old enough to sell.) Of course Junio didn't know his mother's whereabouts or name – any more than she knew his, or what his fate had been; he would have been taken from her shortly after birth.

I wondered what she would think of him, if she could see him now, at nineteen years of age (or perhaps it was twenty, we could not be sure), a handsome married man with a family of his own. It was hard to remember, looking at him today, the piteous half-starved child that I'd purchased from the dealer all those years ago.

'Are you going to stand there all day, citizen?' The bald man who had frowned at us broke into my thoughts. 'Only some of us would like to go and get positions at the feast.'

I had been so busy with my thoughts that I had not noticed that the crowd was shuffling forward by this time, towards the little grove within the grounds where the Imperial temple was. The sevir Augustalis was carrying the phial of blood, to pour out on the altar there; what remained of the entrails, the offal and the brains would be cooked on the altar fire and eaten as a ceremonial collation by the priest. The singers and musicians struck up again, but they were quickly drowned as the crowd – which had been silent – broke into tumultuous cheers and there was much enthusiastic waving of the fronds.

'Well, citizen?' The bald man was sounding more impatient now; I was blocking the access to the aisle.

'A thousand pardons . . .' I squeezed myself into the wall and allowed him to go past, hoping that the talkative trader would depart at the same time, so that I could link up with Junio again.

But my neighbour was not so easily deterred. He was forced forwards by the pressure of the crowd, but he turned to call to me, 'I'll go and do my duty by filing past the shrine, and then I'll try to go ahead and save a place for you. They are already making preparations, by the look of it.'

He waved a vague hand in the direction of the court, where the dismembered bull's carcass was being hauled away, taken off to the temple kitchens to be cooked. Already I could see a group of little temple slaves, at the doorway of the building where the attendants lived, ready with the trestles to set out for the feast.

'Don't trouble! There is my son – he'll need a place as well,' I shouted back. But I could have saved my breath. The man had already been borne off in the throng and my voice was lost in all the noise. I remained pressed against the wall until the crush had eased, and then made my own way down towards the court, looking out for Junio, who had likewise sidestepped from the crowd and was waiting beside a giant statue of the Father of the gods.

He emerged as I approached and fell into step beside me, his face alight with smiles. 'A splendid ritual! Even better than last year.' He gestured delightedly towards the Imperial shrine. 'And what a culminating sacrifice! I hope the god Commodus appreciates the smoke. Myself, I am content to be a mortal and just enjoy the flesh!'

I flashed a warning look. This was a daring joke, if not outright indiscreet. Someone might have been close enough to hear. We were almost the last to join the file and the leaders of the original procession to the shrine were making their way back towards us by this time, so that my patron and his guest were almost parallel with us, though going the other way.

Junio saw the danger and added instantly, 'But what a

splendid basis for a feast. There will be enough for all – although there is a crowd.'

I nodded. 'Enough for everybody here to have a piece – of one of the offerings, if not the bull itself! The temple slaves will see to that. Though it will take a little while for the later beasts to cook.'

He grinned at me. 'So you are wise to have avoided rushing to the front. Trust you to think of clever things like that.'

In fact there was a considerable delay before we had made our duty visit to the shrine, ritually rinsed our faces and our hands and had our foreheads dabbed with altar-ash, so that we could join the crowd waiting at the long table in the court. My companion from earlier had reserved a space and was looking out for me, so Junio and I both went across and we managed to insert ourselves into the narrow gap and find a garland to put around our heads.

Just in time, in fact. The great dishes of cooked meat were being brought into the court, and the sevir muttered an incantation over them before they were taken and shared among the crowd. There is not much decorum at such a public 'feast'. The attendant priest moved down one side of the table, offering the bowl and a muttered blessing to each man in turn. People seized a portion and gnawed it where they stood, followed by a quick swig from the communal cup, while people on the fringes queued to get a share. I ate mine and retired, being careful to keep my toga clean – the temple slaves would bring the bowls of rinsing-water for fingers afterwards, when the final prayer of dismissal had been said.

The trader, who had followed at my heels, licked the last scrap of cooked beef from his fingertips. 'Well, that was very good. I suppose we must thank your Publius Martinus. Though no doubt he'll have more than a taste of it himself – he and your patron will have the better bits. Along with all the rest of the councillors, I suppose. Just as they'll have the best seats at the games this afternoon.' He nodded towards Marcus and the official guests, who were on the dais at the front and had a proper place to sit.

I was about to murmur – diplomatically – that, since they were the ones who had provided all the beasts, of course the choicest portion would be reserved for them, but I was interrupted by Junio tugging at my sleeve.

'Look,' he said. 'That visitor from Rome. It seems as if he's leaving. And the final prayer's not said.'

The trader goggled. 'There's been a message for him, by the look of it. It must have been important, to disturb him here.' He pointed out the crimson-faced young courier who had fought his way unnoticed to the central dais, and was now escorting the Roman towards the outer gate. The crowd stood back to make way for them.

'It's no doubt to tell him that his Vestal Bride's arrived,' I said. 'I understand he plans to present her to the crowd.'

Junio looked stunned. 'You think he'd bring her here? A woman?'

'Why not?' I made a knowing face. 'As a Vestal she's entitled to attend.'

'And claim her as his bride in front of everyone?' The trader's eyes were wide. 'So we would legally all be witnesses?'

I shook my head. 'I gather the formal nuptials will follow afterwards. The bride's uncle is arranging another banquet at his home – no doubt an old-fashioned wedding with vows at the family altar. There'll be witnesses enough. Everyone important is likely to be there.' I was aware of people listening as I spoke, but I was not concerned about discretion now. If Publius had gone to fetch the Vestal, as it looked as if he had, the whole of Glevum would know it very soon and I was rather proud to be the first to break the news.

But it seemed that I was wrong. Though we waited an interminable time Publius Martinus did not come back again. The official party looked at first bemused, and then increasingly impatient, until – after a little whispering among the priests – the sevir rose and spoke the words that showed the feast was at an end. The musicians struck up again, the important guests filed out, and the rest of us were free – at last – to drift away.

As I walked out of the enclosure with Junio at my heels a hand fell on my shoulder. I turned around, to find the trader looking quizzically at me. 'So it seems that you were misinformed? There is no Vestal Virgin after all.'

A palm-frond trader was packing up his stall and must have overheard. He sidled up to us. 'You haven't heard then, citizens?

Well, I'm not surprised. The runner said that he'd been told not to give the message till the man came out here, away from public ears. It would have been a dreadful scandal wouldn't it, if they'd announced that the bull of sacrifice had proved to be ill-omened after all, just at the moment when you'd all eaten it?'

I rounded on him. 'What do you mean, ill-omened? What has happened now? Did that messenger bring news about a problem of some kind?'

'There was a proper fuss. Boy had come running with a message all the way.' He bared his snaggled teeth into a yellow grin. 'That Publius's servant was waiting by my stall and when the man came out, I heard every word they said.'

I saw where this was leading, and I reached into my purse. 'A sestertius if you tell us, and it proves to be the truth.'

The stallholder took the coin I offered him, and tried it in his teeth. When he was satisfied he grinned at me again. 'Well then, I'll tell you, citizen. You're right in one respect. There was a Vestal Virgin – but she has disappeared. That fat Roman has gone to look for her.'

TWO

I boggled at him. 'How could she disappear?'

He shrugged. 'You tell me, citizen. Magic powers, perhaps. I'm just a simple freeman with a market stall. Vestal Virgins are a mystery to me.' He turned his back and returned to his fronds. Now that he had his coin, the palm vendor had lost interest in the dialogue – or perhaps he had really told me all he knew.

My trader friend from the temple had been listening to all this. He cocked an eyebrow at me. 'So there is nothing to wait here for. Should we set off to the games? Or do you think they will be cancelled after this? I presume that Publius will be funding them – and if his sacrifice was not acceptable to the gods . . .' He trailed off.

I knew why he was anxious to hurry to the games, which were another annual component of the birthday celebrations. The amphitheatre was a little way outside of town, beyond the Eastern Gate, and people were already pushing past us to hasten over there, hoping to get the best seats with a view. All seating in the public area was free, and the event was paid for by *decurions* and other providers of the festal animals – so naturally the performance was very popular. But I was not proposing to attend.

I shook my head. 'Watching armed combat is not my favourite sport, especially on an occasion like today when few of the losers are likely to survive.'

He grinned. 'Oh come on, citizen, it makes for better sport. Much more so than the usual tame affairs we see. I know that gladiators are expensive things, and I suppose if I owned a team I wouldn't want them killed, but most of the conflicts that we are treated to round here are designed to be thrilling entertainment, rather a proper battle to the death.'

He was right about the usual local shows. There are always wounds, of course, but – normally – unless the loser shows actual cowardice, most of the vanquished live to fight another day.

I shook my head again. 'It won't be tame today. These games are in honour of the Emperor, and if they are indeed paid for by this newcomer from Rome he will have the final verdict on the fights. I expect that at the end of every bout this afternoon, when the victor looks up to the official box, he'll get the "thumbs-down" signal which seals the victim's fate. No doubt Publius intends to tell the Emperor all about it afterwards.' I did not add the obvious, that Commodus was noted for his sadistic streak, and was known to like a gory finish to a fight.

My trader friend, however, was nodding eagerly. 'So you think the games will happen? Despite what we've just heard?'

'I imagine so. Publius was going to finance them, of course – no doubt in part as celebration of his wedding plans – but even if that fails, Marcus and the other councillors will meet the bill, I'm sure. They wouldn't want to lose favour with the populace. But I doubt that he'll withdraw – most of the money will be already spent. Besides, if the games were to be cancelled, we would have heard by now.'

The man looked doubtful. 'I suppose you're right. Though I'm surprised that the authorities have not made some announcement to the crowd.'

'What? Make an announcement in the marketplace that Publius's sacrifice appears to be ill-starred – and that people had been given ill-omened flesh to eat? The priests could not do that. There would very likely be riots in the street. And what would the Emperor say when he found out that a feast in his honour had been declared bad luck?' I shook my head. 'The sacrifice is over. The bull was accepted by the hirospex and it is too late now. Besides, Publius did not come back into the temple after he was called away so it's possible that the authorities do not even know the news. It's only chance we heard this from the fern-seller.'

My companion considered this a moment, then answered thoughtfully, 'We only have his word for it, in fact. And there has been no announcement . . .'

I nodded. 'Exactly. So, if you hope to get a good view from the public stands, I should hurry there at once.'

'You genuinely do not mean to come?' He sounded quite

amazed. He motioned towards Junio, who had been listening to all this. 'Would your son not welcome a visit to the games?'

I laughed. 'We have already done our duty to the Emperor by coming to Glevum for the temple rite. That is no small thing. Remember that my roundhouse is several miles from town, and my son's is next to it. We have already walked a long way to get here, and – since there is no chance of a carrying-litter on a day like this, far less a hiring-carriage – we'll be walking back again. And we'll have to go the long way, by the military road: we can hardly scrabble down muddy country lanes in these expensive clothes.' It was an exaggeration – I had done such things before – but there was some truth in what I said. A toga is an awkward thing to hurry in, even on the most well-laid of roads, and very expensive to have cleaned, besides. I saw the fellow wavering and I urged again. 'If we stop to see the games we'll be lucky to get home before it's dark – and it isn't safe to walk the forest paths at night. So if you want to see the gladiator, I suggest you hurry on.'

'Well, if you say so, citizen.' And he scurried off.

I turned to Junio, smiling. 'I thought he'd never go.'

Junio watched him out of sight, then turned to walk across with me towards the fountain where we had left our slaves to wait. 'You realize he was hoping to go into the games with you? He thinks your influence with Marcus might have won us better seats.'

The idea made me laugh. 'Then he doesn't know my patron! Marcus is in his most public role today, the senior man in half Britannia. He's very conscious of his dignity. If he deigned to notice me at all on such a day, it would only be because he wanted some service out of me.'

Junio made a semi-sympathetic face. 'And you really do not wish to see the games yourself, father?'

'If I want to see butchery I'll frequent the marketplace,' I joked, then saw the look of disappointment on his face. It was obvious that my son would have liked to go to see the birthday games – of course these things were still a novel treat for him – and for a moment I felt a twinge of guilt. I touched him on the arm.

'The next time there are public games in Glevum, I will

take you there,' I promised. 'You won't have long to wait.
Some aging wealthy citizen is almost sure to die, leaving
money in his will for a gladiatorial show in memory of himself,
and even failing that there'll be elections very soon.'

He brightened. 'I suppose so. There are always contests
then.'

'Usually sponsored by the candidates,' I said, and added
teasingly, 'specially to impress young citizens like you.'

'You mean that it's an attempt to sway the vote?'

'Well, not entirely. Most citizens would claim it isn't just
a bribe. It's a demonstration that the candidate concerned has
a lot of money which he's prepared to spend for the benefit
of the populace.'

'But you do not sound as if you very much approve.'

'I'd prefer to see the money spent on public works like
drains,' I said. 'But I don't suppose that's very glamorous.' I
grinned at him. 'It would disappoint you of an entertainment,
too, since I've said that I would take you. And I'll keep my
word.'

'Although you don't much care for gladiatorial games?'

'In the ordinary way, I quite enjoy the spectacle. I always
like watching a *retinarius* – they show such skill with just a
trident and a net – sometimes against a swordsman with full
armour and a shield. But not on an occasion like today, when
half the combatants are likely to be killed. Still, enough of
that. For now let's find the servants and get home to our wives.
I want to take my toga and these new sandals off – the soles
are killing me.'

It took us a few moments to locate the slaves, in fact, though
usually they were not hard to pick out in a crowd: two little
red-haired lads – who had been trained in Marcus's household
but who had passed to me as a reward for various 'services'
that I had done for him. I spotted them at last, with their backs
towards me, at the rear of a throng of other household slaves,
who – along with assorted beggars and poor freemen from the
town – were huddled in the entrance to a nearby lane, craning
to watch something in the alleyway. The boys were standing
on tiptoe to see between the crowd and they did not notice
the two of us as we approached.

I gestured Junio to silence, then – as he held back – I went up behind the nearer slave and said loudly in his ear, 'Minimus! What is the meaning of all this? Didn't I tell you to wait beside the fountain over there?'

Minimus, who was – despite his name – the taller of the boys, (they had been purchased a matching pair, but he had grown the most) spun around at once and a look of startled horror crossed his face. 'Master! You didn't go to watch the games?' He nudged his companion, and I heard him whispering, 'Maximus! The master's here. And the young master too. Look what you have done! You were supposed to be on watch and warn me when they came.'

The smaller slave whirled instantly round, scarlet with embarrassment and shame. 'I am very sorry, master—' he began.

I cut him off with a gesture. 'I expect obedience, not apologies!' I said, with an attempt to be severe. My wife is always telling me I am too lax with them, and this would be a flogging matter in many households. But I could not altogether blame them for their escapade. On feast-days such as this the town is always thronging with alluring sights, quite apart from the official marches and parades: exotic street performers, jugglers and acrobats, and enticing stalls selling honey-cakes and oatcakes and small crispy rinds of pig. It was all a lot more interesting than standing at a fountain watching water flow, and after all the boys had scarcely moved a dozen yards. I said more gently, 'What is so exciting that it makes you leave your post?'

It was Maximus who answered, his eyes alight with glee. 'Master, you should see it for yourself. There's a magician here – straight from the African provinces, he says – sitting on a mat and doing such things as you would not believe. He makes things disappear. He took a coin in his hand, and blew on it, and then it wasn't there. And that's not all – a moment later he produced it from a woman's ear.'

The crowd had parted slightly (probably in deference to our togas) and I could see the magic-man: a turbaned dark-haired fellow, in a coloured robe, now doing something impossible with a coloured cup and balls. I turned back to the slaves. 'So that's what happened, is it? He turned his charms on you and made you disappear, as well? So you vanished from where I left you and turned up somewhere else?'

If I meant to be ironic it was lost on Maximus. 'A thousand pardons, master,' he said earnestly. 'Please do not be angry. It was all my fault. I saw him when he first appeared, before the crowd arrived. He had a magic cage. One minute there was a pigeon in it, but then he covered it – just a piece of cloth, I saw both sides of it – and when he moved the cover there was nothing there. It was astonishing. I persuaded Minimus to come and watch. If anyone is to be whipped, it is my fault, not his.'

He was so contrite that I took pity on him. 'Well, I suppose no harm was done, and I have found you now. It is the birthday of the Emperor, and for his sake I'll overlook your lapse. Just make sure your mistress doesn't hear of it. And Maximus, when we get outside of town, I'll take my toga off and you can carry it the whole way home as punishment.'

The two boys exchanged glances of undisguised relief but no more was said and I urged our little party away from the magician (who by now was apparently drawing a string of coloured ribbons from his mouth) and through the crowds of bystanders and stalls towards the southern gates, in the direction where our family's two roundhouses lay.

It was hard to walk against the general direction of the jostling tide – visitors were still crowding into town to see the shows – but we struggled to the gatehouse and were preparing to walk through, under the eye of the surly soldier on the gate, when a commanding voice rang out behind us.

'That citizen! The one with the balding head and greying beard. The one with the two red-headed slaves. Stop him for me.'

I felt my heart sink swiftly to my sandal-soles. What had I done now? Had someone heard me whispering to my trader friend, something unflattering about the Emperor? Was I about to be blamed for the failure of the sacrifice? I tried to remember exactly what it was I said. One thing I was fairly certain of: no good was likely to come of it!

The guard on duty had already drawn his sword and stepped towards me. 'You heard, citizen. Stay right where you are. There's someone here who wants to talk to you.'

'Keep him there!' the voice rang out again. 'Don't let him get away.'

Everyone fell back, as always happens when someone is arrested in the street, as if to distance themselves from trouble as much as possible. I motioned to Junio and the slaves to keep walking on – no point in getting them involved as well – and turned to see who my accuser was. I expected to see the bald man who had shushed me at the sacrifice, but the person who was jostling his way towards me through the crowd was someone I had never seen before.

It was a young man, handsome, well-built and imperious, but not a citizen. In fact, his conspicuous red tunic with gold bands around the hem marked him as the private page of some hugely wealthy man – though if he wore a slave disc round his neck ('I am so-and-so, the property of x. If you find me straying, have me whipped and send me back') it was covered by the fur-edged cape. I had seen a similar livery before – my patron sometimes dressed his messengers this way – but I knew most members of my patron's staff by sight. Besides Marcus's taste in pages was more for pretty boys, not threatening and athletic fellows such as this.

He had reached my side by now, and looked me slowly up and down. 'Are you the citizen Libertus? Pavement-maker or something of the kind?'

For a moment I could not answer him, my heart was hammering so hard against my chest. Who was this person? Not one of Publius's men – his escort was arrayed in emerald green. An Imperial spy perhaps? One of the dreaded *speculatores* – the mounted secret agents used by the Emperor to deal with his suspected enemies? We'd seen such men before, even in this corner of the Empire. My blood ran icy at the thought. Was I about to be marched off to some secluded place and found tomorrow with a dagger in my ribs?

His cool dark eyes swept over me again. 'You look like the man that was described to me. Ancient toga and dishevelled hair – and you had the two red-headed servants, too. Is your name Libertus?'

I thought for a moment of making an appeal to the guard. I was a Roman citizen, after all, and the law should protect me from random harassment at the hands of servants, however grand they were. But I could see it was no use. The elaborate uniform had already done its work. The soldier levelled his sword-blade at my ribs and said in a none-too-friendly tone of voice, 'Answer the question, citizen.'

I managed to stammer that it was indeed my name. 'I am Libertus, one of the *clientes* of His Excellence, Marcus Septimus,' I went on, in the vain hope that the mention of my patron's name would deter this stranger from whatever unpleasant plans he had in store. 'I'm sure he'll vouch for me.'

I had unnerved the sentry, he dropped his blade at once, but the young man merely looked at me in some surprise. 'Well, I should think he would. It is on his account that I am seeking you.'

I boggled. 'You come from my patron, do I understand?'

He nodded. 'Indeed. His Excellence was looking for you at the games. He sent his other attendants out to search for you – there and at the entrance of the temple in the forum too – but you could not be found. In the end he sent me rushing over here, hoping I could catch you before you left the town. I am simply grateful that I was not too late – I was only given to His Excellence today, a gift from my previous owner, Publius, and I would not have wanted to fail in my first task.'

'And that was?'

'To find you and bring you back to him. Your patron requires you to attend on him at once. He's waiting at the games.'

THREE

I was escorted swiftly through the town – remarkable how the crowds stood back to let us through once they caught sight of my attendant's dress. My escort said nothing until we reached the entrance of the amphitheatre where the games were being held – they had already started, by the sound of it.

However, Marcus was not waiting for me inside in the official stand, as I had half-expected, but in a covered litter outside the entrance-way. It had been set down on the wide convenient stone block, where litter-bearers sometimes assisted their plumper fares to mount, though there were no bearers visible today. My patron was sitting in the carrying-chair with the drapes pulled back, and as soon as he saw us approach he motioned me to come.

'Libertus, old friend, there you are at last. We've been looking everywhere.' He extended a ringed hand for me to kiss. 'Where did you find him, Fiscus?'

'At the southern gate on his way home, as you suggested, Excellence.' The man replied, making an obeisance.

'Were you really not proposing to attend the games?' My patron frowned at me. I was on my knees before him by this time of course, and I was about to answer but he waved my words aside. 'But never mind all that. Come into the litter. I have something to discuss – something of great importance to the colonia. Fiscus, help him in and then you can keep watch. Move back a pace or two and keep the crowds away. I don't want this conversation overheard.'

The young man was looking quite astonished by all this – the idea that my wealthy patron should address me as 'old friend' and invite me to share his litter was clearly quite a shock. It would have been amusing if I had not known that this open friendliness was almost certainly the prelude to some importunate request: Marcus is always gracious when he wants my services – though I would be happier if he paid in cash rather than in compliments. (This is not ingratitude. Working for my patron is apt to take much time and prevent me from pursuing my usual livelihood, but Marcus is famously careful with his wealth and refuses to 'insult' me by offering me gold. However, when His Excellence suggests that you might serve him in some way, declining to do so is not conducive to one's health.)

Besides, I told myself, there are often other sorts of recompense, though usually ones which do not cost him anything: my two slaves for instance, had come to me this way. So I smiled with an appearance of good grace and climbed into the chair beside him as proposed.

It was rather cramped in there – most litters are designed to carry one man at a time, and it was hard to squeeze into the space at all, let alone to keep my head below my patron's all the time, as etiquette required. However I managed to insinuate myself into the gap between his feet by kneeling rather uncomfortably on the floor. Marcus drew the drapes so that we were curtained off from view.

'Libertus, something very unexpected and dreadful has occurred. It almost made Publius decide to stop the games, but that would have been disrespectful to the Emperor, so we have decided that they should go ahead. He has gone in to start them, as though all was well, but you'll never guess what's happened.'

I could not resist it. 'His bride has disappeared.'

Marcus looked at me – rather as Maximus had looked at the magician in the street – with admiring disbelief. 'It seems she has been kidnapped. But how do you know that?'

'I heard it in the forum,' I answered, truthfully, suggesting by my tone that I was always well-informed.

He was not impressed by this. Indeed, he began to tap his baton against his leg, which was an indication that he was irritated and dismayed, and his tone was sharp and fretful. 'I don't understand how that could come about. I hope the time it took to find you does not mean we are too late. If news of this should get around the town it might call the temple sacrifice into disrepute: that would look like a bad augury and what would the Emperor have to say to that? Yet you claim it's common gossip?'

I hastened to retract. 'Well not exactly that. I happened to be talking to a stall-keeper. He had a stall of palm-fronds near the entrance to the temple enclosure, and he chanced to over-hear the message brought to Publius.'

Marcus frowned again. 'You could identify the man? We'll have him taken into custody – this information must not be allowed to spread. I had supposed that we were safe. It is not general knowledge among the populace that Publius was even intending to be wed.'

I blanched, remembering my stupid pride at knowing some-thing other men did not and the blithe way in which I had passed on the news myself. 'It may be a little late to call the rumour back,' I said, not mentioning my own part in it of course. 'If I have heard it, others will have done. If you try to silence gossip, you will make it worse. Better probably to let the matter rest – if they hear no more about it people will simply assume the stories were not true, or else were exag-gerated as most rumours are.'

My words were interrupted by a loud roar from the crowd in the amphitheatre. No doubt some Thracian fighter had put up a good display.

I saw my patron's eager glance towards the sound and I ventured a diplomatic effort to excuse myself and go. 'It was a good move, for instance, to continue with the games,' I said. 'But will your absence not be a matter of remark?'

He fidgeted. 'Perhaps you're right. I should go back inside and be conspicuous and we'll allow this public gossip to die down naturally. But that makes this matter more confidential than before, which will doubtless make your urgent task more difficult.'

'My task, Excellence?' I felt my throat go dry. I had supposed that I had fulfilled my role by offering advice.

He smiled impatiently. 'But naturally, I have promised Publius that you would find the girl. Or woman, I suppose that I should say, since he has chosen to marry someone of advancing years.'

'But Excellence,' I bleated, 'how can I do that? I've never seen this Vestal – and since she has been in the temple thirty years, I don't imagine many people could describe her very well. Even her family will have no portrait of her face and

even if they did, surely as a Vestal she'll have travelled in a
veil, as any modest Roman matron would have done? Nobody
could swear that they had seen her on the way, or pick her
out if they saw her in a crowd. I understand that Publius went
to look for her himself, but I gather from your words that even
he did not succeed and he is a man of wealth and influence.
If he can't find her how on earth can I?'

'I leave that up to you.' He gave a fleeting smile. 'I'm sure
you'll find a way. You've done such things before.'

I tried to protest that this was different. I didn't know the
woman or the man concerned (they did not even know each
other, it appeared), both of them were strangers to the town,
and the kidnapping – if that was what it was – had not happened
here. But Marcus brushed aside such trivial complaints.

'It cannot be as difficult as you pretend, old friend. She was
seen this morning by lots of witnesses – according to the
carriage-driver, anyway – and the carriage did not stop until
it reached the city-gate. So she was either seized immediately
before she left Corinium, or smuggled from the carriage as
soon as it reached here. As long as you find her in a day or
two – before Publius has to leave – I'm sure you'll find the
bridegroom generous in his gratitude.'

I felt my throat go dry. Not only was I commanded to find
the missing bride, but I was expected to do so in just 'a day
or two'. However, I was not in a position to refuse so I said,
resignedly, 'Very well, Excellence. I have no hopes of this,
but – as ever – I am at your command. If you wish me to, I'll
go straight in and speak to Publius.' At least it would give my
poor numb feet a rest, I thought. My legs were almost dead
with kneeling by this time. I started to get out.

Marcus's firm grasp on my arm prevented me. 'But of course
you can't do that. The populace would see. This whole enquiry
will have to be discreet.'

'So I'll have to wait until the games are over, Excellence?
Obviously I must speak to Publius and I thought you wanted
me to make a start at once?'

'Of course I do.' The baton was tapping on the leg again.
'I suppose I can tell you what Publius told me – that might
give you somewhere to begin . . .' He broke off as his words
were drowned out by another cheer. 'Though I cannot be long.

The fights are underway, and my absence will be noted, if I linger here.'

I was as keen to move as he was. 'What did Publius say?'

Marcus was distracted – it was evident that his mind was already on the games – but he did his best. 'When he got the message, he went outside the gate – the north one, which links up with the east road to Londinium – and met the carriage-driver who was waiting there and who, of course, had sent the messenger.'

I nodded to show that I had understood.

'The fellow was almost inarticulate with fear, but he claims he saw the Vestal into the coach himself and did not know that she was missing till he drew up outside the town. It took him only minutes to secure the horse, he says, but when he went to help her down he found that she was gone – together with her attendant and her dowry box. Of course he sent for Publius at once and also contacted the woman's family – but they sent a slave to say that she was not with them. They were not expecting her until the feast was finished here.'

'After Publius had presented her in public as his prospective bride?'

'Exactly. The father of the family was here in Glevum, at the rites himself, but the rest of the household had remained at home and was preparing for the wedding later on today – but they had heard nothing from the Vestal.'

'Or from her kidnappers? One might have expected a ransom note by now.'

'That is what worried Publius most of all. He fears it may have been a bandit robbery, he said.'

I knew what that implied. The penalty for robbery on the public road is crucifixion, ruthlessly applied, so victims of banditry are usually found dead – thus ensuring that they cannot testify. 'So the bride may be in danger if he does not find her soon?'

'Exactly. But where was Publius to look? He does not know the town. He found the paterfamilias – who was among the official guests of course and was walking to the games – and alerted him, and they came to find me quietly and ask me what I thought.' He looked me in the eye. 'I spoke most highly of your abilities, and obviously since Publius is a guest of mine . . .'

I said nothing and went on saying it.

He made a helpless little gesture with his hands. 'You know, of course, that he's been very generous? Not only the sacrificial bull and birthday games, but he's promising to fund another fountain and some drains. And he gave me Fiscus as a gift. Under the circumstances . . .' He gave my arm a pat. 'I rely on you, Libertus.' And to my astonishment, he pulled the drapes aside and gestured to Fiscus to assist him down.

I scrambled after him, saying in an urgent whisper, 'But, Excellence. What am I to do? You say I cannot speak to Publius.'

'Start with the driver of the coach, perhaps?' he hissed, impatiently.

'Do you know where I can find him, Excellence? Or what he looks like? If he is at the gate, it won't be easy even to discover which carriage-man it was, without asking questions . . .'

Marcus paused to look at me at last, and shook his head. 'That won't be necessary. I believe that Publius had him seized and escorted back to the Vestal's family home, where he is no doubt under lock and key. I am not entirely certain where the villa is, but I am sure that you can get directions to the place.'

'Without attracting more suspicion?' I enquired, trying to restore some life into my feet by stamping them discreetly on the ground. 'If Publius had a driver arrested at the gates, that will have given rise to public comment as it is – without my drawing more attention to the incident and directing gossip towards the woman's home.'

Fiscus, who had withdrawn to stand discreetly to one side, came forward with a bow. 'Masters, forgive me, I could not help but overhear. It is possible that I could assist the citizen. I have some notion of where the family live – my previous owner called upon them yesterday.'

It was impertinent for a slave to interrupt but Marcus offered no rebuke. His face cleared instantly. 'A good suggestion, Fiscus. You'll attend this citizen and show him where to go – treat him as your master till I instruct you otherwise. In the meantime, I must hurry to the games.' He motioned to his other pages, a pair of matching blond boys, who were waiting by the wall, and went to turn away.

I prevented him from leaving by falling on one knee so that he was obliged to present me with his ring to kiss. 'And my own family, Excellence?' I murmured. 'Will you send them word? They will think I've been arrested if I do not return – they saw me detained by the sentry at the gate.'

A look of irritation flashed across his face – the roar from the amphitheatre was louder all the time and he was clearly anxious to be gone – but he said readily enough, 'I'll send one of my pages to let them know you're safe – as soon as they have escorted me into the games.' He motioned me to rise. 'Report to me at my country house, when you get back, and let me know what you have managed to find out. Perhaps tomorrow. I may be late tonight. I am invited to a birthday feast with Publius's family and I've not heard that it's cancelled.'

I got up clumsily. The feeling was coming back into my lower legs, though my foot was still inclined to buckle under me. 'It may take me a little time to reach the house in any case,' I said. 'It is some way to walk.'

Marcus, who never parted willingly with cash, reached into the purse he carried at his waist and seemed about to fetch some money out. Then his face cleared, and he shook his head. 'You can have this litter to take you over there – I have reserved if for my personal use this afternoon. I will send the bearers out to you – I gave them permission to watch the games a while – and when you get to the villa you can send them back to me.'

'And when I have finished there? How shall I get home?'

He waved a lofty hand. 'Doubtless the bride's household have a wagon you could use. You may tell them that I suggested it. Now, be off with you, or it will be too late – for you to ask questions, and for me to see the fights.'

And this time, accompanied by his slaves, he disappeared into the games. A moment later I heard the general cheer that welcomed his appearance in the official box. It was not until this moment that it occurred to me that I had not remembered to ask about the names of the family that I was intending to approach. Fiscus, when I asked him, was no help at all – on his visit to the house he had been whisked off to the back and entertained with watered wine and cheese in the servant's sleeping room.

'They talked about the master and mistress, that was all,' he said. 'They didn't mention names.' An idea so obvious that I should have thought of it.

I aimed a frustrated kick towards the mounting block, but my dead leg almost crumpled under me.

There was an ironic jeering from behind us and I turned to see a little crowd of urchins, pie-sellers and curious spectators who had clearly stopped to watch the unlikely spectacle of a pair of citizens crammed into a litter that was not going anywhere. So much for Marcus's idea of being secretive!

With such dignity as I could muster I got into the chair, and gestured to Fiscus to find the carriers. After a moment, he came back with them. They were visibly disappointed at being forced to leave, but – like me – they could hardly disobey an order from Marcus Septimus, and with very little grumbling they lifted me aloft.

Fiscus had to trot beside the chair, of course, and give the bearers directions where to go, but he was athletic and they were young and strong so it was a good deal quicker than my walking to the place, especially when one leg refused to work. I lay back on the cushions and enjoyed the ride.

It must have been rather less than half an hour before we jolted to a stop and I pulled back the litter-curtains to see that we had halted outside a pleasant country house.

FOUR

t was a compact villa, compared to my patron's vast and rambling one: an attractive single-storey building with two rearward-facing wings, and just a gatehouse and small court-yard in the front, although an adjacent piece of farmland was clearly part of the estate, since a single-cart track led right through the fields to what was presumably another entrance at the back. A half-dozen young land-slaves were leaning on their hoes looking at us with interest from beyond the hedge – till a cursing foreman strode up with a whip, whereupon they turned reluctantly to work.

The feeling had come back into my feet by now, so as soon as my conveyance was safely on the ground I permitted Fiscus to assist me out of it. But before I had taken a single step towards the house the doorkeeper had come out of the small stone cell where he kept watch and – to my surprise – was hurrying to meet us, wearing the broadest smile of welcome I have ever seen.

It was just as well, because he was otherwise a most forbid-ding sight. Unusually for a man who kept the gates (who are most often hairy giants) he was small and squarish, with a bald head that glistened like a wet ballista ball, but what he lacked in size he clearly made up for in strength. His short orange tunic strained across his chest, powerful legs bulged above the heavy boots, the sinews in his arms were like twisted strands of rope and he carried a huge club as if it were a twig. This was a man who could repel unwanted visitors. But there was the smile.

In fact I was so encouraged by this sign of friendliness that I gestured to the carrying-slaves that they were free to go, although I had previously asked them to delay until I was admitted to the house: I had no wish to be stranded miles from anywhere down a narrow country lane. They were obvi-ously anxious to get back to the games and at my signal they picked up the litter and set off at a run.

I turned back towards the gatekeeper, a word of cheerful greeting already on my lips, but as he saw my face the smile dissolved like smoke.

'Citizen.' He fidgeted a little with his club. 'I didn't . . . that is . . . the toga – I should have realized.' He stared from Fiscus and the scarlet uniform, to my much-laundered garments with disapproving disbelief. 'I don't believe I know you, after all. You have some business here?'

My heart sank lower than my sandal-soles. I had been overhasty in letting the litter-bearers go. It did not take an oracle to see the problem here.

'You were expecting Publius?' I asked, pacifically. 'Of course. And no doubt my attendant confirmed you in that thought. He tells me he came here with his owner yesterday. I expect you recognized him, despite his change of uniform.'

The doorkeeper looked distrustfully at me, tapping his left palm with his club meanwhile – so hard that it made my fingers twitch in sympathy. 'I did,' he growled at last, evidently deciding that – since I had Fiscus at my side – I should at least be permitted to explain. 'I saw him running by the litter and naturally I thought that the esteemed Publius and the lady Audelia had come.'

'So that the marriage would take place after all?' I prompted. I hoped to lure him into saying something that would help, by indicating that I knew about the problem with the bride. 'No wonder you were pleased. No doubt you intended to escort them in, yourself – and maybe earn a *quadrans* as the bearer of good news?' I ventured a confidential smile. 'I understand your feelings perfectly. I was once a slave myself.'

He shot me a wry look, as if we shared a secret now, but his manner thawed. 'More than a quadrans, citizen. A silver coin at least. If you had been the bride and groom, it would have been such a wonderful relief, especially to the mistress – but to all of us, as well. I thought for a moment that our problems had all been sorted out . . .' He broke off suddenly, as if he'd said too much and a red flush of embarrassment ran up the hairless neck. He began weighing the cudgel in his palm again. 'But how did you know a wedding had even been proposed? I thought the guests were sworn to secrecy. Were you invited?'

I took a step backwards, more because of the action of his club than because I was offended by his words, but he seemed to acknowledge that he'd sounded impolite.

'Forgive the challenge, citizen, but that is what a doorkeeper is for, especially in a circumstance like this. I ask again, were you invited to the marriage feast? I understood that only a small selected group were asked – just seven of the magistrates and senior councillors – enough to be the witnesses the law demands. But clearly from your clothing you are not one of them.'

Fiscus was looking absolutely shocked at this, but it was evident that the doorkeeper meant no disrespect. He was merely talking candidly, now that he knew that I was once a slave myself. And it was true, my toga's lack of any purple stripe showed that I was not a man of noble Roman birth and – though it was newly-cleaned in honour of the day – it did not dazzle with the expensive spotlessness expected of a candidate in public life.

So I did not bridle and issue a rebuke, as my attendant clearly expected that I would. I simply made a wry face and observed that I was just a simple tradesman-citizen and could not afford to send my toga to the fuller's twice a moon.

Fiscus looked affronted and stared hard at the ground but the doorkeeper made a sympathetic noise. 'In that case, are you some kind of distant relative? I know that there are other branches of the family here in Britannia but I'd heard that – since they weren't people of any consequence – they were either not invited or had declined to come. But if you are one of them, let me have your name and I'll enquire if the mistress will permit you to come in.'

This suggestion that I was of no account was not a compliment either, but – to Fiscus's growing horror – I responded with a smile. Even if the gateman turned me from the door, I wanted at least to lure him into saying something more. I had hopes of learning the family's name, at least, though I dared not show my ignorance by asking him outright. He had already told me – without intending to – that the bride was called Audelia, and I'd also learned much about the household's attitudes.

'I am not a member of the family,' I said. 'I have been sent

here by His Excellency, Marcus Aurelius Septimus, to try to
find out what happened to the bride. My attendant here will
bear me out, I'm sure.' I gestured at Fiscus who briefly raised
his eyes, nodded grimly, and then went back to gazing at his
feet. I turned a wheedling smile onto the gatekeeper. 'Would
it be possible for you to let us in?'

The man looked doubtful. 'Well, I don't know I'm sure.
There's not a slave to spare that I can send to ask. Wait here
and I will go and make enquiries myself.' And before I could
answer he had gone inside the gate and barred the entrance
firmly in my face.

I glanced at Fiscus but he would not meet my eyes. He
would never have endured this kind of greeting in his life, and
was doubtless mortified at finding himself in attendance to a
mere ex-slave. I would have to tell him sometime that – among
my own people – I was a nobleman before I was captured
into slavery. But in the meantime I was glad that he was there.
Without him, I suspected, I would have been turned away
before I'd had the opportunity to say a word.

There was a short uncomfortable silence while we stood
there in the lane and I was just beginning to calculate how
long it would take us to walk back to the town, when the
doorman reappeared. From the haste with which he opened
wide the gate and ushered us inside, I deduced that he had
been reprimanded for not admitting us at once. The name of
Marcus Septimus had no doubt worked its charm.

The gatekeeper was all obsequious helpfulness now, as he
led us through the court. 'I am sorry, citizen, that there is no
page to show you in. The whole of the household is in disarray
not knowing whether there will be a wedding feast or not – or
whether the whole banquet will be cancelled after all. But I
see there is a maidservant waiting at the door, she will escort
you and show you where to wait. My mistress will be with
you in just a little while.'

The slave-girl was a timid, skinny little thing, in an orange
tunic far too big for her, but she contrived a little smile and
led us shyly in. She took us down a central passage from the
portico to the central atrium, a large room where there was a
mosaic of a pool – in imitation of the real ones which they're
said to have in Rome – though of rather indifferent

workmanship, I thought. Normally this was a place where one would wait, but today it was a hive of domestic industry: a senior slave was supervising the fuelling of lamps and the arrangement of sweet-scented herbs around the family altar in a niche, while a group of slave-boys struggled with the weight of a table and more couches for the dining room beyond.

The folding doors were thrown open to the rear to reveal a pretty little colonnade where troops of garden slaves were also hard at work, sweeping the pathways round the court with bundles of bunched broom, and garlanding the outside shrines and statues with fresh flowers. Other servants were hurrying to and from a separate wooden building to the rear – evidently the kitchen, from which mouth-watering smells were beginning to emerge – carrying pails of water and great trays for serving food. The chief slave looked up and bowed as we walked by but none of the others acknowledged us at all, as our slave-girl led us through the atrium and into a small study to the right.

It was not a large room and it was already full with a cupboard, boxes and a set of open shelves which must have held at least a dozen manuscripts in pots. The top of a handsome wooden table by the window-space was covered too, with opened letter-scrolls, clean bark-paper, an iron-nibbed pen or two, little containers with the elements for mixing ink, two oil-lamps, and – at the very front, as if it had recently been used – a stylus, and the kind of stamp-seal and wax that ladies (not having seal-rings) sometimes used to seal the ties on their fancy writing-blocks, though there was no such wax-tablet here that I could see.

A folding stool had been set up beside the desk and the maidservant suggested shyly that I should sit on it, but indicated that Fiscus – to his visible dismay – should stand and wait outside the study door. No question of entertainment in the servants' room today.

'I will bring some wine and dates for you,' the slave-girl ventured, rather timidly. 'The mistress won't be long.'

'Thank you for your help,' I murmured, as she turned to go. I saw the doubtful smile that briefly lit her face, and realized that she was very rarely praised. That gave me an idea. I motioned to the girl that she should shut the door. 'You could help me further,' I said, when this was done and I was sure that Fiscus could not overhear. 'I am a stranger to the household and I don't know the names. Perhaps you could tell me?'

She misunderstood me, her thin cheeks aglow. 'They call me Modesta, citizen.' She seemed astonished to be addressed at all.

I would have to do better, without alarming her. 'Thank you, Modesta,' I answered with a smile. 'You have done very well. It is not your normal duty to greet visitors, I think? No doubt the usual attendants are with your master in the town?' I was only guessing this, from her awkward manner, but it seemed that I was right.

She blushed still brighter. 'Exactly, citizen. I am just a sewing-slave who mends the garments here, and I do not usually have anything to do with guests. But I am not wanted to help prepare the feast so they have released me to come and show you in. You bring word from the master?'

'Not exactly that.'

'The mistress will be disappointed then. She sent a message to her husband, an hour or so ago, to ask him whether the banquet was likely to take place – but up to now there has been no reply.'

'Yet she has gone on making preparations just the same? Even if there is no wedding for you to celebrate?'

I'd mentioned the wedding to see what she would say, but she just shrugged her skinny shoulders. 'My master holds a banquet every year in honour of the Imperial holiday. Everyone knows that. Lavinius's feast is quite a famous one, and if it was cancelled the mistress is afraid that the Emperor might get to hear of it.'

So the master was called Lavinius, I thought. That was a little victory, at least. 'I see. So she thought it might be dangerous to cancel everything?'

An eager nod. 'That's why we were hoping that you brought a message back. We should have heard by now.'

My imagination made a sudden leap. 'She sent a written letter – a wax tablet possibly,' I said, thinking of the stylus I'd noticed earlier.

The slave-girl coloured. 'It was difficult for her. She can read, of course – I think it's wonderful the way she understands all the inscriptions on graves and everything – but obviously she doesn't often write. When would she have occasion to? But I heard her saying to the senior slave that she didn't want this message to be delivered verbally: it might be overheard, and we'd have the whole town knowing what the problem was. She sealed it up and gave it to the last remaining page and told him to run the whole way in with it.'

It seemed that I was not the only one to think discretion was the safest policy! 'Then perhaps her letter hasn't reached your master yet,' I said. 'It would not be easy for the message-boy to interrupt, if the official party was busy with the games.'

She looked at me distressed. 'You mean, perhaps the master doesn't know about . . . the troubles with the wedding?'

I remembered what Marcus had told me earlier. 'He does know that his daughter has disappeared,' I said. I was about to go on to explain how he, too, was trying to keep that knowledge from the general populace but the girl let out a cry of pure dismay.

'Little Lavinia? She's disappeared as well? When did this happen? How did you hear of it? Is that what you have come for – to tell us about that?'

I was as surprised as she was. 'Lavinia? I thought the bride was called Audelia?'

The small face cleared a little. 'So she is. But . . . oh, I see! You said you did not know the family!' She saw my face and gave a little giggle of relief. 'Lavinius Flaccus is not the father of the bride. Did you suppose he was? He is just her uncle – or at least he is the husband of my mistress, who is Audelia's aunt.'

'Aunt?' I echoed, rather stupidly.

'Her dead mother's sister, as I understand. Both of Audelia's parents died of plague in Rome some years ago, and Lavinius is her nearest living male relative – though she doesn't need one as a legal guardian, of course, as other women would.' My error had cured her of her timidity, and she was savouring the unaccustomed joy of knowing something other people didn't know. She rolled her eyes to heaven. 'Being a Vestal Virgin must be wonderful. She didn't even need anyone's consent when she chose to marry Publius – though of course Lavinius would have given it at once. He and my mistress are absolutely thrilled.'

'So Audelia was to be married from her uncle's house?'

'But it is not her uncle's. You really didn't know? This whole estate belongs to Audelia herself. Her father left it to her when he died.'

I was astonished. 'Although she was a girl?'

She nodded. 'She was an only child. Of course, as a Vestal Virgin, she could officially have managed everything herself, but she was still living in the temple then, so she installed her uncle to take care of it for her.' She gave her timid smile. 'So now I've explained things for you, shall I fetch this fruit and wine?'

'Just one more moment!' I said, urgently. My thoughts were in a whirl. If this house belonged to Audelia herself and she was due to marry, what would happen then? Surely it would come to Publius as part of her dowry – even Vestal Virgins lose their status when they wed. So what would happen to the uncle who was living here? Would he and his family be obliged to leave? Had I stumbled on a reason why somebody should wish that the prospective bride should disappear?

The girl was staring uncertainly at me, expecting me to speak. I cleared my throat. 'Lavinius was content with that arrangement, I suppose? Surely – since I understand he is a wealthy man – he has his own affairs? No doubt including substantial property elsewhere.'

'Ooh, certainly!' She glanced around, as if she feared the walls were listening to all this, then dropped her voice and grinned, showing a set of little pointed teeth. 'He's got a town house in Venta, over to the west – that's where I was born. But this arrangement was convenient to him. He didn't have a country villa anywhere near here – only a tract of forest and a stone-quarry – and it suited him to be a little closer to the docks.'

That made a difference to my theory, of course. The man would clearly not be homeless after all, but . . . 'And now he'll lose all those advantages?'

She stared at me. 'Of course, you wouldn't know. He has some land adjoining this, which my mistress – Cyra – brought him as a dowry when she wed, and they are building another house on that. It would have been competed by this time, in fact, if it wasn't for the rain that we've had recently.'

Any hopes that I had found a motive for a kidnapping had vanished more completely than the gatekeeper's smile. But I was struck by what seemed an odd coincidence. 'Land adjoining this? You don't mean the farmland that I saw outside the gate?'

She did her shy giggle at my ignorance. 'Of course not. Though it was once all one estate. Cyra's father left her the other portion when he died.' She saw my puzzled face and went on patiently. 'He was Audelia's grandfather, of course – he had two daughters and no other heirs – and his land was subdivided between the pair of them.'

It was the obvious explanation, when you thought of it. I was about to say as much when the door was thrust open and we were interrupted by a shrill, reproving voice.

'Modesta, why are there no refreshments for our guest? Go, see to it at once. How dare you stand about! This is no time for idle gossiping! I'm sorry, citizen, the child is not accustomed to receiving guests. When Lavinius gets home, I'll see that she is whipped!'

FIVE

I stood up, almost scattering the writing-implements from the tabletop. I was ready to defend my young informant but the slave-girl had already scuttled from the room. The newcomer – who, like me had left her attendant waiting at the door – swept towards me with hands outstretched.

This was very clearly the mistress of the house. The high quality of the dark blue stola which she wore and the lighter blue embroidered over-tunic were evident even to my untutored eyes. Her purple slippers were of finest kid, the soft leather cut into a latticework of leaves which would have made my Gwellia sigh with jealousy. Yet in one respect my wife was much the more fortunate of the two.

The woman before me was not handsome, even for her age – she was far too thin and angular for that – and there was no sign that she had ever been a beauty in her youth. Her face was lined and sallow under the whitening arsenic-powder that she wore, though she had done her best to give some colour with wine-lees on her lips and a touch of enhancing lampblack painted round the eyes. The lustrous black hair, coiled into a fashionable chignon on her head, was all too evidently a wig, and wisps of her own greying mousy locks crept out from under it. Her form was tall and bony and her long-fingered hands so wrinkled, pale and fleshless that they almost seemed translucent as she held them out to me. I noted a very handsome jet-stone in her ring as I bowed over it.

'You have a message for me, citizen?' Her face was unsmiling and, glimpsing the smirking handmaiden behind her at the entrance-way, I wondered how much of my conversation with Modesta had been overheard.

However, it was too late to think of that. 'You are Cyra, wife of Lavinius?' I murmured to the ring, mentally thanking Modesta that I knew the name, at least. 'I am the citizen Libertus. But I bring no message from your husband, I'm afraid. My patron Marcus Aurelius Septimus instructed me to come.'

No answer.

I straightened up and met an icy glare. 'I was just explaining all this to your maidservant. I'm very sorry if I caused her to delay, but – far from failing to look after me – she was attempting to understand my task. Please do not punish her on my account.'

The shrewd eyes thawed a little, but the manner was still as unbending as a sword. 'And why should His Excellence instruct you to come here?' she said, without the shadow of a smile.

'He hopes that I can help you to find your missing niece.'

'I see!' She gestured to the female attendant that I had noticed at the door. 'A stool here, slave. I will listen to what this man has to say.' The girl came gliding in, and from behind the table took a second folding seat, which she placed for her mistress in what little space remained. Cyra sat down and – dismissing the slave-girl with an impatient wave – indicated that I should do the same. 'If you can find Audelia, citizen, I will offer a private blessing-tablet to the gods for you.'

Encouraged, I assayed a tiny joke. 'Offering information would be more use to me,' I said.

She did not smile. 'I don't know what useful information I can give. I have not seen my niece since she was two years old and I was not a great deal older – seven or eight, perhaps.' She saw my startled look. 'My sister, of course, had moved away from home and was living with her husband in Londinium by then.'

I was doing a little calculation in my head. It was not uncommon in Roman families for a daughter to be married at fourteen years of age, but even so – allowing for the birth of Audelia . . . 'Your sister was a good deal older than you, then, I presume?'

Some might have thought this was a compliment, but the look that Cyra gave me would have withered stone. 'Nine years my senior. Not so very much. My mother had more children in the years between – all boys – but the women of my family are not good at sons, it seems. Only we two females survived. My father was always cursing that he had no male as heir, though to have his granddaughter accepted as Vestal Virgin was some slight consolation to him, I believe.'

'Yet your father did not send his own girls to serve the hearth-goddess?'

She gave a bitter smile. 'He would have liked to. There is no doubt of that. But a Vestal Virgin must be perfect in all ways – physically as well as morally of course – and my sister had poor sight, the result of a spotted fever when she was very young. They would not permit her even to enter the lottery for a place.'

'And you?'

She gave a thin-lipped smile. 'They would never have accepted me, even if I had been fair enough of face to qualify. My poor mother died in bearing me and a girl must have two living parents – both freeborn Roman citizens – to be accepted at the shrine. So you see, we were not good enough! That only encouraged my father in his view. He did not regard daughters as of much account in any case. Indeed – perhaps because I cost my mother's life – he could hardly bear to have me in the house.'

'Yet he left you property, I understand?'

'How do you know that?' She shot a glance at me. 'Your wealthy patron told you, I suppose?' I did not disabuse her, and she went swiftly on. 'As it happens, that report is true – though I cannot see what concern it is of yours, or what this has to do with the disappearance of my niece.'

'If Audelia was kidnapped, as her bridegroom fears,' I said gently, 'the wealth of her family may have much to do with it.'

That sobered her. 'I see. I'm sorry, citizen, I concede you have a point. Forgive me if I spoke more sharply than I meant. It was my father—'

We were interrupted by a tapping at the door, and Modesta reappeared with the promised tray of fruit, and a jug of something that looked like watered wine – a Roman drink of which I am not particularly fond. She set this down before me and I waved aside the drink, but – not wishing to seem churlish – I selected a few grapes before I turned back to Cyra.

'Your father . . . you were about to say, I think?' I prompted, tipping back my head to bite from my grape-bunch as I'd seen Marcus do.

'It was at his funeral that I last saw my sister and her family.' She had begun to fidget with the items on the desk, lining up the seal-stamp and the little pots of soot, gum and vinegar, like a rank of soldiers, as though this would somehow help her to control her evident emotion. 'And afterwards, on the steps of the basilica, when the will was read.'

'And you two girls inherited his lands?'

She gave a rueful smile. 'This part of it, at least – the rest of his fortune went to distant male relatives in Rome. Even then, as the younger sister, I got the smaller part, and of course my inheritance was managed for me by a male cousin, till I wed. My sister was married – as I said before – and already had a child, so she got the villa and the larger piece of land, though in return she had to swear that she would offer Audelia to the Vestal temple to be trained, if there was no son to take charge of the estate.'

'I take it there was not?' I bit into a grape.

Cyra shook her head. 'She bore a boy infant, three years afterwards, but it did not live and afterwards my sister did not conceive again. I told you that my family was not good with sons.'

I could not answer for a moment. The fruit – like my hostess's tone – was uncomfortably sour. 'But you do have a daughter, I believe.'

Cyra got abruptly to her feet and turned away, as if to hide the hurt and anger on her face. 'To the disappointment of my husband, citizen. Of course I was lucky that he agreed to marry me at all – my inheritance was hardly generous, scarcely enough to make a decent dowry. For a time, I feared I'd never wed. Fortunately my guardian found Lavinius for me. He was a widower, whose first wife had been barren and he was prepared to take me so he could have an heir. I did provide one, in the end, though even then it took me many years – and many sacrifices to the gods – to bear a child that lived. I believe that otherwise he would have cut me off in a divorce. Of course, with my ill-fortune, it turned out to be a girl and now I've had to hand her to the Vestal temple, too.'

'She has gone to be a Vestal?' I was genuinely surprised. Modesta had spoken as if the child was young, but a Vestal novice must be six years old at least and cannot be more than ten. I did a calculation in my head. If Cyra was five years older than her niece, who had just completed thirty years of

service at the Vestal House, then – even if Audelia had joined
the Vestals young, and Cyra's daughter was joining very late
– Cyra must have been all of thirty when the child was born.
No wonder the babe had seemed a present from the gods.
'Another provision of your father's will?'

She shook her head. 'This was my husband's doing. It was
the one way a daughter could bring esteem to him, he said,
without the necessity of giving half our land as dowry payment
to someone else's son. Of course my father had given him the
idea.'

'So you sent her to the shrine,' I said.

'Not I, citizen!' The voice was icy cold. 'It was a shock to
me. I begged Lavinius not to let her go. But he formally offered
her to the pontifex, who came and ritually dragged her from
my knee, and it is the priest who is accompanying her on her
way, not us. So my daughter is not legally even a member of
this family any more. My only living child, after years of
barrenness. All my other children died in infancy – perhaps
it is a family failing in some way. But she is on her way to
the temple as we speak.'

'I see. But surely her place is not yet a certainty? Did you
not say something about a lottery?'

She gave a bitter laugh. 'If a well-born citizen offers his
daughter to the shrine, and she meets the criteria of perfect
form and two living parents of sufficient degree, she is usually
accepted without the need for drawing straws – especially if
a dowry is provided with the girl. As of course it was. Lavinius
saw to that. My daughter will take the same sum with her
thirty years from now, when she retires, but until that time the
Vestal House will have the use of it.'

'Just as her husband would have done if she had wed,' I
murmured.

Cyra cast a furious glance at me. 'And now she never will!'
She gestured to Modesta to fill the empty cup which was still
lying used on the tray, and when it was brimming she picked
it up herself. That was astonishing enough: it is not customary
for a well-bred Roman matron to drink wine at all, except at
a banquet – and especially not before a male guest in the
mid-afternoon – but Cyra raised the cup and, far from sipping,
drained it at a gulp. 'So I'll not see her again. I won't survive

another thirty years and my husband will never take me to the
Vestal shrine. If I had borne a son, it would be a different
thing.'

I could not like this woman – she was bitter and resentful
– but I couldn't help feeling some sympathy for her. I tried
to turn the subject to more cheerful things while, of course,
continuing to probe. 'But when she returns she will be provided
for. Not only will she have her dowry sum to spend, and of
course the famous pension which the state provides for retired
Vestals, but I believe that there will also be a house for her.
You are building on that piece of land, I think?'

She brightened, just a little. 'We are. It is a much finer villa
than this one, too. You must have seen it, as you travelled
here?'

I hadn't. I had ridden in the litter with the curtains drawn.
But I did not tell her that. All I said was, 'It must be close to
finished.'

She almost smiled. 'There are a few rooms to plaster and
a bathhouse to complete, but we could move in tomorrow if
my husband chose. Indeed we might have done so earlier,
except that Audelia wished to hold the wedding here. I believe
that Publius intends to take her off to Rome, to meet what
family he has, as soon as they are wed – and we will certainly
have moved by the time that they return. Supposing that you
find her. Where will you begin?'

I could not confess that I had no idea, but that was how I
felt. If I had harboured any notion that there might have been
a motive for this family to want Audelia gone – or even dead
– it seemed that I was wrong. However, there was still one
avenue that I might explore. 'I understand that you have the
carriage-driver in the house? The one who was driving when
she disappeared? Perhaps it would be possible for me to speak
to him?'

The violence of her answer startled me. 'Publius sent him
back here – though why I cannot think. The fellow is clearly
a liar and a thief. I told my husband before we hired him that
the man was dangerous – I did not like the look of him at all
– but of course Lavinius took no notice of my fears.'

'You knew the fellow, then?' I was thinking so hard about
the problem that I plucked off another grape.

'Well, not exactly knew, but he had been here to the house. He took Lavinia to Corinium, of course.'

I could make no sense of this. 'But I thought—'

Cyra cut me off. 'My daughter was most anxious to see the bride before she wed, but the pontifex insisted that today – as soon as the birthday feast was over – he must take her to the shrine. So we found a compromise. She couldn't travel in the same carriage with the pontifex anyway, of course, for the sake of decency, and Audelia was due to spend last night in Corinium. So it was arranged that Lavinia should leave here yesterday and spend Audelia's wedding-eve with her and learn a little about Vestal life.'

'At the official mansio, I suppose?' I asked. A Vestal Virgin would surely merit preferential lodgings at the official inn. I knew the mansio at Corinium. I determined to call there and ask questions if I could.

'A Vestal Virgin at a military inn? Of course not, citizen.' Her tone of voice dismissed the fine official inns as though they might be dens of vice. 'We chose a respectable private household known to my husband from his visits there. They let out rooms sometimes. They did have other guests last night, they said, but the wife gave up her own room and thus they managed to accommodate Lavinia – who drove there in a hired *raeda* yesterday.'

'And the same driver was to bring Audelia back here? Rather than use the temple coach to bring her all the way?'

She gave a wry smile. 'Lavinius suggested the arrangement himself. He found a driver with a raeda for hire, who was to take Lavinia to Corinium, to the lodging-house. The pontifex was to join her in the temple there today, and tomorrow my daughter was to travel on towards the shrine, using the Vestal *pilentum* which Audelia had used, while the raeda brought the bride the last few miles to us. It saved a double journey for both conveyances and – as my husband pointed out – the cost of hiring the raeda any further than he must.'

I nodded. 'So your *raedarius* was to bring the bride back here? Or rather to Glevum to meet up with Publius?'

She nodded. 'That was the disadvantage of the scheme. Being a hired raeda, and not the Vestal coach, it could not enter the town in daylight hours. But Audelia consented very willingly – this was all arranged before she left the shrine – and she arranged to meet Publius at the games. My husband thought it would create a pretty little spectacle to crown the day. She would make a public entrance there – they always have a symbolic seat for Vestals anyway – and Publius would announce the nuptials to the crowd. Then the raeda could bring them both back here to solemnize the wedding before our banquet guests, and we would pay the raedarius his dues.'

'A handsome fee?' I queried. I was a little doubtful of this raedarius.

Cyra clearly shared my thoughts. 'We would have paid him well. It was not a very complicated task we asked of him, but he seems to have failed to look after my niece or her possessions either. Worse that that. My chief slave believes the fellow had been plotting for this all along – hoping to receive a portion of the ransom, he suggests. I'm bound to say he's half-persuaded me. Who else would know the value of his passenger? This can't be an accident. The deepest dungeon in the jail is too good for men like that. I don't know why Publius did not send for the town-guard and have the fellow arrested and locked up in the town.'

'I gather this happened at the public gate, where there would be dozens of people looking on. Possibly Publius hoped to be discreet.' I wondered suddenly whose suggestion that had been.

'Discreet! It could hardly have been less discreet, from what I hear of it. The raedarius was bellowing to everyone around, swearing by all the gods that he was innocent, and didn't know that she was missing till he was at Glevum gates.'

I bit the grape I'd selected. It was particularly sour and I began to wish I had a little wine to gulp. 'So how did the raedarius get here from the town? I presume he did not drive?' I managed to say through teeth that had been set on edge.

She shook her head. 'He came here in our gig. It was waiting at the gates to bring Lavinius home – he is too old to walk from Glevum now – and apparently Publius saw it and recognized the slave-boy who was driving it. He had already travelled in the gig the other evening when he came here to dine, and of course the gig-slave knew Publius by sight. So, when the patrician told him to tie the raedarius up and bring him here, the boy obeyed at once.'

'Tie him up? With what?'

'With his own tunic-belt, I understand. He had to gag the captive and bind his feet, he said, otherwise the fellow would have jumped out of the gig. But talk to the raedarius yourself. Modesta will take you when you have finished those.' She gestured to the grapes.

I needed no encouragement to desist from eating more. I put down the remainder of the bunch and got quickly to my feet. 'Madam, I will go to him at once, and not detain you further. You have been most helpful. Thank you for your patience – if you still intend to have a banquet here tonight you must have much to see to in the house.'

Cyra extended her ringed hand to me again. 'Then I will leave you to your questioning, and see if there's a message from my husband yet. I sent him a letter asking what I am to do about the preparations for the feast. I hope I get some sort of answer very soon. I'd better send the gig back to wait for him, I suppose.' And still frowning, she stalked out of the room, with her personal attendant trailing after her. Fiscus, who was still positioned at the door, peered in to see if he was wanted now.

'Come with me, citizen.' Modesta beamed at me. She seemed to regard me as her personal charge. 'I will attend you. Your servant can wait here. I'll come back for the tray.'

I had no trouble in accepting that, and motioned to Fiscus to stay where he was, to his evident dismay. Meanwhile the slave-girl led the way across the atrium again; it was looking very handsome, now the garlands were in place and all the lamps were lit, though slaves were still burnishing the bronze statues as we passed. Watched by a dozen curious pairs of eyes, we went out to the courtyard, round the colonnaded walk and out through the back gate into the stable-yard.

When we were safely out of sight and sound of everyone, Modesta turned to me and whispered, confidentially, 'I hope that fruit was not too horrible, I'm sure it tasted sharp, but the chief slave said the best was wanted for the feast.'

I was emboldened by the little confidence. I answered with a smile. 'It is of no account. But there is one thing that slightly troubles me. If your master has a private gig to use, why did he hire a raeda to take his daughter yesterday? Would it not have been far safer to have used his own?'

She giggled, clapping a skinny hand across her mouth. 'Oh, citizen, you haven't seen the private gig. No more than an open carriage, with a single wooden seat – apart from the driver – and it has no roof. They could never have sent Lavinia all the way in that, much less expect a Vestal Virgin to ride home in it! Supposing it had rained? It would have made a public spectacle of her. In any case, there was too much luggage to get into the gig and – of course – there was Lavinia's nursemaid travelling with her too.'

'She did not have a manservant to guard her on her way?'

She grinned at me. 'She will have one from tomorrow, when the pontifex arrives. As to yesterday, my master chose this carriage driver most especially, because he was particularly young and strong and could protect them if he needed to. Fierce-looking too – or so the mistress said. She didn't like him from the start. She's had him shut in there.'

She crossed to a long low building which was clearly the sleeping-quarters of the slaves. I half-expected her to go inside, but she passed the door and made for a smaller outbuilding nearby, with a row of stout doors along the length of it.

Outside the last door she stopped and looked at me. 'He's in here, citizen. I'll undo the bolt.'

SIX

The room revealed was a sort of storage area, with not even a window-space of any kind – nothing but bare walls, rows of heaped-up bulging sacks, and a floor of trodden earth from where a youngish man was blinking up at me, clearly blinded by the sudden light. He was lying rather awkwardly on his left-hand side, on a narrow strip of floor between the nearest piles of sacks. His hands were tied behind him and his feet were fettered to a stout iron loop that was set into the wall.

I took a step towards him and he tried to lift his head, but fell back with a groan. I saw that the rope which bound his arms was also tethered to the ankle-chain, so that he could not move or ease a single limb without experiencing agony. The shoulders of his tunic were stained with stripes of blood. Someone had whipped him savagely, by the look of it.

'What do you want? And what are you doing here? You're not Lavinius.' His voice was weak with pain, but he was sullen too. 'Have you come to torment me a bit more?'

I was aware of Modesta, behind me, craning to look in. I gestured her to stand a little further off and moved to squat down on a lumpy sack where he could see my face. Inside, the room was dank and smelt strongly of something old and vegetal: overripe turnips or damp nuts, perhaps.

'I've come to ask about your missing passenger. She was a Vestal Virgin, as of course you know, and a most important person. Far more important than either you or me – you cannot expect her relatives to simply let it pass.'

With a painful effort he turned his head away (almost the only part of his body that he could move at all) and maintained a stubborn silence. It was a foolish gesture, in the circumstance – anyone from the household would have had him flogged for it – but I could not fault his spirit or his bravery.

I tried again, though I was talking to his averted cheek. 'You were responsible for delivering her safely to her bridegroom, and in that you failed. You can hardly be surprised if they have locked you up.'

In fact I felt some sympathy with the prisoner. This was a miserable place to be chained up but, judging by the hoop to which the ankle-chains were fixed and the expert way that his bonds had been arranged, he was not the first to be incarcerated here. This was clearly where errant household slaves were held while they were awaiting serious punishment. Most large establishments have some provision of the kind – though in general offenders do not have to share their prison with stores of vegetables.

The captive muttered sullenly, 'I've already told them everything I know. I saw the wretched woman get into the seat and put the shutters up – that was the last I saw of her.'

'And you drove straight to Glevum after that?'

No answer.

A sudden inspiration came to me. This man was almost certainly a Celt – as I was myself – but here was I approaching him in formal Roman dress. I could not tell for certain what his clan might be, because he wore the now-ubiquitous short brown Roman tunic instead of traditional Celtic breeches made of tribal plaid, but he was fairish and I guessed that he came from the local Dubunni. I, of course, had been captured further south and dragged to Glevum by a slave trader, so our respective dialects were no doubt different, but I was fairly sure that he would understand me if I used my native tongue and I hoped he might be more inclined to answer if I did.

But first I had to win his confidence. 'Modesta,' I said, rising to my feet. 'Fetch the chief slave and tell him to come here, and bring a knife to free these bonds a bit. I cannot usefully question a man who is in too much pain to speak.'

The girl looked startled but she scuttled off.

I squatted on the sack beside the man again and said softly, in Celtic, 'Raedarius, I too have been given an unwelcome task. The bridegroom and my patron – who are hugely rich, important men – have charged me with finding out what happened to the bride. If she didn't come to Glevum, she must be somewhere else, and if I can find her (which I am very doubtful of) it might be possible to get you out of here.'

A moment's silence, before he answered in the same tongue. 'You would do that, citizen?'

'For a fellow Celt. Especially if we prove you had no part in it. But I can't do anything if you will not assist. So I ask a second time – did you come straight to Glevum, when she'd got into the coach?'

He made a huge effort and turned his face to me again. When he spoke, his voice was tight with pain. 'I'd like to say so, citizen, but it is not quite true. I've thought about it half a dozen times. She was sitting in the raeda, I assisted her myself, but then I had to go upstairs and get her other box. It was a large one, very heavy – full of gifts she had been given, I believe – and she wanted it to ride inside the coach with her. She already had her jewel box in there for security.'

I nodded. Carrying valuable goods inside was not unusual – most travellers did it if they could as it helped discourage thieves. 'So you went up for the box?'

'Exactly, citizen. And that was the last time I can absolutely swear to seeing her, because the box was so heavy that I could not manage it. I had to send for two of the house-slaves to bring it down for me. Her handmaiden watched them put it in the coach while I saw to the horse.'

I interrupted him. 'Ah, the maidservant, who disappeared as well? So she was with Audelia in Corinium? You can vouch for that?'

'Of course she had a maid there,' he said, reluctantly. 'An important lady like that would not travel far alone. Indeed, for several days – apparently – she had a mounted guard as well.'

'So what became of him?'

'He left this morning – going the other way, I understand. She had left some things behind the day before and the rider was sent back to recover them.'

I felt at once this was significant. 'It must have been something of great importance!' I exclaimed.

Despite his discomfort he managed a wry smile. 'She seemed to think so, citizen. She was quite distraught. A pair of special wedding slippers, I believe it was. She did not discover the loss till after we arrived last night, I understand, when she went to show them to Lavinia and found they were not there.'

Wedding slippers! I had not expected that, I had been

imagining the loss of jewels or gold. But this was a more endearing picture of Audelia. Although she was marrying so late, she would be a virgin still – Vestals who infringed their vows in that respect faced an appalling death – and like any first-time bride, naturally she'd want the special trappings of the day. The shoes would be especially important to a Vestal, too, since most of her other clothes looked like a bride's in any case.

I remembered the only time that I had seen a Vestal was when I was in Londinium once. I had actually commented that she looked dressed for marriage, then: the same special hairstyle divided into six, the light-coloured stola and the carefully knotted band around the waist which can only be untied for a husband – or a deity. It was explained to me that these were all adopted when the priestess joined the hearth as a sign of her being spiritually wedded to the shrine. So only the distinctive saffron-colour of the bridal veil and shoes, instead of the white versions which she usually wore, would mark Audelia's marriage-day. 'No wonder the poor woman was distressed at leaving them behind,' I said.

'It was the maidservant who was to blame for it, of course,' the driver said, moving his shoulders slightly as if to ease the ache. 'The Vestal was so proud of them, and so excited that she was at last to be a bride, the girl was sent to get them from the box at every stop they made, to show them off. Only this time, it seems she forgot to put them back.'

I looked at him suspiciously. 'How do you know all this?'

'Puella, the maidservant, told me so herself.'

'You talked to her?'

He made a woeful face. 'That box took up so much room there was no space for her inside – there was less room in my carriage than the one they'd had before – so she had to come and ride with me on the bench-seat in front.' I realized that, although speech was agony, he was now keen to help me if he could. 'Of course, she swore that it was not her fault – she'd put the shoes back as she always did – and someone must have moved them afterwards.' He caught his breath in pain. 'But of course she couldn't have. Took them out to look at them herself, I rather think. They were finest leather and quite exquisite, she said, a parting present from a grateful, barren

wife for whom the Vestal had once offered sacrifice – and
who had then gone on to bear a son. Audelia was heartbroken
to find that they had gone.'

'Had Puella been guilty of such a lapse before? Indeed, had
she been with the Vestal very long?' I was suddenly suspicious.
It occurred to me that attendant servants at a shrine are usually
slaves of the temple as a whole, and not owned by any individual. I wondered how much Audelia knew about her careless
maid.

'Acquired for the journey, as I understand. A gift from
another grateful supplicant, which only made the situation
worse. Puella was a pretty little thing, but you could see that
she was terrified. She'd been promised freedom when she got
here, I believe, and obviously she feared that she had lost her
chance and that a fearful beating was awaiting her instead. I
think she was quite glad of the excuse to ride outside with
me, despite the fact that it was raining heavily.'

These wedding shoes were interesting me. Was it possible
the maid had left them out deliberately? Or had she packed
them, as she claimed she had, and someone else had really
moved them later on? But either way, what purpose did it
serve? And then it struck me: it removed the guard.

'Who suggested that Audelia should send the rider back?'
I asked.

It was more and more painful for him even to draw breath.
'Citizen, I fear I cannot answer that. I was in the stable,
sleeping near my horses as I always do, to keep an eye on
them. By the time I was sent for the decision had been made.'
He winced. 'Have you nearly finished with your
questioning?'

'Not quite. If we hope to find Audelia you must tell me all
you can. You did not think it strange that they sent away the
mounted guard?'

He took a sobbing breath. 'Not really, citizen. I was there
to guard her the remainder of the way – after all I had
guarded Lavinia until then. And anyway, what else was there
to do, if Audelia really wanted to have her slippers for the
marriage feast? If the rider set off at first light there was a
good chance that he would manage to retrieve the shoes in
time, especially if he brought them directly to this house: a

man on horseback can travel twice as quickly as a coach.
It wasn't my idea, but if I'd thought of it, I might well have
suggested it myself.'

It seemed a cruelty to ask him any more, but I had no choice.
'So where had Audelia left the shoes?' I asked. 'Another
lodging-house? I understood that she had only assented to this
stop, because the owners were known to her uncle's family.'

'There were other stops, of course. It took her several days
to make the journey from the shrine, I understand.'

But of course it had, I thought. It's not as if she were an
Imperial messenger, with relays of fresh horses every mile or
two. 'A Vestal pilentum is notoriously slow and dignified,' I
said. 'I suppose he would have to stop somewhere overnight
each time. Doubtless the family had arranged it all.'

'Glad to stop too, I shouldn't be surprised, in an old-fashioned
coach like that. I saw it in the stable-yard and had a look at
it.' Talk of his trade brought animation to his face. 'Two horses
– like a raeda, but much more cumbersome. A little bit more
padded, but extremely slow.' He was so engrossed that he
almost tried to rise, only to sink back with a painful groan.
When he spoke again, he sounded more subdued. 'Puella said
they stopped at several households on the way – most of them
friends or distant relatives of Lavinius. It was all arranged
before they left the temple, anyway. A Vestal Virgin doesn't
stop at common inns. But I can't tell you anything about all
that. I only collected her at Corinium.'

There was a movement at the doorway and Modesta sidled
in, looking in astonishment at the pair of us speaking in a
language which she clearly didn't understand.

'Well?' I said in Latin. 'Have you news for us?'

'Citizen, the steward's on his way,' she said in the same
tongue. 'I thought you ought to know. There has been a message
that the banquet will take place after all. The master and the
bridegroom are already on their way, Publius managed to use
his influence and borrowed a carriage to bring them here as
soon as the games ended. They will not be very long. When
they come, I'll bring them out to you.' She darted me a timid
little smile. 'Don't let the master catch you talking foreign
languages, though, or he'll think you two are plotting and
chain you up as well.'

The raedarius made an outraged, strangled sound. 'But . . . !'

I kicked his leg to warn him that he should hold his tongue. I knew what he had been tempted to retort: that Latin, if anything, was the foreign language here, and that what we were speaking was her ancestral tongue, but it is not wise to voice an argument like that – especially if you are at the mercy of a high-born Roman at the time.

I need not have worried. The captive took my hint and said not another word until the maidservant had sketched a bow and scuttled off.

SEVEN

turned back to the prisoner. 'You heard her, raeda-driver. We don't have very long.' I leaned towards him, settling myself more firmly on the sack. 'And the facts are against you, as you must see yourself. Let's just go over all of it again, in case there is something extra that comes into your mind.' I was convinced that he was hiding something, but I could not see what. 'You saw Audelia get into the coach, but when the slaves brought down the box you set off without checking that she was still a passenger?'

He looked at me helplessly. 'I didn't have to check. I knew that she was there. She was talking to some other people who had come out of the inn – they said goodbye to her and I heard her voice calling to tell me to drive on. And that was it. When we got to Glevum, she had disappeared.'

'There were no unexpected hold-ups on the way?'

He shook his head. 'None that I can think of,' he said reluctantly.

'Not even for a moment? Not of any kind at all?'

I saw a look of resignation cross the anguished face. 'Well, now you come to mention it, there was one incident. It was only a few moments, and I cannot see how anyone would have the chance to seize her then, but we did have to stop at one point to let some troops march by.'

So why had he attempted to disguise the fact? The stop made sense, of course. Marching soldiers always have priority – that is why the Romans built the roads, and why they are always called the 'military routes' – so all civilian traffic must wait till they go by: it is only by concession that we can use the roads at all. But of course a marching cohort draws the eyes of any spectators, which might create an opportunity for a kidnapper to seize a passenger while everyone's attention was elsewhere. Yet marching troops are subject to orders from Imperial command. A kidnapper could hardly have arranged that in advance. Or could he?

'And you did not get down to check your passenger and let her stretch her legs?' I knew from Marcus that this was sometimes done.

'I sent the maidservant,' he muttered, painfully. 'But she came back and said the removable shutters were across the window-space, and that was a signal that her mistress did not wish to be disturbed.'

'The shutters were in place?' The fact was news to me. 'This did not surprise you? It must be dark in there.'

He was so startled by the question that he tried to lift his head. 'You are clearly not a raeda-driver, citizen. It's just what you'd expect. Most ladies prefer to travel with the shutters up – it keeps the rain out in the wet, and in the dry it keeps the dust at bay.'

I mentally conceded that this might be true. I once heard my patron's wife say something much the same: complaining that on a journey from Aqua Sulis, when they'd hired a coach, the jolting and darkness make her feel quite ill, but it was a price worth paying to keep out the dust.

I was aware that I was uncomfortable myself, from sitting on something damp and lumpy in the sack. I moved my weight again. 'You did not urge Audelia to get down and take the air?'

The driver answered readily enough, although the effort still made him catch his breath with pain. 'This was a priestess, citizen. I would not presume to urge her to do anything, and obviously she would not want to let herself be seen. You don't meet many Vestal Virgins on the road. Common people would have crowded round to gawp when we were forced to stop, even if she'd simply had the shutters down.'

'Supposing that she was really in the raeda at the time.'

'But citizen, where else could she possibly have been? If anyone had snatched her, I would certainly have seen. I didn't leave . . .' He tailed into silence.

'You didn't leave the raeda? That is what you were about to say, I think. And then you suddenly thought better of the claim. You did leave the carriage for a moment, then?'

His voice, which had not been strong at any time, was faint and laboured now. 'I suppose I shall have to tell you, citizen. At the time there seemed no harm in it. It was only for a

moment, and I left the maid in charge – just while I crossed
the road to buy a basket for my wife.' His eyes beseeched me.
'Don't tell Lavinius this, or he will have me whipped to death.
I am newly married, and we expect a child, and . . .'

'The basket?' I persisted.

'The hold-up happened at a crossing point, where there are
several little rundown cottages. At one of them there lives an
ancient crone who from time to time picks osiers from the
stream and weaves them into baskets which she sells at the
front door. Lavinius had paid me half the money in advance,
and . . .' He trailed off again.

'So you went and bought one, leaving your precious
passenger unguarded and alone?'

His tone of voice was almost piteous. 'It cost no extra time.
We had been obliged to stop in any case and it only took an
instant – I didn't even stop to haggle with the crone, I just
paid what she was asking. And there seemed to be no harm
– when I got back Puella was still sitting in her place, terrified
of moving or making any sound lest her mistress should awaken
and find more fault with her. I even asked her whether everything was well – and she said it was exactly as it was when
I had left.'

Which might be a very clever choice of words, I thought.
I was more and more interested in this serving-girl. 'And when
you got to Glevum and found Audelia gone, this girl went
missing too? At the same time you think?'

He gave a painful shrug. 'I didn't see her vanish, either.
She was on the raeda at the front with me and I told her to
stay there and watch my basket while I let the horses drink
and went and tied them up. I only left her for a moment, while
I was doing that. When I came back she was no longer on the
cart. I supposed that she had gone to open up the door, but
when I got round there I found the bride had gone.'

'And Puella?'

He looked uncomfortable. 'She was nowhere to be found
– and neither was my basket. I could not believe my eyes. I
looked in all directions but there was no sign of them. I did
not know what to do, so I found a passing messenger and sent
the news to Publius at once.'

'You did not search for them?' I was incredulous.

'Where could I begin? I asked around, of course, but none of the other drivers had noticed anything – they were more interested in the wine-stall that was opening up outside the gates. Of course a slave-girl with a basket is not remarkable, especially on a feast-day like today – but a Vestal Virgin would have raised an eye or two. The two of them had simply disappeared – and Audelia's jewel box with them.'

'And what about the box that was inside the coach?'

'Still in the raeda, as far as I'm aware. Not even a skilful kidnapper could have taken that – it was far too heavy for anyone to move without attracting huge attention to themselves. I tried to tell Publius about it being there, but he would not listen – just had me gagged and bound and dragged away – though I think he left a servant to keep an eye on things—'

He broke off as a squeaky voice interrupted us. 'Citizen?' It was Modesta once again. I got uncomfortably to my feet and went towards her, feeling rather stiff and aware of a damp patch on my toga, where I had been sitting on the sack.

'Have you brought the chief slave to free this man?' I enquired.

She was staring at me goggle-eyed. 'He's on his way here now. And the master and Publius have just arrived so they are going to come and speak to you themselves. Here they are in fact.'

I looked where she was pointing and saw a small group of people now approaching us, coming from the direction of the house. There were two 'purple-stripers' – wealthy Roman citizens in patrician dress. Each of them was accompanied by a page while, dancing along a step or two behind, attempting the near-impossible feat of keeping up with them while simultaneously bowing at every other step, was the beaky steward that I'd noticed in the atrium earlier.

The chief slave had lost his air of cool authority and now seemed to be explaining something to his owner earnestly, with frantic gesticulations of his hands. He turned to Modesta. 'Your mistress requires you. You're wanted at the house.'

She gave me an apologetic glance, as if reluctant to leave me unattended, but she scuttled off and I turned to meet the newcomers.

I recognized the stouter citizen as Publius, from having seen him at the feast, but I realized that I had also seen Lavinius before. He was not a resident of Glevum, of course – and therefore not a member of the local curia – but I had noticed him from time to time at the basilica, consorting with various important councillors. He was not an easy man to overlook: a strikingly tall, thin individual, whose patrician hawk-nose was made more prominent by sharp, clean-shaven cheeks. With his balding head and fringe of whitish hair, he might have been good-looking in a Roman kind of way, except that age had given his shoulders a slight stoop and his face an expression of ill-disguised contempt for lesser men.

He was turning that expression in my direction now. 'You are this pavement-maker I have been hearing of?' His voice was low and colourless, but strangely echoing, like someone speaking in a sepulchre.

I had learned from long experience how to respond to wealthy men like this. I dropped immediately down onto one knee and bowed my head as though I were truly as low in status as his words implied. 'The citizen Longinus Flavius Libertus, at your service, mightiness,' I murmured. It was a pretence at grovelling, but in fact it made a point. I was a Roman citizen and therefore entitled to respect – as my formal use of the full three Roman names was deliberately designed to emphasize.

Lavinius, however, was not impressed by this. He waved a bony hand in vague dismissal of my words. 'Well whatever your name is, pavement-maker, do get up from there.' As I clambered stiffly to my feet, he ran a pair of faded pale-blue eyes over me, from my now-grimy toga to my greying hair. 'Your patron, Marcus Septimus, commended you to me and seems to think that you might be of help. I suppose he knows what he is speaking of, although to look at you, I must say I'm surprised. If we are dealing with armed kidnappers and bandits, as seems probable, I can't see what use a man your age will be. I had expected someone with a bit more strength to him.' He made a little tutting sound against his perfect teeth. 'Still, it is not for me to question what His Excellence suggests. I have agreed to allow you to assist. I think you understand the problem – my niece has disappeared. Where exactly are you hoping to begin?'

It was hardly an encouraging start to dealing with the man, but I dusted down my toga and said doggedly, 'By having this raeda-driver's bonds released a bit, so I can question him. I sent to make the request to your steward earlier.'

The long brow darkened. 'So I understand. Though I can't imagine what you hope to gain.' He looked at the raedarius, lying helpless on the floor. 'This wretch is culpable of care-lessness at least, and possibly much worse. More sensible to have him tortured till he tells us everything.'

I said (as I have said to Marcus many times), 'Flog him and you may force an admission out of him – some men will agree to anything you choose, simply provided that the torturer will stop. However, I am more concerned with getting at the truth – that is the only way to find your niece alive.' Even supposing that she's not already dead, I added inwardly, though I knew better than to voice that thought aloud. Lavinius was already looking unconvinced.

It was Publius who unexpectedly came to my support. 'He may be right, you know, Lavinius my friend. I've been witness to such things in Rome. Evidence extorted is not always true.'

I could see Lavinius wavering, and I pressed the point. 'What I need from this raedarius, you see, are little details of the trip – perhaps things that did not seem important at the time, but which in retrospect may be significant. He tells me, for instance, that they had to stop to let a legion of marching troops go past. That might be the place where the kidnapping took place, and not in Glevum as we thought at first—'

'So,' Lavinius interrupted curtly. 'Why ease his limbs for that? It seems to me that a modicum of pain has already spurred his memory.'

'If we loosen his bonds there may be more that he recalls – a man can't think clearly about details like that when his mind is focussed on his suffering.'

'Have them cut the bonds, Lavinius' Publius urged. I'd obviously swayed him by my argument, 'I'm willing to try anything to find Audelia. And what is there to lose? This pavement-maker has already learned something that we did not know before. Nothing that your steward's flogging managed to obtain has, up to now, been of any use at all.'

I turned to my unexpected ally with a smile. 'Respected

citizen, if you are really willing to try anything, the really useful thing would be to have this driver take me to the place where he was compelled to stop because the troops went past. If he can identify the spot, it is possible I can discover something there. Though there is still the question of the maidservant—'

Lavinius's snort of outrage interrupted me again. 'You can't mean that you expect me not just to loose the bonds – though, Jove knows that is extraordinary enough – but actually to let this fellow go? And more than that, to give his raeda back and actively encourage him to drive away from town in it? Citizen, you have a very strange idea of how Roman justice works.'

Actually I had a pretty clear idea, and I could see that I was likely to end up in court myself – charged with conspiring to help a prisoner escape – if I persisted in this argument. I was about to say that I'd abandoned the idea, when Publius again spoke up in my defence.

'Perhaps we should try it his way, Lavinius, my friend. There seems to be very little else that we can do, and this is at least something positive. The place where the raeda stopped might well be relevant, but it will not be easy to identify the spot, unless the driver is there to point it out. And, as the citizen suggests, the easiest way of him achieving that is for the raedarius himself to take him there. I'll bear responsibility, if trouble comes of it.'

I was warming to this fellow, despite his podgy pompous looks. Perhaps it was his open nature which had won Audelia. I would have liked to ask him how he came to know his bride, but Lavinius was already saying angrily, 'I can't agree to that. It was the pavement-maker citizen who suggested this, and he alone must be responsible. I think the whole idea is ludicrous, but you are the bridegroom, and my guest besides, so of course the choice is yours. If you wish me to indulge this citizen in his unlikely plans, then I must comply. But only if the pavement-maker will pledge a hundred *aureii* on the driver's safe return.' He cast a triumphant, cunning look at me. 'And I give him fair warning that if he lets the man escape then I will drag him through the courts for full payment of the debt – and the value of whatever jewels were lost as well.'

I gasped. A hundred aureii was a huge amount of gold

– more than I had ever set eyes on in my life, and certainly a good deal more than my whole estate was worth. The mere suggestion took my breath away. Of course I realized that Lavinius was perfectly aware of how I would react, and this was simply a way of making sure that I declined the trip. But before I had recovered my wits enough to utter the legal formula required to refuse a bargain and so make it void, my defender Publius had intervened and was clapping me on the shoulder with a friendly smile.

'Well then, pavement-maker . . .' Before I realized what was happening he had seized my unsuspecting hand and thrust it into Lavinius's bony grasp. 'There! You have shaken hands and I have witnessed it, so the contract between you now has legal force. Come, steward, cut the driver's bonds and let him go.' He turned to Lavinius with his chubby smile. 'If His Excellence Marcus Septimus has such confidence in our mosaicist, then I am inclined to act on his advice – and if he is right there is no time to lose. The sooner he finds out where the stop took place, the faster my dear bride is likely to be found.'

EIGHT

To say that I was utterly appalled by this does not come close to describing how I felt. I was literally speechless with dismay. Not only was I legally compelled to bring the driver back, on penalty of a small fortune in gold coins, but I was also apparently expected to set off at once – when it was already the middle of the afternoon – to a town that was fully twenty miles away, with not the slightest prospect of getting back that day. Whatever else, I'd not intended that.

'But my family, mightiness,' I burbled. 'They won't know where I am. Besides, it will be dark in only a few hours and I have no money for an inn. What am I to do when I get to Corinium? Or do you expect me to sleep beside the road?'

Lavinius gave me his icy pale-blue stare. 'Citizen, I have complied with your request.' (In fact he hadn't – the driver was still bound.) 'After that – as far as I'm concerned – the matter rests with you. If there are resultant problems, that's not my affair. Perhaps you should have thought the matter through a little more.' He turned to the steward, who was hovering nearby. 'Slave, do as this pavement-maker says. Cut this scoundrel's bonds then go and fetch the iron-smith to strike the fetters off his feet. If he tries to run away, arrest the citizen.'

The steward stepped forward and drew out a long knife from his belt. He pulled the driver roughly up onto his knees, causing him to groan in agony and, propping him in that position against the sacks, began – none too gently – to hack at the rope tethered between the feet and hands. As he worked, the pressure on the bonds was visibly increased and I could see the driver biting his lip to stop himself from crying out. Then the tether snapped and the captive, suddenly released from being tensioned like a bow, toppled over and fell forward on the floor.

The steward kicked him over on his side and knelt to cut the belt that bound the hands.

'You need not let the prisoner go entirely,' Publius put in. 'He does not have to drive his raeda yet – that's still outside of Glevum anyway. In fact he does not have to drive the thing at all. Lavinius, you could send them in your gig. There would be just room for both the prisoner and Libertus at a pinch, and that way you could keep the man in bonds throughout.'

That was quite an intelligent idea: not only did it appease Lavinius, it might save me a good deal of anxiety besides.

Before I could voice this, the raeda driver spoke up from the floor – unbowed as ever, it appeared. 'The box containing all Audelia's wedding-gifts is still inside my coach – at least I hope it is – and I imagine you will want it back? There would be not room to take that with us in the gig.'

It earned him a savage thump across his back from the steward. Lavinius scowled at the prisoner's impudence, and Publius looked affronted at this challenge to his words. For two *quadrans*, I could see, he would wash his hands of this.

I did not wish to lose the only ally that I had, so I gave him what I hoped was an ingratiating smile. 'Citizen Publius, with the greatest of respect, that raeda is the last place that Audelia was seen. I would like to stop and take a look at it. There may be signs of struggle, or some other sort of clue. Perhaps – as you suggest – the gig could take us to the gates, and then we could go on in the raeda after that. The man you set to guard it could travel on with us, in the front so that the raedarius couldn't run away. The gig meanwhile, could bring the box back here.'

Publius frowned. 'The slave I left on guard is not mine to command. He was borrowed from the pontifex, and will be wanted in the temple later on tonight, I'm sure.'

'Then Fiscus, perhaps, could help me,' I ventured, hopefully.

'But he was only lent to you to be a guide, I think. Marcus Septimus expects him to be here when he arrives. I'm sorry, Libertus, you will have to watch over the raedarius yourself. I only wish that I was free to come with you, myself, but I cannot desert the birthday feast tonight, at which Lavinius is kind enough to have named me as chief guest. Perhaps, in the circumstances, the gig is good enough. We can arrange to have the box brought here another time.'

I was not anxious to travel all those miles in a crowded, bouncing, open gig. I had an inspiration. 'But, supposing that we find Audelia?' I said, praying that the raedarius would not betray my confidence in him by running off. 'We would need some comfortable way of bringing her back here. She certainly couldn't travel with us in the gig.'

Publius looked approvingly at me. 'You are quite right, mosaic-maker. That is unthinkable. You may let the prisoner drive the raeda, when you get to it. In the meantime, steward, do not free his hands. Time enough for that when there's an extra guard.'

The steward had already sat back on his knees and stopped sawing at the rope while he listened to all this. He glanced towards his owner with an enquiring look.

Lavinius nodded at him, clearly dismayed at this usurpation of his authority, and equally clearly unable to resist. 'Very well. Let it be as Publius says. Bring the wretch to us when his feet are freed.'

'Immediately, master!' and with a parting shove to the unfortunate raedarius the slave got to his feet and went bustling away, no doubt to find the smith.

'We should instruct the gig-slave what to do. The man will want fresh horses, I expect.' Lavinius was suddenly all brisk efficiency, evidently determined to resume command. He turned to his attendant boy. 'Page, go and find the gig-slave and tell him what's required. Publius, my friend, we two will go into the house and wash our feet and I will have someone bring some dates and wine.'

He had pointedly not invited me and I hesitated, not certain what to do, but Publius gestured to me to accompany them. 'Libertus must come with us so we can devise a plan. If he does discover something I want to know at once, and we must make arrangements for sending messages.'

Lavinius scowled, but signalled his reluctant agreement with a nod and led the way back through the gate towards the house, though he made a point of taking Publius on ahead and talking to him in an undertone, making certain that I could not hear and leaving me to trail behind them with the remaining page.

In the colonnaded garden Publius stopped and turned to me.

I was warming to this patrician more and more by now. He may have forced me to a bargain which I could ill afford but this was clearly not the outcome of ill-will – simply the failure of a hugely wealthy man to understand how much a hundred aureii seemed to humbler folk.

He illustrated the gulf between us by his next words, too. They were addressed to Lavinius but they were meant for me to hear, and once again seemed an attempt to help. 'About accommodation, is it not the case that Marcus has a second town-house in Corinium? Given his very high opinion of his protégé, surely he would not object to Libertus staying there?'

In fact I knew my patron would be appalled at the idea. The place was shut up when he was not there, with only a handful of slaves to keep it clean and aired. Besides, I am a simple tradesman, not a Roman patrician. It is true that I did stay at his country villa once, when I was ill and he required my services, but I am not the class of guest he usually invites. The notion of my simply arriving at his Corinium town-house unannounced, demanding food and somewhere warm to sleep, was quite unthinkable.

How could I explain this to a man like Publius? I shook my head and followed him inside as a smirking Fiscus held open the door of the atrium for us, smiling at his erstwhile master and ignoring me.

'Respected eminence,' I muttered to Publius, once I was in the room, 'I am a citizen of very humble rank, and though my patron is very kind to me I could not presume upon him in this way. The house is closed and providing hospitality for me – or any unexpected guest – might be difficult. In any case the servants do not know me there and, without a letter from His Excellence himself, I doubt that they would even let me in.'

The atrium was full of flowers and scented oil, and servants were already setting a pair of fine carved stools – one ebony, one ivory – on each side of the little table by the wall. Publius seemed to take this as his right, and sat down on the nearer one, saying with a smile, 'Would it help if I wrote a letter to the house myself.'

'What would be really helpful,' I said urgently, crouching on a lower footstool which Fiscus pointedly had set for me, 'would be for me to stay at the lodging-house where Audelia stayed last night and where she changed coaches with Lavinia. I might learn something very helpful there.'

Lavinius had already settled on the ebony chair, dropping his cloak where the slave would pick it up and said, with a sneer, 'They would not take a stranger they did not expect – they require a letter sent on in advance – that is the very reason that we chose their services. It keeps out the common class of travellers.'

A thoughtful frown crossed Publius's pudgy face. 'Suppose I wrote a letter to them, instead, explaining who I was, and gave it to Libertus to carry to the house. I am quite sure they would admit him then.'

Fiscus expressed his evident disdain by raising one eyebrow at Lavinius, but our host did not respond. He turned to the house-slave who was already at his side with a silver salver piled with cheese and grapes: I would wager the hundred aureii that these would not be sour. Lavinius selected one and signalled for some wine, before remarking smoothly, 'The pavement-maker said he had no money for an inn, I think. And this one is not cheap.'

Publius selected a piece of proffered cheese. 'I was prepared to offer a reward – or even pay a ransom – for Audelia's return. I daresay I can undertake to pay for this. I will stop there and settle matters personally, on my way back to Londinium. Perhaps I could even stay there overnight myself, instead of using the military inns as I did on my way here. Courtesy of the provincial governor, of course.' He smiled at me. 'Of course, if Libertus is successful in his search, I will have my bride with me by then. So, Lavinius, if you would arrange a wax writing-block for me – or a sheet of bark-paper and some ink – I will compose a note. I have a seal-ring, if you have some wax. Fiscus can fetch the materials, perhaps, if your slaves are—'

He broke off as Modesta came rushing in, aghast. 'Master.' She flung herself breathless at her owner's feet. 'Your pardon, master, for disturbing you. There is a man on horseback here, whom I think that you should see.'

Lavinius made a lofty gesture with his long thin hand. 'Doubtless one of the early banquet guests.' He turned to

Publius with a knowing smile. 'This isn't Rome, you know.
A lot of humbler people don't have water-clocks or well-
positioned sundials, even now. Sometimes people find it very
hard to judge the hour – especially if they know good wine
awaits them here.'

Publius responded with the expected laugh, but Modesta
did not smile. 'But Master, it isn't you that he is asking for.
He insists he wants Audelia – no one else will do – and he
won't believe me when I say she isn't here.'

The two patricians exchanged a startled glance, then
Lavinius said sternly, 'Show the fellow in.' Modesta hurried
off to do as she was told.

Publius put his cup down, half-troubled, half-relieved. 'This
must be a contact from the kidnappers. Or perhaps it is a trick.
Do you think, Libertus . . . ?'

I never heard the rest, because at that moment the slave-girl
reappeared, accompanied by one of the most enormous men
I'd ever seen.

NINE

This newcomer was perhaps not quite as old as I am, but certainly he was no longer young. All the same his presence filled the room. He was not simply hugely tall, he was big and muscular, with a neck that was almost wider than his head and massive thighs like the trunks of well-grown trees. His arms were brawny and in one gigantic hand he held a ridiculously dainty leather bag, which made his fingers look enormous by comparison. His short-cropped head was rounder than an earthen cooking pot and his face, which was baked to terracotta in the sun, was weather-etched with lines. He wore big boots, a yellow tunic and a heavy riding-cape. Modesta had said he was a horseman. I found myself feeling a little sorry for the horse.

He looked around the atrium and acknowledged the presence of our togas with a bow. 'Greetings, citizens.' He made another vague obeisance towards all three of us, as if two of the company were not marked out by patrician purple stripes. 'Which of you gentlemen is the master of the house?' His eyes were small and darting and I saw that he was missing several of his teeth. Not a man I'd care to argue with.

Lavinius stepped forward, all cold authority. 'I am Lavinius, the paterfamilias of this household and the uncle of that Audelia whom – it seems – you seek. She is not here, as I believe you have already been informed. However, in her absence you may speak to me. What is your business here?'

The rider's tanned face split in an astonished grin. He would have been ugly, even with the teeth, and the crinkles of amusement creased his wrinkled face still more. 'I don't think you can help me this time, citizen. I was sent to bring her these. I don't think they would fit you particularly well.' He opened the drawstring of the bag and brought out a pair of yellow wedding shoes, which he dangled by the laces between one finger and a thumb as though they had no weight.

I could see at once what Puella, the missing slave, had meant.

They were the most beautiful slippers I have ever seen, the
soft dyed leather cut into an intricate design of flowers and
butterflies. The colour was extremely delicate and the soles and
lacing so beautifully fine that the whole seemed worthy of an
empress or a queen. They had not been worn, so the donor
who had given them as an offering to the Vestal at the shrine
must not only have paid a handsome price for them but
somehow contrived to have them specially made to fit Audelia.
No wonder the bride-to-be had been keen to show them off.

It was clear to me by now who this intruder was. 'So you
are the mounted guard who escorted Audelia to Corninium?'
I said at once, though it really was not my place to interview
the man. Publius looked at me, much as my slaves had looked
at the magician in the town, as if I had produced a ribbon
from my ear.

The horseman grinned. 'All the way from the Vestal temple,
citizen. Escorting people is my trade these days. Retired auxiliary cavalryman Ascus at your service, gentlemen.'

Lavinius coughed, to indicate that he was in command.
'Retired, but not a citizen? How did that come about? Did
you not get your citizen's diploma when you left the cavalry?'

Ascus shook his pot-shaped head. 'Took a wound, and had
to leave the force before I'd served my term. Nineteen years,
instead of twenty-five. But I used my pay-out to obtain a horse
– as you can see – and when I had recovered, I made another
life. So here I am. Armed and ready to fend off robbers on
the road.' He looped his other massive thumb and finger
through his belt, pushing the cloak back to reveal the cudgel
at his side. 'Of course I am only a civilian now, so it is illegal
for me to carry a sword or dagger on the road. But a simple
bludgeon is usually enough to deter would-be thieves and
attackers on the road.'

I could imagine that. If I were a bandit, that cudgel – in his
hands – would certainly have dissuaded me.

Lavinius though, was scowling at all this. 'But not this time,
it seems. Do I understand that at Corinium you abandoned
my poor niece?'

The massive shoulders shrugged. 'I am a hireling, citizen.
I do as I am told. She hired me in the first place and I was at
her command. She sent me back to get the shoes she'd left

behind – and I have done so, as you can see yourself. I told her it was foolish to go on alone – not in so many words, you understand – but she would not listen. She's a determined lady, as no doubt you know, and she wanted her slippers for her wedding day. Said that the goddess Vesta would protect her; Vesta and that idiot of a driver who brought Lavinia to the lodging house.' He looked around. 'Did she not tell you this? I thought I'd find her waiting and impatient for her shoes, but I suppose she was weary and has retired to rest. Not surprising really, jolting all that way in such a springless cart. Still, she promised to reward me if I got here before the feast, so one of the servants had better take these up to her.' He put the slippers back into the bag and held them out.

No one moved to take them.

For the first time Ascus looked discomfited. 'Well, surely somebody should tell her that they have arrived? Not that she'll be specially impressed, I don't expect, though I have ridden like the hounds of Dis to get them here in time.' He thrust the bag towards Lavinius. 'It wasn't easy following her directions to this place, either. Several times, I had to stop and ask the way.'

Lavinius snatched the leather bag and glared at him. 'So you haven't heard what happened to my niece? When your famous bludgeon was not there to help?'

The giant looked at him. The smile had vanished, but the creases in the face deepened even more. 'She had some misfortune when I wasn't there? She surely wasn't set upon and robbed?' He struck his forehead with the heel of his hand. 'Dear Mars! I knew it was stupid to let her go alone. They took her jewels, I suppose? Great Jupiter, mightiest and best! She promised me reward – a very handsome jet and garnet ring she had with her – and now I suppose I won't get paid at all.'

Publius got to his feet, impatiently. 'Never mind the jewels, my friend, the bride herself has gone – apparently kidnapped from the raeda on the way. And her maidservant has disappeared as well.' He glared at Ascus, whose mouth had dropped open in astonishment. 'I wonder they didn't tell you all this at the gate.'

'They wouldn't tell me anything at all. I almost had to force my way inside, before the gatekeeper would call the slave and have her announce to you that I was here.'

The idea that the unhelpful gatekeeper had met his match was enough to make me smile. Publius rounded on me instantly.

'You think that this is somehow comical?'

'I was simply thinking, respected citizen,' I said quickly (I did not wish to lose the best support I had), 'that the arrival of this rider makes things easier. He is a guard by trade. He can accompany us to Corinium and if we find no information there tonight, tomorrow he can take us to where Audelia left the shoes. I'm very anxious to ask questions of the household there.'

Lavinius frowned. 'What point is there in that?'

I had forgotten that he had not heard the full story of the shoes. 'I suspect the loss of the wedding shoes was no mere accident – I believe that they were deliberately taken from her box, precisely in order to divert the guard.'

Publius looked surprised. 'I expect you're right. She had mentioned in a letter to her aunt that she had been given wedding shoes. I wondered at her neglecting to take care of them. If you don't find Audelia by tomorrow, either at the stopping-place or at the private lodgings in Corinium, of course you must go and find this other house. And Ascus is the perfect man to take you there. He has been there before, so he knows where it is – and he will be known to them so they will let you in. And if you discover anything, he can bring us word at once. A single horseman can even ride by night, if he takes care.'

Ascus flashed a look of concentrated hate in my direction. Not surprisingly, I thought. The man had been riding since daybreak as it was, and was no doubt hoping for a well-earned rest, but my intervention meant that he would now have to set off again. Hardly a recipe for making friends. Yet I needed his co-operation.

I tried to think of some way I could repair the fault. 'Revered Lavinius,' I ventured, turning to my host who was looking furious at this whole affair. 'Would you consent to send this horseman to the servants' hall and have him given some refreshment there?'

Publius applauded this at once. 'He will be in want of

something, naturally – and a fresh horse as well if you can spare it, Lavinius my friend. Ascus can retrieve his own mount when he comes back here again. The creature that he came on will be tired by now. It must have covered many miles today and speed is essential if we hope to find my bride. The sun is in the west and there is much to do. Lavinius, I'm sure you have something in your stable that will serve.'

Another shrewd suggestion, I thought inwardly. That would certainly ensure that Ascus did return and not simply vanish when he had the chance. But Lavinius's expression, which he directed straight at me, was now as venomous as the rider's glance had been. He was clearly furious that he was asked to lend a horse. But he gave a curt nod to his slave, 'See to it, page.'

'Instantly, master.' The boy set off at once. He was halfway to the door, when his owner called him back.

'Not so quickly, you worthless son of a washerwoman. Wait till I have finished speaking or I will have you whipped. Take this horseman with you, and see that he is fed. And find out what has happened to that idle steward, too.'

'At once, master,' the young unfortunate replied. 'This way, horseman,' and he led Ascus out.

Lavinius opened the leather bag again and took the slippers out. 'What should I do with these? Are they *nefas* – accursed – do you think?'

Publius took them from him and murmured with a smile, 'But of course we must keep them till Audelia is returned. And the pavement-maker here is going to rescue her. Is that not so, Libertus?'

I gave a pallid smile. 'I will do my best. But there is one thing that rather troubles me. If Audelia has been seized for ransom, why have we not heard? You would expect her captors to send us their demands. But there has been no word.'

'If she was captured where the raeda stopped,' Lavinius said, dismissively, turning back to the tray of dainties, 'the kidnappers would scarcely have had time to contact us. They may, indeed, have simply let her go, when they discovered who their victim was. The penalties for laying hands upon a Vestal are so terrible, they may have wished to wash their hands of it. In that case, no doubt, she will come here soon enough.' He picked out another tasty morsel of the cheese and popped it fastidiously into his mouth. 'She is a woman of some determination in her way. It is even possible she has refused to tell the bandits where to send.'

I doubted this. Any kidnapper would have methods of compelling her to speak, methods which I did not care to think about.

But Publius was already saying, with a smile, 'I know that you still believe that this is an accident – mere chance meeting with highway robbers on the road. But Libertus seems to think that this was all a plan, and the kidnappers were well aware of who she was. I trust that he is right. It would mean that they expect that we will ransom her, in which case we can hope she's still alive.' He turned to me. 'Who do you suspect of planning this?' he asked.

'The person I would like to talk to is her maidservant,' I hedged. 'She was with the raeda when it got to the gates, and only disappeared when it had stopped. Yet it's by no means certain that Audelia got that far. I'm quite convinced the missing slippers were taken from the box, either by the maidservant or by someone else. She could lead us to the truth, I am convinced of that.'

Publius nodded. 'If they knew about the slippers, they knew she was to wed.' He frowned. 'Although it was never publicly announced. It was to be a sensational surprise when I announced our betrothal at the games. Your idea, I think, Lavinius.'

I'd already wondered whose suggestion it had been. But all I said was, 'And it seems that someone also knew her route and when she would be passing. Which suggests it must be somebody she knows?'

Lavinius snorted in his cup, derisively. 'Well, it wasn't one of us, if that is what you are trying to suggest. Publius and I were at the birthday feast, and Cyra and the house-slaves have been here all the time – and there are dozens of witnesses to that.'

Publius paused in the act of sampling the wine. He was looking troubled. 'Besides, if it were a member of the family, Audelia would recognize her captors, wouldn't she? That would be no use.'

I shook my head. 'I am not sure that is true. Cyra told me, when I first arrived, that she had not seen Audelia since she was a child – and I expect the same is true of most of her other relatives unless for some reason they visited the shrine. She has been in seclusion at the hearth since she was young and Vestal Virgins have no portraits made.' I turned to Lavinius. 'But if she was kidnapped – and we can't be sure she was – we must find somebody who knew her face. You were her agent as I understand. Have you, for instance, seen her recently?'

'How dare you, citizen?' Lavinius's face was black with rage. 'I have been as tolerant as possible. But this whole suggestion is preposterous. Am I to be questioned by a mere mosaicist?'

I stood my ground. 'Respected citizen, I was not accusing you. I simply need a description of Audelia.' I said it meekly, but I enjoyed the chance to add, 'How else am I going to look for her?'

'He is right again you know, Lavinius.' Publius motioned to the slave to pass the grapes and cheese. He took a handful. 'And I can't help him. I've never seen the bride.'

Lavinius looked from Publius to me and back again. 'Oh, very well,' he grumbled. 'I'll tell you what I know, but it's not very much. I've only met her once. She is of slightly more than middling height and fairly slim – as to more than that, I really cannot say. Her face was half-covered with a Vestal veil, of course, since she was not acting as a priestess at the time and was in public in the presence of a male, though I have the impression that her hair was fair.'

'But you have met her? Was that recently?'

'I have been in constant touch with her, of course, but in fact we only met a moon or so ago. I went to Londinium on private business and saw her – with a chaperone – to discuss affairs, mostly with regard to her retirement from the hearth. Of course, men aren't permitted right inside the shrine, we had to make arrangements to meet outside in the court. But I'd recognize her voice, and I'm sure that she'd know me.' He downed his wine as if he wished to swallow me, as well. 'I can't accept your theory, that this was deliberate. There were rebels in the woods a moon or two ago, and they take random hostages to build their coffers up. There is your solution, if I am any judge. Besides, Audelia stayed only with relatives and friends throughout her journey from the shrine. You surely don't suggest that one of us – her family – has kidnapped her for gain?' He took another cube of cheese and bit it thoughtfully. 'We would be the ones to pay the ransom fee! Not even you would think that we extort things from ourselves?'

It was clear that the cheeseboard was not going to come to me, though I was hungry now. I'd had nothing but a sour grape or two and a tiny portion of sacrificial beef since I left home at dawn. I began to wish I'd gone with Ascus to the slave-quarters. I got stiffly to my feet.

'Lavinius, I am trying to assist. Not all members of your family are as rich as you. I understand that there are poor relations elsewhere in Britannia who were not invited to the wedding feast. They might be happy to extort a price. Not personally, of course. A man may plot a crime and arrange for someone else to carry out the deed. And as to demanding money from yourselves – did I not hear Publius say that he was prepared to offer a reward or pay a ransom for Audelia's safe return? That's not family money.'

Publius surprised me. 'But I'd pay it, willingly. I have experienced this sort of thing before. My second wife in Rome was captured on the road – I had sent her to my country villa to escape the plague – and, you may be interested to know, it was a full day before they got in touch. I think they wished me to be so desperate that I would instantly comply with their demands.'

'And did you?' I was still more thoughtful now. If Publius was known to have paid a ransom once before . . .

Publius laughed. 'In a sense, I did. I used Egyptian gold to pay them – it can be exchanged in any marketplace of course – but I took care to mark the coins. I alerted the coin-inspectors for several miles around, and when the culprits tried to use the money, they were caught. I had them crucified. Scarcely an encouragement to a repeat attempt, if that is what you are thinking, citizen.'

That was, of course, exactly what I'd thought. I was about to answer when the page returned, with a flustered steward hurrying after him.

'Master,' the chief slave said, bowing low before his owner and ignoring us. 'The gig is now prepared and the chains have been struck off the raeda-driver's legs, though I have left his hands in bonds. If this citizen –' he nodded in my direction – 'is ready, they can leave at once.'

Publius was already on his feet. 'Then if you can provide me with a wax tablet, Lavinius my friend, I will write the letter that I promised straight away. Fiscus will bring it out to you when you are in the gig.'

'In the meantime,' I said pointedly, 'I will find Ascus and tell him that we're ready to depart – perhaps Modesta could accompany me, since Fiscus has another job to do, and maybe she can find me a piece of bread as well.'

Lavinius seemed likely to protest at this but Publius seized me warmly by the arm. 'Let it be as you suggest. Then go, Libertus, go – and may Jove go with you. Good luck in your quest. Send me a message if there's anything further I can do to help.'

I nodded thankfully and bowed myself away, together with Modesta who looked thrilled to be my choice. Lavinius made no objection, but he had turned quite puce. He looked so angry at Publius taking charge, and so frustrated at being overruled, that I could almost have believed he was about to burst.

It did not augur well for the festivities tonight. I did not envy Marcus and the others in the least, and was actually glad to leave the room.

TEN

The slaves' sleeping-quarters was one cheerless narrow room, with two lines of straw mattresses set on the floor: males on one side, females on the other, I assumed. There was a long trestle table just inside the door and Ascus was squatting at it, ridiculously large on a low three-legged stool, gnawing on some bread and gulping water from a cup. He scowled when I came in.

'What now? This is the slaves' room, citizen. You have no business here.'

'On the contrary. I have come to tell you we are ready to depart.' There was a corner of the loaf remaining on the board, and a large knife beside it. There was no one to prevent me and nowhere obvious to sit, so I cut myself a slice and ate it where I stood. Modesta saw what I was doing and found a drinking-cup, filling it for me from the water-jug. I raised it to the horseman in a mock-salute and said, between mouthfuls, 'We are commanded to leave as soon as possible.'

Ascus made no attempt to hurry. He took another bite. 'A fine task you have got me landed with. I am now obliged to escort you to Corinium. If Lavinius – or whatever his name is – was not a purple-striper and likely to have important magistrates as friends, I tell you, citizen, I would refuse to go. You don't need my protection – who would set on you? You haven't got anything a thief would want to steal.'

I swallowed the remainder of the bread. It was dry, but sustaining, and the water helped. 'Have they not told you?' I explained about the raeda-driver. 'Your task is to make sure he does not escape. You claimed that riding guard was your profession, didn't you?'

He thumped his cup down on the tabletop and glared at me again. 'And that's another thing. Who's going to pay me for my services? No one has paid me for the slippers yet, though I was specially promised a reward.'

I put my own drinking-vessel down more gingerly. 'The

contract for the wedding-shoes was with Audelia. If we find her, you can hold her to her word. Otherwise I think Publius has agreed to foot the bill. So if you are ready, horseman?' He flashed the teeth he did have in an unpleasant smile. 'It seems I have no choice. So, citizen, what are we waiting for?' He shambled to his feet, and almost before I'd had time to collect my wits he was out of the slaves' quarters and striding through the yard.

I hurried after him. The gig and its driver were already at the gate, and as we approached I saw the raeda-driver squatting in the carriage on the floor, his hands still bound behind him. He looked up and saw me and gave me a weak smile. 'Well, citizen, I did not believe that you could get me out of there – except to be bundled to the torturers. I am obliged to you.'

The gig-driver whirled around and flicked his whip across the bloodstained back, making the raeda-driver gasp in agony. 'Silence, scum! I heard the steward tell you, you are not to speak – and as long as you are in my gig, I'll see that you obey. If I hear another word from you, I'll use my whip again.' He turned to me, all bland politeness now. 'So, if you are ready, citizen.'

I nodded and clambered up beside him in the gig. The raeda-driver took up so much floor that there was scarcely room for me to squeeze into the seat – a gig is not designed to carry extra passengers – but I contrived somehow. I looked up to find Fiscus grinning in at me, holding out a writing-tablet which was tied and sealed.

'Don't drop it, citizen, as you're going along. That's my ex-master's private seal,' he said, disguising insolence as legitimate concern and exchanging glances with the gig-driver.

A slave had appeared from the stable-block by now, leading a large, recalcitrant black horse. It was a sullen looking animal, shimmying sideways on the rein with wildly rolling eyes, but at least it looked big enough to carry Ascus as was obviously planned. It did not look a comfortable mount, the Roman saddle on its back appeared to worry it. Ascus, however, took one look at the beast and – to my astonishment – vaulted his huge form into the saddle like a child. He leaned forward and rubbed the creature's glossy head. It quieted at once.

'If you are comfortable, citizen . . .' the gig-slave said to me, but he'd already jerked the horses and we were on the move. Comfort is not ever possible in a small, springless carriage along country roads and he was determined to see that there was none. Our speed was such that we constantly jolted up and down so I was obliged to hold on with my one remaining hand – the other was attempting to protect the precious seal. That was difficult enough, but the presence of the prisoner made it infinitely worse. At every bump and pothole he lurched into me and, unable to support himself, his whole weight fell against me and pinned my legs painfully against the seat. Ascus, riding alongside us, saw my predicament and grinned, showing his remaining and discoloured teeth.

No conversation was possible, of course, and – aside from the rattling and jolting of the gig, and my occasional inadvertent grunt of pain – it was a silent drive to town. Never had so short a distance seemed to take so long, and it was with enormous pleasure and relief that I saw the town walls appear.

However, the journey was not over even then. The games had obviously finished long ago, but the gate area was still crammed with carriages and carts of every kind, and citizens in togas were pouring from the town – most of them evidently on their way to dine, if not with Lavinius himself, then at one of the many other Imperial Birthday feasts. There were other, more humble, pedestrians as well, including the travelling stallholders by the look of it – I recognized the palm-seller among them – making for the carts and wagons they had left outside the gates. Some of the crowd were clearly a little worse for wine: the wine-stall was still open just outside the gates, and it was evident that it had done a roaring trade.

I thought it was going to take some time for us to force our way through this jostling and excited crowd and find the raeda, but I had reckoned without Ascus. He urged the horse forward, right into the throng, and people fell back instantly on both sides, lest they be trampled on. The gig-slave simply drove into the space, and in a few minutes we were right up at the gate.

We clattered to a stop. 'Which is your raeda, scum?' The gig-slave raised his whip and grinned unpleasantly.

The raeda-driver looked helplessly at me. Answer, and he would be whipped for speaking when he'd been forbidden to; fail to answer and he would still be whipped – this time for refusing to comply. It is the kind of cruel dilemma often used to taunt a slave but it is not often that a servant can employ the trick himself, especially against a freeborn man who would normally be his superior in rank. But the gig-slave had the excuse that he was obeying orders from above, and was enjoying this. I recalled what Cyra had told me earlier about how he had brought the prisoner home at Publius's request, additionally bound around the legs and feet, ostensibly to prevent the chance of an escape but certainly ensuring a help-less, bruising ride. It occurred to me that the gig-slave would have relished the opportunity.

'Well?' he was demanding of his captive now. 'What do you have to say?'

The raeda-driver raised a weary head and seemed about to speak, but at that moment Ascus cantered back, scattering the people as he'd done before. 'I've found your carriage. I recog-nized the horses, they were stabled beside my own in Corinium last night. That flabby fellow over there was guarding it just now.' He made a gesture with his massive hand to where a pudgy slave in temple livery was hastening through the gate. 'I've sent him to his masters, to his great relief. The raeda is all right. The shutters are still up, but I have looked inside and there's a box.' He grinned at the raedarius. 'You are fortunate. On a feast day like today, when the town is full of rogues, it would not have been surprising if it had disappeared. Let's get the gig over there, and get it loaded on.'

'When we've released the prisoner's arms,' I said.

The horseman grinned again. He reached into the lining of his riding-coat and produced a wicked-looking knife.

'I thought you said you weren't permitted . . .' I began.

'This is for dining purposes, if anybody asks.' He flashed his gaps at me. 'But I dare say it will serve for other purposes.' He leaned into the carriage as he spoke, and sliced the bond in two, as effortlessly as though it were another piece of bread.

The raedarius stiffly moved his arms round to the front and eased his aching shoulders with an attempted shrug. A new bloodstain instantly appeared on his tunic, as though the movement of his back had opened up the wound. I was stiff from jolting, and I ached in every limb and it was difficult for me to climb unaided from the gig, still clutching my precious letter in my hand.

But he managed a wan smile as he joined me on the ground. 'It is as well the horseman is so big,' he said to me, in our own tongue again. 'We could never have moved the box out of the raeda otherwise. That's it over there.'

He walked so painfully and stiffly that people turned to stare, but he seemed oblivious of the attention paid to him. It was not until we reached the raeda that I understood. He did not stop to look inside at all. He made for the two horses and began to coo to them, whispering and stroking their dark flanks, almost lover-like. 'Have you had food and drink my lovelies?' They whinnied up to him.

Ascus was watching all this with a frown. 'What did he stand accused of?' he said privately to me.

'Failing to take care of Audelia and her maid,' I answered. 'And failing to account for any kidnappers, or give any other explanation as to where she'd gone.'

Ascus looked thoughtful. 'She must have been coerced. The last time that I saw her she was happy as could be – thoroughly delighted to be a bride at last.'

'That is why I wished to look inside the raeda,' I agreed. 'To see if there were any signs of force – scratches, or damage, or any sign of blood.'

He nodded. 'I'll move that box for you. What's happened to that gig?' He gestured to the gig-slave. 'Get that over here. And be quick about it. We haven't got all day. This citizen wants to look inside the coach.'

The gig-slave, who'd clearly thought he had a friend, looked mystified at this but brought the carriage up. He leapt down from the driving-seat and gazed inside the coach. 'That's an enormous box.' He put a hand to it. 'And very heavy too.'

Ascus had dismounted. 'I'll put it on the gig.' He took for granted he could handle it, and doubtless he was right. But I prevented him.

There was something about the nature of the box and its excessive weight that made me say, 'Before you move it, let's have a look inside. There might be something of importance there.'

The top had been secured with a heavy lock, but that did not stop Ascus. He used the knife again, this time as a lever, and pushed the lid ajar. But even before he'd fully opened it, the smell had reached me and I knew what we would find.

There was a body in it. A headless body, by the look of it. Ascus did not wait for a command, but reached into the box and pulled it out.

The corpse had been a woman, that was clear at once. Her arms, which had been forced behind her back, proved to finish in mere bloodied stumps where both of the hands had been brutally removed. A woman dressed in a distinctive garb.

Ascus looked at me. 'Seems as your journey will not be needed now. We seem to have found the missing Vestal after all,' he said.

ELEVEN

I stared at the poor, mutilated, lifeless thing which dangled from his hands like some grotesque stuffed doll. Hard to believe that it had once been a living woman, with hopes and dreams and aspirations. Clearly an attractive woman, too. If this had indeed been Audelia, I thought, she did not share the angularity of her aunt.

The form, or what one could perceive of it beneath the Vestal robes, was slim and shapely still, and the bare legs and ankles (though mottled purple with pooled blood where they had been pressed against the box), were well-formed, shaved and slightly muscular.

I wondered at that for a moment, but then remembered what I'd been told when I was in Londinium – that Vestal Virgins sometimes walked for miles to gather the spring water that featured in the shrine. I had not seen it for myself, of course, but I had heard of it: flowing incessantly into a bowl which, in turn, spilled out into a pool to be siphoned back again, so that a priestess or worshipper who washed her hands, in accordance with the ritual, washed them in pure running water every time. To let the water fail was to infringe the vows, so the reservoir was reverently topped up every day. No wonder that this Vestal – if that was what she was – showed signs of constant gentle exercise.

But . . . 'Why cut off her hands and head?' I said the words aloud. 'Unless the intention was to disguise the identity of the corpse?'

The gig-man, who had been standing goggling at my side, looked pityingly at me. 'And leave the rest of her in that distinctive dress? What sense is there in that? More likely it was to make the body fit into the space. Must have been a fairly tight squeeze as it was.'

Ascus looked surprised. He hoisted the corpse above the open box, and gauged the volume by dipping it inside and pushing down. He turned to me. 'I believe he might be right.

There's not a lot of room – and if the head was on, you couldn't close the lid.'

I had to admit there was some force in that. 'But why remove the hands?' I persisted. 'That would hardly help to get the body in the box.' I was about to press my theory of disguised identity, when I realized the fundamental flaw. That could hardly be the explanation here – one wealthy woman's hands look much like the next. Unless this was some arthritic ancient crone, or hard-working toil-worn slave (which clearly it was not, the rest of the body was too well-fed for that) the hands were surely quite irrelevant. It was not as though you could classify people by their finger-shapes, and we didn't know what Audelia's looked like anyway. 'So what could anyone hope to gain by doing that?' I said aloud.

It was the raedarius who answered. 'After her jewellery, citizen, I shouldn't be surprised. Whenever this was done they must have wanted speed, or they might have been discovered. Easier to hack the finger off than struggle with a ring.'

The gig-driver rounded on him instantly. 'So you know all about it? And you had this box riding with you all the way?' He smiled, unpleasantly. 'I knew that we should not have set you free.'

'Of course I did not touch the Vestal,' the raedarius protested. 'I place far too much value on my life! Anyway, I'd no idea that she was in the box. It's just that I've come across the same thing once before – two unhappy corpses, that I found in a ditch, who had been stripped and robbed by highway thieves. They'd also had their hands and feet removed to steal the golden toe and finger-ornaments.'

'And you were there that time as well!' The gig-man sneered. 'Is that a coincidence? I wonder if the master will think so when he hears? I have my own ideas – and I'd like to know where you've hidden the jewels you cut from her.' He glanced at Ascus, certain of support. 'Will you seize him, horseman, or should I call the guard? I daren't lay hands on him this time – he is a freeman and I am just a slave and I have no authority from my master or Publius to take him prisoner again. And . . .' He looked contemptuously at me. 'It's clear this citizen will take no steps at all.'

Ascus surprised me. He put down the headless corpse, letting

it collapse into a heap upon the street, then turned towards
Lavinius's slave and stood towering over him. He was twice
as big as the gig-boy, and looked as if he could swallow him
for lunch so I was not surprised to see the young man flinch.

The ex-cavalry-man put a giant hand under the gig-slave's
chin and forced the young slave to look up at him. 'Listen
here, young man! Take care whom you accuse. You think
you're very clever, but you know nothing of the world. Any
man can murder, for profit, for revenge – that much I will
grant you. But to take a knife to some helpless female and
cut bits off her – that takes a special kind of ruthlessness. And
I will tell you this – the raedarius clearly is not that kind of
man. You saw what happened when I cut him free – he was
more concerned about his animals than anything else. If he
had known what was hidden in the box, would he have ignored
it and been so happy to let me open it? Besides, a man who
cares that much about a horse is not likely to cut women into
pieces, in my view.'

The gig-slave was attempting in vain to get away. 'But you
heard what he said about the hands . . .'

'Exactly!' Ascus said. 'And what he says is true – I've seen
it happen on the battlefield, myself. People are always plun-
dering the dead. And not just cutting off their rings and amulets
– but whole torcs and helmets, and even pairs of boots.' He
let go of the boy, who stumbled back and rubbed his face.
Ascus turned to me. 'So I find the explanation very probable.
And Audelia did have finger-rings, I told you earlier. She
promised one to me.'

I nodded. 'Though that was in her jewel-box, I believe you
said? She wasn't wearing it?'

Ascus looked shifty. 'That's true. And the jewel-box isn't
here. Though there is something in here, now I come to look.
I don't suppose . . .' He leaned across the corpse – paying no
more attention than if it were a dog – and plunged one massive
hand into the box. 'Nothing significant. It is only cloth.' He
drew out a folded piece of delicate material dyed a saffron
hue. 'This was underneath the body. I did not see it before.'

'That must be Audelia's marriage-veil,' I said.

He flipped it by two corners so that it half-opened out. It was
beautifully embroidered with gold and silver thread – butterflies

and flowers, as if to match the shoes. 'It answers the description that I heard of it,' he agreed.

'I'll give you two *sesterces* for it,' said a cheeky voice. 'Cursed by being with a corpse or not.'

I turned around. I had been so transfixed by our discovery that I had not realized it, but we had attracted quite a little crowd of curious spectators, many of them slightly the worse for drinking wine.

'Make it three sesterces,' the speaker said again – a fat, florid tradesman with a pockmarked face. 'It's a handsome offer. You won't get more than that. Come on, citizen, she won't be needing it. And I won't sell it locally – I'll take it somewhere else. I know a bride-to-be who will be pleased to have the veil – she doesn't need to know that it belonged to someone dead.' It was clear that he'd decided that I must be in charge – I was wearing the toga after all – and he pushed his face towards me, reeking of cheap wine. 'You can't tell me that you want to put it on the pyre. All that work, it would be such a waste. It's not even damaged, she's hardly bled on it.'

There was an outbreak of ragged cheers at that and cries of: 'Go on, citizen.' But I hardly noticed them. I was staring at the speaker. 'What did you just say?'

He sighed theatrically and spread his hands apart. 'Three sesterces and one denarius. That's my final offer, citizen. I can't make a profit if I give you more – even on stitching of pure gold and silver thread.'

But I wasn't listening. 'She hasn't bled on it,' I echoed, stupidly. 'Of course she hasn't! Or on her vestments either!' I turned to Ascus. 'You see what that implies? Someone cut her hands and head off after she was dead. Quite a while afterwards – or there'd be bloodstains everywhere.'

He stared at me. 'I do believe you're right. I should have thought of that.' He opened out the veil to examine it. 'This was underneath her all the time, but there's hardly a sign of a bloodstain anywhere.' But even as he spoke, something brownish-green fell out and fluttered to the ground. He bent to peer at it, pushed it with his foot, then said dismissively, 'That isn't anything. Just a piece of leafy twig. Caught in the hemming by the look of it.'

'That might be important, all the same,' I said reprovingly. 'For instance, it might give us a clue as to where the girl was killed – or put into the box. Could you get it, gig-boy, and save my poor old back?' I placed Publius's precious letter in my toga-folds, where it would be supported by my belt, and held out my hand.

'If you insist, citizen.' The gig-boy gestured the trader to stand back, and bending down, picked up the piece of twig. But instead of handing it to me, he took one look at it and dropped it instantly as if it burnt his skin. All the colour had drained out of his face.

'Well?' I held my hand out more insistently.

He shook his head and went on shaking it. 'I'm not touching that. Where's that lucky charm I saw tied on the coach? It's not a proper deity, but it'll have to do.' There was a crude wooden trinket-doll tied to the raeda – the sort of talisman that travellers sometimes use to ward off evil spirits on the road. The gig-boy scooped it up and pressed his lips to it and I saw him mouthing some kind of hasty prayer. Then he let the charm go and said shakily, 'That's the only good-luck incantation that I know. I hope it is enough.'

'Whatever is the matter?' the raedarius asked.

'Oak leaves and mistletoe,' the slave said, breathlessly. 'That's what the matter is. Though it explains the mystery, doesn't it? I am sorry I accused of taking part in it. These were not ordinary robbers and murderers – though that would be bad enough. This is the work of those accursed Druids.' His voice was getting high and faster all the time and it was clear that he was panicking. 'They didn't cut her head off to put her in the box, they cut it off to hang it in their accursed grove – no doubt a Vestal Virgin was a special prize – and only their dark gods know what they wanted with the hands.'

At the mention of the Druids, the forbidden sect, there was a frightened murmur from the onlookers and even the florid trader stepped back a little way.

I confess that a cold shiver had run down my own spine. It was more than possible that the boy was right. Oak leaves are everywhere, of course, but mistletoe was not a common plant round here these days – and when it was found it was almost never picked because of its association with the sect. It had become an evil sign, regarded as a curse: the symbol of the forbidden cult of Druids, who – as the gig-slave said – famously cut off the heads of enemies and hung them onto trees in a grisly offering to the gods.

But it was not only their treatment of dead enemies that made the Druids so much feared. Their priests were rumoured to disembowel living men, in order to read the message of the entrails, and there were ancient stories of huge man-shaped structures, built of wood and filled with people who were burned alive to pacify the gods. It had all served to put the cult beyond the law. The Romans frowned on human sacrifice and, besides, their own troops were often the ex-owners of the heads. To be a Druid follower these days was a capital offence.

Despite this – or perhaps because of it – the religion flourished still, mostly in dark, secret places in the woods. I am not a follower – although I am a Celt – preferring the simpler ancestral deities of streams and woods. All the same, I have seen a sacred grove; one of the few outsiders who have done as much, and lived. It was an eerie place, its gruesome oak trees draped with mistletoe and hung with rotting skulls, displayed as a kind of ghastly sacrifice. The stuff of nightmares, just as rumour said. And there were other rumours, even more unspeakable, which spoke of what would happen to those that crossed the cult. No wonder that the gig-boy was so terrified.

I reminded myself that there were other aspects of the Druids, too – fine artefacts and learning, poetry and healing arts. I bent down stiffly and picked up the sprig of leaves myself. As I did so, I pricked my finger on something in the leaves.

A strand of wool had been tied around both stems to make a tiny sprig, and a small metal pin was still threaded through the stalk, showing where it had been deliberately pinned onto the veil. As I sucked my finger, I realized what this meant. The presence of this greenery was not an accident. Someone had fixed it there on purpose, as a deliberate sign of connection with the Druids. The gig-boy was quite right.

I wondered what Lavinius and Publius would say when they heard this. It might be kinder not to tell the groom, in fact, because what might have happened to Audelia in Druid hands,

before she died, was horrible to consider. I wondered if I
should examine the corpse a little more to see whether my
worst fears were justified, but decided I could hardly do so in
this public place. In any case, I reassured myself, such an
examination of this body was not appropriate. This had been
a Vestal Virgin after all, and intimate inspections were likely
to be cursed if carried out by any man at all who did not
happen to be a pontifex. I sucked my hand again, hoping that
there had not been poison on the pin.

'Citizen?' an urgent voice said in my ear.

I turned. Most of the crowd had drifted back a little way
– frightened off by the discovery of the mistletoe, no doubt
– but I found the florid trader still hovering nearby with a
curious companion not very far behind.

I was about to demand a little more respect for what was
clearly the body of a woman of some rank and tell them to
go away, but the man forestalled me. The pock-marked face
came very close to mine. 'I formally withdraw the offer, citizen.
If Druids are involved, I want no part in it.'

'You quite sure?' his companion enquired. 'Your customer
won't know.'

'You can't take chances. There might be a curse. How do
you think I got these marks?' He was still murmuring. He
turned to me and pointed to his nose. 'Once bought a blanket
that was cheap because it had been wrapped around a sickly
cow. More than likely the animal was hexed. Next thing I
know, I had caught a pox myself – and lucky to survive it,
everybody said. So – as this man is my witness – I formally
withdraw my offer for the veil.'

I shook my head at him. 'I did not agree to sell it,' I said,
impatiently. 'And I would not have done, whatever price you
offered. This is the body of a Vestal, as you see – and hence
clearly a woman of very wealthy birth. We have come to take
her back to her family for proper burial – and her vestments
with her. So move away. That's all there is to see.'

Neither of them budged. Indeed, the larger crowd, becoming
curious, was edging close again. Ascus picked up the hapless
corpse and put it in the box, draped the veil around it where
the head should be, then turned to face the gogglers, fingers
in his belt.

'Have you no fear of omens, any of you fools?' he demanded
in a roar. 'It is a sacred feast-day – and what have we here?
A murdered woman – and a Vestal too – hacked about and
with Druid symbols tucked into her clothes. And for double
measure, she was to be a bride. What kind of luck do you
suppose that sight will bring? And yet you idiots want to stand
and stare at it?'

Even the florid trader turned bloodless at the words and
there was a general murmur in the crowd.

'I saw a donkey carrying *hipposelinum* yesterday,' I heard
someone remark, 'I should have known there would be trouble.'
He spat on a finger and rubbed behind his ear, in the age-old
gesture to keep evil thoughts and influence at bay. 'I'm going
to go and make a sacrifice at once, to ward the evil off.'

People were already starting to disperse, though mostly in
the direction of the wine-shop, I observed. I grinned at Ascus.
'That was well expressed. Shall we move the corpse into the
gig?'

The raedarius however, motioned us to wait. He was staring
at the box. 'They can't have done this when the raeda stopped
to let the troops go by,' he mused. 'Someone would have
noticed, and it would have taken far too long. And I saw
Audelia get in the coach, myself. It must have happened since
it's been standing here.'

Ascus shook his head. 'I don't see how it could have. The
box was under guard. I saw the man myself when we arrived.
I told him that he was relieved and sent him on his way. A
servant from the temple.' He turned to the gig-slave. 'You
must have seen him too? I suppose it was the same one that
Publius set on watch?'

The boy was still whiter than a piece of fullered cloth, but
he nodded shakily. 'It was the same slave, I am quite sure of
that.'

'Though, I suppose he might have moved in the meanwhile,'
I said. 'You recognize the man. You go inside the gate and
tell him to come here, so I can question him.'

The gig-slave was only too anxious to obey – anything to
distance himself from Druid signs and corpses, obviously – but
the pock-marked trader had overheard our talk.

'I can save you the trouble. I've been here all day – that's my stall over there. I had the raeda in my sight since it first came. I watched this raedarius draw up at the gates and saw him send a messenger inside – obviously to tell somebody that he had arrived.'

I had a sudden memory. 'There was a slave-girl sitting on the seat with him,' I said. 'Did you see her depart?'

He frowned. 'I think I might have done,' he said. 'But I was far too busy watching him.' He gestured at the raedarius as he spoke. 'It was obvious that something was amiss – the way he kept on looking in the carriage as if he could not believe his eyes. And then a moment afterwards, a citizen came out and this fellow was carried off in bonds – everyone was naturally staring by that time. So I noticed when the temple slave was put on guard. It isn't a normal thing for them to do. I wondered why, but he wouldn't tell me, though I came across and asked. But I did discover that there was a box – I managed to get a look inside the coach.'

'And since he'd placed a temple guard on it, you reasoned that there was something very valuable inside? Which is why you made your offer for the veil?' I suggested. I had been surprised by the amount of money offered, at the time.

Colour came flooding back into his cheeks and he gave me a wry nod. 'It did occur to me. A man must take what chances he can get. Of course I didn't know about the body at that time – but neither did the patrician, obviously enough – so I reasoned that if it merited a temple slave as guard, there must be something very special in the box.' He essayed a little grin. 'That's why afterwards I kept an eye on it. Well, naturally I did! And I can tell you this: whoever put that body in the box there must have done it somewhere else. Nobody else came near the raeda all the afternoon. And the guard did not leave it. I'd stake my life on that. If that slave had gone anywhere I'd have had a better look myself, but he didn't give me a moment's opportunity. But here's the slave in question, just coming through the gate. You can go and ask him, but he'll tell you just the same.'

TWELVE

glanced in the direction that he was indicating and saw the pudgy slave in temple livery hurrying back out through the gate. I stepped towards him.

'Excuse me,' I said politely. 'I believe you are the slave who was asked by Publius to keep watch on the—'

He brushed my words aside as though I were a slave myself. 'Indeed I am, and I sincerely wish that I were not. I might have been excused this irksome duty otherwise. I am off to the household where he is staying now, so please excuse me, I have work to do. It's miles to the villa, and I don't know where it is.'

It was impolite of course. From any other servant such rudeness to a citizen would be a flogging crime, but temple slaves are prone to see themselves as servants of the gods and therefore not subject to merely mortal rules. Besides, I wanted to gain his confidence.

'You are going to the household of Lavinius?' I gestured to my companions who were by this time loading the box into the gig. 'In that case, friend, we may be of help to you. We have his gig-man with us, and he is driving back. He has that large box to carry, so there won't be room for you, but he could travel slowly to guide you to the house.'

I did not point out that it was effectively a funeral-carriage now. It would make no difference to Audelia, I thought, whether she travelled swiftly home or not – and personally I would prefer that the journey took as long as possible. It would give me time to set off for Corinium, before Publius could change his mind and call me back. After all, I had been commissioned to bring back his bride for him, and once that was achieved I had no formal contract with him any more. In fact, once he discovered her mutilated body in the box and found out that Druids were apparently involved, I was sure that he would fear a curse and want to distance himself from the whole family as soon as possible. But I'm a stubborn man and the presence of the mistletoe intrigued me very much; I was more anxious than ever to discover the truth.

And this self-important pudgy slave might help me. 'Let me take you to the gig-boy,' I suggested, with a smile.

My attempts to woo his friendship were ineffectual. He made an impatient noise. 'There is no time for that. I have a message from the pontifex which must get there as soon as possible. I have been told to find a hiring-carriage which will take me there, my master is using the temple coach himself. He still intends to go to Corinium tonight, it seems – though it is long past noon and he will barely get there before dark.' He looked around. 'There doesn't seem to be a carriage for hire anywhere,' he fumed. 'I would expect to find several hereabouts at this time of the day.' He nodded in the direction of the hiring-stable close nearby, where they customarily let out carriages and drivers for payment by the mile.

He was so full of outraged self-importance that I almost smiled. 'There may not be one available today,' I pointed out. 'With the Emperor's birthday and this evening's feasts, perhaps they have all been previously engaged.' He frowned. 'Then it will have to be a carrying-litter, I suppose . . .' he began.

Suddenly it struck me. I had been so busy trying to win his confidence that I had missed the real significance of what was being said. 'But why would the pontifex change his mind about going to Corinium tonight? You said he was "still going there". What did you mean by that?'

The puffy face turned pink. 'It is a matter of the utmost delicacy, citizen. A temple matter, I think that you could say.' He gave me a bland smile. 'Now if you will pardon me . . .' He moved as if to leave.

'It wouldn't be about that missing Vestal Virgin, I suppose?'

That stopped him in his tracks. Pink turned to scarlet. 'How do you know that?'

I ignored the question and asked one of my own. 'Has the temple had some kind of message from the Druids?'

His plump brow puckered into puzzled folds. 'What have Druids got to do with it?' He gazed into my face, then said as though he read the answer there, 'You don't mean that they have taken her away? Great Jupiter! I'd better go and let the high priest know at once. He's just had the message that she'd disappeared, but if he knows they've captured her, it may be that he won't go to Corinium at all. Then he can go and give this message to her family himself.'

He was already turning to go back through the gate but I caught him by the dark red fabric of his sleeve. 'Wait just a moment. What do you mean by that? Surely the high priest has known this news for hours? And wasn't he going to Corinium to link up with Lavinia . . . ?' I trailed off, seeing the expression on his face. 'Lavinia is missing?' I said disbelievingly. 'Is that what you are saying? She's disappeared as well?'

He pulled his tunic roughly from my grasp. 'I can't discuss the matter, citizen.'

'Oh, but you can!' I said. I pulled out Publius's letter and waved it at the slave. 'I have been charged by the family to find out what I can – as this letter would tell you, if you want to break the seal and check?'

He shook his head as I had known he would. Breaking the seal on a fastened writing-tablet was a serious affair, especially when the writer was a citizen of note. But Publius's insignia was unmistakeable.

'I believe you, citizen. I recognize the seal and you obviously know much about the matter anyway,' he said with a great deal more respect than he had shown me up to now. 'So I'll tell you what I know.'

I waited.

He ran a nervous tongue around his lips. 'The pontifex was to set off for Corinium, as you seem to be aware, to link up with the girl Lavinia and escort her on the rest of her journey to the Vestal House. It is highly inconvenient at this time of day, but her parents were generous and it had been specially arranged. He was ritually preparing for the journey when a messenger arrived with a missive from the guest house where she had stayed last night.'

I nodded. 'With her attendant, as I understand?'

'An aging nursemaid who had served her all her life. She was the one who first raised the alarm. It seems that once her cousin left the house, Lavinia went and shut herself away, resting and fasting in an upper room, preparing herself quietly for her new life at the shrine. But at shortly after noon she called out to the nurse – who had been set to sit all morning just outside the door – and sent down for a simple meal of bread and milk. The nurse went down to get it instantly, of course, and she and the lodging-keeper's wife went straight up with the tray. But when they tapped the door there was no answer from within. The boarding-house woman pushed the door ajar . . .'

'And found that Lavinia wasn't there?' I finished, almost unable to believe the words myself.

He nodded. 'They thought at first the girl was in her bed – there was a lump underneath the covers, it appears – but when they went to shake her, they found it was just clothes, piled up to give the impression of a human form. And there was a rope of twisted bedding dangling from the window-space down into the court, which in turn, gave out onto the road. They searched, of course, but no one had seen or heard the girl.'

'And the nurse?'

'The loading-keeper had her seized at once and locked away, awaiting questioning. She's quite distraught, of course, but it does not seem that she has very much to tell. She was in sight of the inn-servants all morning, anyway.' He gave me a rather quizzical look. 'I know you mentioned Druids, citizen, but this business does not sound like Druid handiwork to me. It looks more as if Lavinia has contrived to run away.'

I had to admit that it did look probable. Yet there were objections. 'But where could she run to? Her father would hardly consent to have her back. The best that she could hope for – if he was merciful – was to be sent into exile to some barren isle with nothing to her name. But I don't think mercy is his speciality. He might even sell her into slavery; he would have legal cause. She has disgraced the family – broken her parents' vow and made a mockery of them. It would be the talk of Glevum for a moon – and that's not something her father would lightly tolerate, if I am any judge.'

He took a moment to consider that. 'The pontifex supposed that – being only six years old – she would run home again but Mars knows you are right. Lavinius is not obliged to have her back, and the temple would not take her after this – of course – not without Lavinius making it worthwhile. But from what you say it's much more likely that he'd cast her out and then her fate would be deplorable. But surely his daughter would have realized that?' He paused. 'Or perhaps she did, since there's been no sign of her.'

'So where would she have gone? She has no family in Corinium – otherwise she and Audelia would have lodged with them, of course, as Audelia had done in other places on the way. She can hardly walk unnoticed around an unknown town alone – a well-dressed wealthy child like that – and she won't have any money to pay for lodging-rooms. Besides, according to the raedarius over there, she was excited about her future life.'

'Dear Jupiter. I do believe you're right. Perhaps somebody did take her captive and smuggle her away, and deliberately arrange the room to make it look like flight. Though if so, they must have watched the house and seized the moment when the poor nursemaid was not sitting on the step and when none of the other servants were about. If it was not Lavinia acting by herself, this must have been meticulously planned.' He frowned at me. 'What makes you think the Druids might have been involved?'

I glanced towards the gig, where Ascus and the others had by now arranged the box and were in the act of putting back the lid. 'It rather looks as if they laid hands on her aunt,' I said.

He had not seen what was in the box, of course, and his voice was casual. 'The bride of Publius, who did not appear?'

'Exactly.'

The pink eyes widened. 'I did hear a rumour that she hadn't come, but I thought it was just gossip, or perhaps she'd changed her mind. I didn't know that she was taken off by Druids. But you think it is connected?'

'Two disappearances in a single day – both of them Vestals, or very close to it – and taken both from Corinium, by the look of it. Hardly a coincidence, do you suppose?'

He nodded. 'You are right. I'd better go and tell the pontifex. If the Druids have captured the young woman, we must think again. If she had simply run back to her family as we had supposed, her service to the temple might just have been excused as childish nervousness – given sufficient extra dowry – just as a shy bride can be forgiven for unwillingness on her wedding day. But this is different. Obviously the Vestals will never have her now – this is too bad an omen for a novitiate. Too bad for almost anything, in fact. There will most likely be a ransom to be paid, if you're to get her back, and even that won't be the end of it. She'll carry the stigma of bad luck all her life. Perhaps her parents can arrange a match for her, something quiet in a year or two – some older man who'd be glad to take the dowry she would bring and is not too worried about her history.'

I noted that he had subtly washed his hands of her: the words 'if you're to get her back' had made that very clear. 'But you'll still inform her parents?' I enquired. 'After all, the pontifex was to take charge of her.'

He shook his head. 'Not until this evening. So it's no longer our affair. And you should be the one to tell them, surely, citizen? If you are going back to the villa with the box, and you are somebody the family trusts.'

I had to smile inwardly at his view of my role but perhaps I had led him to suppose I was a trusted friend. 'I am not returning to the household,' I explained. 'I am charged with travelling to Corinium – just as the pontifex had arranged to do. And I must leave at once. So I am afraid you will have to deliver that message for yourself – as you were ordered to – unless you wish to send it by the gig-driver?'

'It hardly seems fitting, but perhaps I could.' But he was tempted. I could read it on his face.

'He is already carrying serious news,' I urged. 'About the likely involvement of the Druids. We've just discovered that. And in that connection, you could help us, perhaps. I know that you were asked to guard the raeda through the day – did anyone come close to it or speak to you at all?'

'Only some pock-faced trader who tried to look inside, obviously bursting with curiosity. But I knew my duty. I sent him away. I told him nothing. Did you think I would?'

'And you did not for an instant leave your post? Not even to . . . ?' I waved towards the large pot just outside the gates, where someone from the wine-shop was busily engaged in providing urine for the fuller's shop. 'Or to eat and drink? It was a long time that you were standing there.'

He shook his head and gave a grimace that might have been

a smile. 'When you work at the temple, citizen, you learn great self-control. Some of the ceremonies can go on for hours. And as for food and water, today's a fast for us, until we celebrate the birthday feast tonight with a special meal at the temple slave-quarters.'

'So nobody could possibly have tampered with the box?'

'Not without my knowledge, citizen. And I saw nobody.' He was emphatic now.

'Very well,' I said. 'Thank you for your help. Now if you would like to go over to the gig and pass your message on, I will take the raeda and set off at once. It is a long way to Corinium and when I get there I have to find the house.'

'Can't you tell them for me, citizen?' the slave began, but Ascus was already striding towards us by this time.

'The gig is ready, citizen, and the raedarius is waiting for your orders to depart.'

I turned to the temple-slave who was boggling at the giant. 'Then I will leave you to pass your message to the gig-driver. I think we've finished here. Very well, Ascus, help me to my seat. On the front of the raeda with the driver would be best – then you can call him and we'll be on our way.' I beckoned to the raedarius and he came across while I let Ascus hoist me to my seat.

'Are we ready?' the raeda-driver asked, climbing gingerly aboard and picking up his whip. I nodded my assent. Ascus had vaulted up onto his horse again, and was already clearing a path for us through the now thinning crowds. I took a last look back.

In the distance I could see the gig with the box wedged into it. The temple-slave saying something to the gig-driver, who looked up and waved frantically at us.

I made a swift decision and waved politely back. I had not told my two companions that Lavinia had gone. I would tell them later – when we were on our way. Otherwise, I feared a mutiny.

I settled in my seat. 'Lead on,' I called to Ascus, and we rattled off.

THIRTEEN

It was a long journey to Corinium and for the first hour, at least, an uneventful one. The roads were almost empty and we travelled fast until we reached the crossroads where the basket-weaver lived.

We had hardly exchanged more than a few shouted sentences till then – the rattling carriage drowned them and the wind of our passage whirled the words away – but now the raedarius slowed the cart and turned towards me, gesturing with his whip towards the place. 'Do you still want to stop there, in case anything was seen while I was at the stall, or has the discovery of the corpse made that unnecessary now?'

I thought a moment and decided that I wanted him to stop. I signalled to Ascus to rein in his horse and we left him holding the raeda while we walked over to the stall. It was a simple lopsided table piled with osier baskets of every shape and size and stood outside a tumbledown cottage in a weed-strewn patch of ground, where hungry chickens pecked for food among straggly cabbages. Behind the stall a warty woman was sitting on a stool, weaving yet another of her wares.

She looked up and watched us warily as we approached, her face as thin and sharp as any of the dried stems that she wove. She exuded a strong smell of sweat and cooking-smoke. But she seemed to know the raeda-driver. She gave him a doubtful smile.

'Why, Ephibbius, are you back again?' She gestured to his bloodstained tunic. 'You've been whipped, I see.' She glanced evilly at me as though she thought I might have wielded the lash. 'Brought a customer?'

I shook my head. 'We are on our way back to Corinium. I hoped to have a word with you, that's all. About that basket which you sold him earlier, when he drove his carriage past . . .' I nodded to where Ascus had the raeda in his care.

'That so, citizen?' She picked up a knife and began to trim the ends of the osiers set around the frame, with savage little movements that emphasized her words. 'Well, don't you come complaining and bringing giants here. He doesn't frighten me. If that basket handle's broken, it's no fault of mine.'

'Broken?' This was unexpected. I glanced at Ephibbius, since that seemed to be the raeda-driver's name. I wondered how the woman came to know – he had certainly not mentioned it to me. However, the word sounds rather like the Greek for 'horse', so it may have been a nickname she had just thought up for him. I used it anyway. 'Did you know that, Ephibbius?'

She put the knife down, and began to thread another willow-strand into her handiwork. 'Well, of course, he did – that's why he sent it back. But it won't do any good – I told the slave-girl that. Perfectly all right when it left here, it was. Must have been something that she did to it. Silly child put too much weight in it, I expect.'

I stared at her. 'What slave-girl do you mean? What are you talking of?'

She looked up at me, her hands still busy with her work. 'Don't come here in your toga and start harassing me. You are a citizen. You must know the law of sale as well as I do. *Caveat emptor* – let the purchaser beware. Ephibbius bought the basket he contracted for. If he gave it to that maidservant and she broke it afterwards, that's no concern of mine.' She gave him a sly look. 'And him telling me he bought it as a present for his wife!'

'But I didn't give it—' the raedarius began.

I interrupted him, 'Not now, Ephibbius!' I turned back to the hag, suddenly realizing the implication of her words. 'Are you telling us you have seen the girl again? The one who was with him?' I hazarded a guess. 'She brought the basket back?'

The woman pursed her lips and gave an affronted sniff. 'Supposing that she did? I told her – same as I told you. Not my responsibility if the handle broke. She should have been more gentle – stuffing it so full.'

'Full of what?' I wondered. From the account that I'd been given earlier, Puella had no possessions of her own.

'Wild watercress!' the hag said, with a contemptuous sneer. 'Isn't that what Ephibbius gave her the basket for? Trying to sell it, from the looks of it – though Minerva knows who'd want to buy it around here. If we want it, we go and pick it for ourselves. There's plenty of it, off the beaten track.'

I frowned. Collecting watercress to sell? This sounded less and less like Audelia's maidservant. If Puella had been fleeing to escape a punishment – as the raedarius supposed – she would never have deliberately drawn attention to herself by coming to the basket-woman to complain. She would have known the risks she ran by calling here again – being recognized and handed to the authorities. There would be more than a mere flogging to be fearful of – the penalty for a slave who ran away was very often death. As to my own theory, which I'd briefly held, that the girl had run away because she knew what was hidden in the box – it was clearly false as well. Unless Puella had done the deed herself (in which case she was doubly certain to avoid the chance of being recognized) seeing the body would certainly have frightened her too much – knowing that the murderers were somewhere still at large and might do the same to her, if only to ensure she held her tongue. I could discount the whole idea. No female who had seen that mutilated corpse would idly stop in a deserted spot to gather watercress.

I shook my head. 'There must be some mistake. It was the same basket, you could swear to that?'

She snorted. 'Of course I could. I'd know it anywhere. It had a piece of blue-dyed thread around the joint. I put it there to cover up the . . .' She broke off. 'To make it stronger,' she corrected hastily. 'It was the one I sold to Ephibbius, all right. I should know my own handiwork, I hope. Anyway, I recognized the girl.'

That would have been my next enquiry. 'You're certain of that too?'

She sat back on her stool and grinned gleefully at us. 'So you didn't send her here? Well, by all the gods! Steal it from him, did she? Lure it from him and then run away? Well, I am not surprised. Used to getting her own way in everything, that one, you could see that at once – the way she was looking up at him, I knew what sort she was. Pretty face and pretty figure – knew how to use them, too.'

'You noticed her when she was here with Ephibbius before?'

'Well, you could hardly miss her, sitting where she was.

Made you wonder what she was doing, riding up the front with him – especially in the rain – instead of travelling with her mistress in the coach. But when I got a look at her, I knew what sort she was.' She nodded knowingly. 'He'll know better, another time perhaps – letting a pretty girl wheedle a present out of him – and him telling me that he had bought it for his wife.'

'But I didn't . . .' Ephibbius began again.

I shook my head at him. Her view of his character was not important now. 'But you've seen this servant since. How long ago was this?'

She screwed up her face. 'An hour or two, I suppose. The sun was over that elm tree over there.' She gestured to the place.

I was disappointed. 'It couldn't have been her. She was in Glevum close to the end of the birthday sacrifice. She could not possibly have walked here in the time.'

The sneering look came back. 'Who said anything about her walking here? She was riding on a cart. Ogling the owner, as you would expect. Seemed to be a farmer carrying some hay. Bribed him to carry her – or that is what she said, though she called it "paying him", of course.'

'But she had no money. She was a serving girl!' I exclaimed.

'Well, you may say so, citizen, but she had cash all right. Plenty of it, too. I saw the purse myself. Offered me a quadrans to put the handle right, but when I said that it would take an hour she wouldn't wait, because the farmer came over to tell her to get back on the cart.' She had picked up her work and started weaving the osiers again. 'His place is on the far side of Corinium, he said, and if she wanted to get there before dark they'd have to go. He'd promised her a dry bed in his stable overnight.'

I looked at Ephibbius with a puzzled frown. This was more and more perplexing. If this really was Puella, as the woman seemed to think, why had she been so eager to impart the details of her future whereabouts, which would make it easier to hunt her down? It made no sense at all.

The woman saw the frown, and misinterpreted it. 'With the horses, so she told me,' she said gleefully. 'And she was proud that she'd agreed a price – though I have my doubts that money

was what that farmer had in mind. I saw how he was looking
at her while she talked to me – worse than Ephibbius, if that
is possible. I wonder what the wife will have to say when he
gets home.' She broke off, with a leer. 'In any case, citizen,
what is that to you? It wasn't your purse, was it? She told me
that her mistress had given it to her.'

It was Ephibbius who spoke then. 'Her mistress gave her
nothing – and I can vouch for that. The servant was in trouble
for having lost some shoes, and was expecting to be punished.
When we arrived in Glevum . . .' He exchanged a glance with
me and obviously thought better of what he'd planned to say.
'When we arrived in Glevum the servant disappeared.
Obviously she took the money from her owner when she fled.
So now the family want her. We're here to look for her.'

The woman seemed singularly unmoved by this account.
The warty chin wobbled in a mirthless laugh. 'And what about
the letter? Did she steal that too?'

The raeda-driver and I exchanged a look, and said in unison,
'What letter?'

That changed her attitude. She put down her weaving and
got slowly to her feet, wafting the scent of burned grease round
us as she moved. Her fingers closed around her trimming-knife.
She was a tiny woman, no higher than my chest, but her hard
life had clearly toughened her. With her knife clutched menac-
ingly against her skinny breasts she was more intimidating
than many a full-grown man.

'Now see here, gentlemen. I'm a self-respecting trader and
I want no trouble here. I thought that you were honest and
had simply come to complain about that basket, but it seems
I'm wrong. I don't know what your game is, but this I'm
certain of, if you had been sent here by her owner's family,
as you said you were, you would know that she had a letter
from her owner round her neck, to the person she had served
before.'

I shook my head. 'Her owner's dead,' I said.

The knife-blade faltered slightly. 'Well, that slave-girl
doesn't know that – and it will break her heart. She was
promised manumission as soon as she got home.'

'Home? But her home was to be Glevum.'

A shrug. 'Well, that is where you're wrong. Somewhere

near Calleva, as I understand. That Vestal she was travelling with – to whom she had been loaned – had sent her back again, and given her the letter to prove she was entitled to be travelling alone and to have her slave-price money with her in a purse. I know there was only a woman signatory, but she was a Vestal Virgin apparently, so the document had force.'

I stared at the woman. 'How do you know all this?'

The basket-maker looked aggrieved. 'She showed me the letter – a proper little vellum scroll, no bigger than my hand. In a wooden cover, like a locket, specially made, I'd say.'

'And you read this yourself, though the text was in Latin?' It was clear I doubted it. It would be astonishing if she could read at all.

Her eyes avoided mine. 'I looked at it.' A brief affronted sniff. 'So, perhaps I couldn't read the words, but I know a proper seal when I see one, and this had one all right – though it was already broken when I looked at it. I understand she'd shown it to the farmer earlier, though I doubt that he could read it either – if it came to it.'

'So why are you so confident of what the letter said?'

She looked at me with something very near contempt. 'Citizen, what kind of idiot do you take me for? I had it read, of course. Do you think I would have let her drive off in that cart, if I had thought she was a runaway? There was a mounted soldier passing and I called him over here – he looked at it and read the words out loud to us. I was slightly disappointed, to tell you the truth; if she had being lying I'd have had him lock her up and tell the authorities in Glevum where she was – in case the owners were offering a reward. But the letter asked the public to assist her on her way – so, of course, I had to let her go.' She gave Ephibbius a crafty sideways glance. 'I'd even have swapped the basket, if she'd asked me to. You can't cross a Vestal's wishes – it would be appalling luck.' She sat down at the table and picked up her work again.

'But she didn't ask you to exchange the broken one?'

She shook her grizzled head. 'Just got onto the cart and they set off again.'

'I suppose the farmer was reassured by what he'd heard?'

'In fact, I don't think he was altogether pleased. I wonder if he might have had the same idea as me, and had planned to hand her in when he got home – or demand all her money to keep her secrets safe. However, once he learned that she was truly free to travel on her own, and had the protection of a Vestal Virgin too, he could hardly argue. He treated her with more respect, I noticed, afterwards.' She glanced up at us again. 'But you should have known that, if you really represent her owner's family. Though the woman's dead, you say?'

I shook my head. 'I was right the first time. This has all been a mistake. Thank you for your help.' I gestured to Ephibbius. 'Let's be on our way. Unless you want to buy another basket for your wife?'

He shook his head grimly and we went back to the cart. Ascus listened gravely as we told him what we'd learned. He used his giant hand to scratch his head. 'This gets more and more bewildering!'

Before we moved off, I told them about Lavinia's disappearance too. Additional disturbing and perplexing news could hardly make much difference to us now, I thought.

FOURTEEN

It was growing late before the walls of Corinium came into sight, and almost dark by the time that we drew up at the gate. We stated our destination to the guard and he allowed us through – together with a dozen heavy-loaded carts, of the sort which are usually banned from moving in cities during daylight hours. Corinium, being a market town, is more relaxed than some – Glevum, for example, is extremely strict, because of the constant military traffic passing through – but none the less these clanking carts had been held back till dusk and our progress was exasperatingly slow as we followed them into the darkening streets, which were of course too narrow to let us pass or turn.

It had not occurred to me, although it should have done, that the address we were seeking might be hard to find. I have been accustomed, in unfamiliar towns, to staying in the official inns, or mansios, which are built to serve officials and the Imperial post and so are always conveniently placed at or within the gates. This house was simply a spacious private home, which occasionally supplemented the owner's income by accepting paying guests, and though I'd heard it had a stable-block and court attached to it, I was surprised to learn that the entrance lay down a fairly narrow lane, at the town-wall end of a little line of shops. Fortunately, my companions had both been there before – though even then the raedarius passed the entrance to the alley once and had to drive all the way around the block again.

When we did arrive it was to find another problem awaiting us. The gate into the stable-court was bolted, the windows shuttered and the front doors firmly locked. There was not even the glimmer of a candle anywhere. This was something I hadn't bargained for – although of course the owners were not expecting us. Granted, many thrifty tradesmen living in the town – not having social lives and banquets to attend – retire at sunset and rise again at dawn, thereby saving heat and lighting fuel, they claim, but it was barely dusk. One would have expected some evidence of life. Even in the thrift-iest establishments there are always chores which cannot easily be done in working hours, and generally people require a little time to eat. Perhaps the owners had gone out, I thought – though surely in that case there would be slaves at least? I knew that there were at least two at the establishment, because they had carried the fateful box downstairs.

We knocked and shouted, but to no avail, and I was just beginning to wonder what to do, and whether I should go to the mansio after all, when a shutter opened at a window-space above and an indignant head poked out.

'What do you mean by coming here and making such a din?' The grizzled head and irritated tone suggested that this was the owner of the property. 'This is a respectable household and we are all abed.'

'Already gone to bed?' I echoed, in astonishment.

My amazement must have been evident in my tone. 'We have been busy. It has been a wearing day,' the man said, snappishly. 'Now that you know that, kindly go away. I don't know who you are or what you want, but we are not receiving anyone tonight. If you have business with us of some sort – as I suppose you must – then come back in daylight like anybody else.'

'But I've come to ask for lodgings,' I began, 'I understand you—'

The head shook forcefully. 'Then you've come to the wrong place. We don't take passing trade.'

'I have an introduction . . .' I brought out the writing-block and waved it hopefully towards the window-space – as though he could possibly have read it from up there, even in good light.

He was not impressed. 'I'm sorry, citizen.' He did not sound apologetic in the least. 'I don't know how you came to hear of us, but you've been misinformed. It's true we do take people now and then, but that's by prior arrangement only and even then we only deal with families we know. You'll have to look elsewhere.' He turned as someone with a lighted taper came into the room.

'What is it, husband?' said a female voice.

'Don't get excited, wife. It isn't what you hoped – no news of the young lady you were concerned about. Just some stranger looking for lodgings for the night. Don't worry, I've told him we aren't able to oblige.'

There was a moment's hissing conversation, and then a curly dark head joined the grizzled one – only a shadow now against the taper's light. A plump face looked down self-importantly at me. 'All our rooms are technically taken anyway.' She reached for the shutter. 'Try the mansio.'

'So I take it that Lavinia has not returned?' I called, before she had time to shut the window-space on me. She froze – the hand that rested on the shutter seemed to turn to stone.

'What do you know about Lavinia?'

'I was sent here by her family,' I said, though that was not strictly the answer to what she'd asked. 'And this letter of introduction is from the man who hoped to marry someone else you know, her cousin Audelia who stayed here yesterday.' I didn't mention what had happened to the bride – time enough for that news when we got inside. The town would be full of rumours tomorrow as it was – there was at least one listener loitering in a doorway opposite.

There was still no movement from the householders to come and let us in. I had an inspiration, suddenly. 'If you need further confirmation, ask Audelia's bodyguard.' I gestured to Ascus, who was waiting in the shadows by the court-gates, with the horse. 'No doubt you recognize him? He's noteworthy enough.'

The woman brought the candle and leaned out to look. When she saw Ascus she gave a little cry. 'Dear Mars, Trullius! He's telling us the truth. That is Audelia's bodyguard – I'd know that giant of a horseman anywhere, and by the gods I do believe that's her raedarius too – the one that brought Lavinia here and took Audelia on to meet her groom today.'

Ephibbius acknowledged this with a little bow.

She turned to her husband and thumped him on the arm. 'Trullius, you old fool! Can't you even look to see who you are talking to! Get downstairs at once and let these people in – tell the stable-slave to have the horses seen to and the stable-bed prepared, and I'll get something for this citizen to eat. He obviously comes from the family, as he says, and we are in enough trouble with them as it is.'

He muttered something which I could not hear.

'We'll manage! We'll keep the attic room in case the girl comes back, and he can have my bed, like that couple did last night. I'll just have to sleep in the servant's room again.' She gave him a sharp push. 'Well, get downstairs, what are you waiting for? Don't keep them in the street. You want the whole neighbourhood to know what's happening? We're entertaining half Corinium as it is.'

She was right. Shop doors and window-spaces up and down the lane were opening and people were peeping out of them, though when the side-gates opened and a scruffy slave appeared, waving Ascus and the raeda through into the court, the spectators appeared to lose interest in the scene.

The grizzled husband had come down himself to greet me at the doorway of the house, still dressed in the patched under-tunic he'd been sleeping in. He had draped a worn blanket around him like a cape, but he could not hide the dreadful burn-marks on one arm. He carried a lighted oil-lamp in his uninjured hand as with one bare foot he held the door ajar. 'Come in then, citizen,' he mumbled grace-lessly. 'I've sent a slave to get the fire alight, and my wife will find you something, if you want to eat.' He gave me a searching look. 'Though that may cost extra, at this time of night.'

I brought out Publius's writing-block again. 'It will be taken care of,' I said, loftily. 'I'd be grateful for some food. And my companions too. None of us has eaten anything since noon.' Much longer in the case of the raedarius, I realized, though I'd not heard him complain.

My host took the letter in his damaged hand – though he clearly found it difficult to grasp anything with that charred and withered claw – and peered short-sightedly at it, holding the scratched message so near the lamp I feared the wax would melt. However, what he saw appeared to satisfy his doubts. He looked up and nodded. 'This way, citizen.'

He ushered me down a passage to the right into a small room with a dining-alcove in the wall, complete with a table, a bench and two small stools, and lighted by a pitch-torch in a holder in the wall – rather like a common mansio, in fact. No fancy dining-couches on offer here! I wondered what

Audelia and her cousin thought of that! He motioned me to
sit down on the bench. 'My wife will be with you—'

'I am already here!' She came bustling in. She was much
younger than her husband, as I could now see by the lighted
taper which she held, and she might have been pretty if she
had not been so plump. Unlike her husband, she had found
time to dress, not only in a proper day-tunic to cover up her
legs, but she'd also managed to tie soft sandals on her feet and
thrust a fashionable band around her tousled hair. She gave me
a sly smile, obviously conscious of her ample charms. 'I am
Priscilla, at your service, citizen. Now, I have a little stew of
pork and leeks prepared, which I've put back on the fire, and
I believe there's still some bread and pickled fruits as
well . . .'

'Pork-stew would be excellent,' I said, with truth. It was,
in fact, unlooked-for luxury. I had expected bread and soup
at best. A meal of that quality must have been prepared with
Lavinia in mind. 'And you'll feed my horsemen too? They—'

She was so anxious to reassure me that she cut across my
words. 'Naturally, citizen. There is bread and cheese for them,
such as we usually provide, and I've had the stable-slave make
up a bed for them. Generally these fellows like to sleep beside
the horse.' She snuffed her taper out to save the wick.

I nodded, more because this accorded with what Ephibbius
had said than from any commendation of my own. The woman,
though, seemed visibly relieved that I was satisfied. 'Trullius,
go and give instructions to the kitchen-girl. Get her to bring
this citizen a plateful of that stew, the moment it is hot enough.
Make sure it doesn't burn. When she has done that, she can
take something to the stable for the men.'

The husband nodded. 'He's got a letter. Publius will pay.'
He lifted his oil-lamp to light his way and shuffled out towards
the rear part of the house.

'Nonsense, you old fool!' the woman bellowed after him.
'Of course we cannot charge him, after what's happened here.'
She turned to me. Her words came in a torrent. 'It's not our
fault, you know. We did everything according to instructions we
received – and a Vestal Virgin's wishes, even a prospective one,
are not to be ignored. When the girl demands that she be left
alone, to make quiet preparation for her new life at the shrine

– surely no one would expect us to do other than obey? I would never have gone into the room at all, except that she sent her nursemaid for a tray of this and that, and I had to help the woman take it up. Of course we thought the child was just asleep – worn out with her travel and excitements still to come. Even her nurse was unwilling to barge in on her, having been instructed otherwise, but – when we kept on knocking and getting no reply – in the end we had to force our way inside.' She paused dramatically.

I nodded. 'And when you did so, Lavinia wasn't there? Only a pile of clothing in the bed, to give the impression of a human form, I understand?'

She pursed her lips. She'd obviously been hoping to make a tale of this. But she was not silent long. 'We made a search, of course – she couldn't have got far, she had only sent down for the tray not half an hour before. But she'd obviously climbed out through the window-space, across the lower roof and down into the court – we found a blanket twisted into a kind of rope, and being young she could have swung down easily – though we can't find anyone who saw her doing it. And we couldn't find her in the streets, although we looked. Even went to the forum temple in case she had gone there – and of course they sent a message to the Glevum priests at once. They will not have her to be a Vestal now, so if that is what she wanted, she has got her wish.' She shook her head. 'But why would she run off? She seemed so enthusiastic about her future lot.'

'You think so?' If that was true, it was significant.

'She was so excited that she could hardly speak. Wanting Audelia to show her how to pray and make a proper Vestal sacrifice. Got quite proud and haughty about it, if you know what I mean. Boasting that in a year or two, she would be so important that a convicted criminal who crossed her path could be pardoned execution if she gave the word. The only thing that seemed to worry her at all was learning that she'd have to have her lovely hair cut off – beautiful red curls, she was so proud of them – but Audelia said they always shave the heads of novices. Hardly enough to make her take the risk of running off and bringing the wrath of the gods – or everybody else – upon her head.'

That set me wondering. Suppose the child hadn't run off of her own accord at all? A pile of clothing was no proof of anything – a kidnapper could contrive that easily enough to make it look like a simple childish prank. Besides, if the girl was going to run away why wait until midday? It would have been easier to do it hours before, when the house was busy with the morning chores and there was more daylight left. Unless, I thought suddenly, something had happened to give her a sudden fright, like a recognition of a Druid threat, perhaps? Some member of the household might have some idea. 'I would like to talk to your servants, anyway,' I said aloud.

The woman sniffed. 'If anything, it is the nurse you want to question about this – though she claims she was on watch outside the door all day and never left, except to come down for the tray. If you want to see her, she's under lock and key – I've locked her in the slave-cell till someone comes for her. Though perhaps I should have called the town-guard and had her put in jail. I wasn't certain what to do with her.'

I waved all this aside. 'I shall have to speak to her, of course. In the meantime, I have questions to ask you.'

'I might have known we'd be suspected of complicity! You're from the family, and I'm sure that they blame us,' she fretted. 'But truly, citizen, there's nothing I can add. Oh, dear Mars!' She pulled out a stool and sat down heavily. 'And we were so excited when the Vestal Virgins came. Going to make our fortune, that was – we told half the town – and now look what's come of it.'

She was interrupted by the arrival of her husband, who by now had put an over-tunic on and was personally carrying my supper on a tray – a bowl of steaming stew, some garum in a pot, a hunk of bread, a metal goblet and a jug of watered wine – and the lighted lamp was on the carrying board as well. He managed this by holding one end of the tray and supporting the other against his damaged arm and he set it down by sliding it along the board with practised ease. The stew smelt wonderful. He took a spoon out of a pocket in his belt, rubbed it on his hem and handed it to me. Then he stood back, self-importantly.

His wife had clearly no wish to have him listening to our talk.

'You'd better go and offer a little to the gods – this meal was intended for a priest and a priestess. We can't be taking unnecessary risks.'

He looked reluctant but he took up the lamp and shuffled off to do as he was bid. She motioned me to eat, but even as I spooned warm stew into my mouth she was already launching into speech.

'You see how the Fates have treated this household, citizen? We used to have a splendid business making pots – he had his own kiln in the courtyard and lots of wealthy customers. But then he had a nasty accident, and now he really can't make pots at all – though he refuses to admit it, and still tries from time to time, with the consequent waste of good materials.'

'So you've had to turn to taking passing guests?'

She nodded. 'Usually genteel females travelling on their own who do not want to use the common inns and are not entitled to use the mansios. It does not happen more than once or twice a moon, so it's a precarious living in a general way. So when we were offered this opportunity, we seized on it at once. A Vestal in the house? We thought we'd make our fortune, when the news got out.' She shook her head. 'Now I wish Lavinius had never heard of us.'

I ignored the garum and dipped the bread into the stew. 'I heard that he'd arranged it. How did he come to know you?'

'He used to be a customer when we were selling pots. He heard that we were reduced to taking guests and sent a slave to check that we were suitable. I understand it was his wife's idea, in fact – she wanted somewhere safe for her daughter to come and meet Audelia overnight, since there are no family members actually living in this town.'

'Mmm-hhh!' was all I managed, though I was listening. I swallowed my mouthful. 'Had the cousins met before?'

'I don't believe so, but you would not have guessed. They had such a pleasant evening – they shared a room of course – and they got on so well. I believe they would have talked and laughed all night, if the bride had not needed to get up at dawn and go on to Glevum to be wed. I hope that she'll be happy.' She glanced at me. 'You didn't see her wed? No doubt you had to leave before the wedding feast.'

'You didn't hear that the marriage never did take place?' I said, unnecessarily. The truth of that was clearly written in her face. 'It was thought that Audelia herself had disappeared. I thought the news would certainly have reached you by this time.'

She boggled at me. Speech almost failed her, for once. 'Disappeared?' The big eyes widened. 'Believe me, citizen, we had no idea at all!' A look of sudden panic spread across her face. 'But she left here safely. There are witnesses to that. If she didn't get to Glevum, no one can blame us.'

I was almost loath to tell her. 'I'm afraid that isn't true. Audelia did get to Glevum, but by that time she was dead. Savagely murdered by the look of it.'

The woman jumped up and seemed about to scream but I prevented her. I put my two hands on her shoulders and forced her to sit down. 'This is private information. Do not share it with the slaves. Whoever murdered her is clearly still at large, so the fewer people who know of it, the safer for us all. But tell me. You must have seen her leave? Did you see anything suspicious at the time?'

She shook her head. Her plump face had turned white and she was clearly shaken to the core. 'Nothing at all. I told you, she left here in good health. I saw her get into the coach and so did everybody in the house – except Lavinia who had said goodbye, received a blessing, and was already at her prayers. But Lavinia's nursemaid and the other couple too. They all went down at dawn to see Audelia leave and wish her happiness – as of course you do when you are speaking to a bride.' She was twisting her tunic in her fingers now.

'This other couple?' I had heard before that there were other people in the house, but I had imagined they were simply unrelated guests. 'Were they acquainted with Audelia, then?'

There was a curt laugh behind us. 'Oh indeed so, citizen. More than acquainted. They were her relatives – though fairly humble ones.' It was the husband who had come in unobserved and had clearly overheard this last remark.

'Don't tell him any more,' the woman said. 'Audelia is gone. Oh dear Mars, what will become of us? I wish by all the gods that she had lodged with them, as she originally planned, and I hadn't talked you in to having them stay here.'

I turned to Trullius.

He sighed. 'I could wish my woman didn't talk so much, but since you've heard the half of it you'd better hear the rest. No, don't tell me to be quiet, wife! If he's come here from the family, he had better know. It's quite true, citizen. I think Audelia might have sought to stay with them, till Lavinius put a stop to that by arranging things with us. When he did so, she wrote privately to me, asking me to find a room for them as well.'

'And you agreed to that? Against her uncle's preference?'

He looked defiantly at me. 'Why not? As a Vestal, she outranks him anyway, and a priestess's wish should always be obeyed. Besides, she was prepared to pay me very handsomely and her uncle had not forbidden them to meet – although she hinted that she'd rather that he did not hear of it. Though in the circumstances, I suppose he'll have to know.'

'Dear Mars! He will blame us for everything, without a doubt.' The woman wailed. 'I don't know why Lavinius should object to them, in any case. Nice, gentle people and perfectly polite.'

'Not rich enough to suit Lavinius,' the husband said. 'That's the front and back of it. But they didn't seem to mind. Said that they wanted to come to Corinium anyway, and would take advantage of the trip to visit the slave-market and get a slave or two.'

I was very interested in these poor relations of the bride. 'Where are they now? I may wish to talk to them.' I absently poured myself a little watered wine.

'I can tell you where they live. It's only a few miles' journey to the east of here. I had to send a letter to say we had a room.'

'I only wish she'd gone there after all,' his wife said, tearfully. 'It would have made a convenient stopping-place for her. Personally, I think it was their child that prevented it. The girl is afflicted – deaf and dumb since birth.'

'And allowed to live?' I was surprised at that. Most afflicted Roman children were exposed and killed at birth, saving their family the embarrassment and expense of raising them.

'The parents did not realize for a month or two, and by that time the mother had got attached to it. So they did not leave it out to die or feed it to the dogs – though they could still have done so until the child was three. Instead they made a pilgrimage to every shrine there is, including the Vestals, to offer sacrifices and petition for her health.'

'So Audelia knew them?'

'I believe she did, but then the mother died. She had been frail and ailing since the birth, and in the end the worry was too much for her.'

I paused in my enjoyment of the stew. 'But I thought . . .'

'That was his first wife, citizen – this is the second one. I don't believe Audelia had met her before,' Trullius told me, in a patient tone.

'Though it would have been a good idea if she'd gone to the shrine herself,' the woman said. 'She's delicate as well. Look how the journey here distressed her. Completely wore her out. She was forced to go to bed and rest for several hours until Audelia arrived, and even then I hardly heard her say a word. Of course she has that child of his at home to worry her.' She broke off suddenly. 'I'm sure that's why Lavinius refused to let Audelia stay with them, and why he did not ask them to the wedding-feast today. It's enough bad luck to cross a leper or a blind man on the street before your marriage day. To share a household where a deaf-mute lives would be a dreadful portent for a bride-to-be.'

The man laughed. 'Nonsense, wife. Paulinus and his wife are not rich and powerful enough to suit Lavinius, that's all. Just simple people living on a farm. I don't believe the theory of the evil auguries. It did not alarm the bride-to-be to meet them here—'

She cut him off. 'But Trullius – dear Mars! Perhaps it should have done. Audelia is dead. Did you not hear him say? I still can't believe it.'

'Dead!' He was clearly shocked. 'That news I hadn't heard.' He glanced sheepishly at me. 'We did get a message from the temple in Glevum just before you came – brought by the same courier who took the news about Lavinia from here. He carried the answer that, since Lavinia was no longer in the house, the high priest would not come to Corinium tonight, and when he did come, would no longer call on us.'

So that was the explanation of the stew, I thought. 'After all your preparations?'

He shuffled awkwardly. 'The man did mention that Audelia had not arrived at the birthday games as planned, so I'd heard that before you came – but he said that it was generally assumed, by those few who knew that she was coming there, that she'd been kidnapped by brigands and there'd be a ransom to be paid.'

The woman started to her feet again. 'You didn't tell me that!'

'I know I didn't, wife, I thought to save you more anxiety – we had enough troubles of our own to worry us. But nobody told me that Audelia was dead.' He turned to me. 'Are you quite sure of that?'

I drained my cup. 'I'm absolutely sure. We found the body in her travelling box. The work of Druids, by the look . . .' I said no more. The woman had fallen in a faint upon the floor.

FIFTEEN

Trullius looked at me. 'I knew there would be trouble. Taking in Vestal Virgins – even retired and prospective ones – is not appropriate for the likes of us. I knew it was certain to offend the gods. I said so to my wife! But she wouldn't listen. And now look what's happened!' Before I could stop him he had seized the jug and dashed the remainder of its contents in her face.

Priscilla stirred and moaned. He reached down and used his good hand to haul her to her feet. 'Come on, wife, I will help you to your bed. You have had too much worry for one day as it is. Anyway there is nothing further we can do tonight.' He hoisted her upright and would have hurried her away if it had been up to him.

But, she shook him off and sat down unsteadily on the stool again, resting her head between her hands. When she had come to herself a little more, she looked up breathlessly. 'I may not be a Vestal, husband, but I am not a fool. I run this rest-house just as much as you, and this concerns us both.'

'All this talk of Druids is not fit for women's ears,' he said. 'Go to your bed – I'll see to matters here.'

She shook a stubborn head. 'I want to find out what's been happening – and it's obvious I can't trust you to tell me what you know.' She turned to me. 'So, what befell Audelia, citizen? If it's not so disturbing that it spoils your meal.'

I had eaten every morsel of the stew by now but she was still deathly pale and I really did not welcome telling her the details of that shocking corpse. I procrastinated, picking up a crust of bread. 'I'm sorry that I caused you such distress,' I said. 'The news that Audelia had disappeared – as we supposed – was discovered this morning, before the games began. Knowing there had been an exchange of messengers between here and Glevum, I naturally assumed you knew at least as much as that . . .' I tailed off, apologetically.

She cast a furious look at Trullius. 'And so I would have done – if my husband had seen fit to tell me anything.'

Trullius spread his one good hand in outraged innocence. 'And have you fainting at the news?'

'I would have done nothing of the kind! Ignore him, citizen. A little while ago you told me that Audelia was dead, and did I faint at that? Of course I didn't. But I thought we were talking about a robbery gone wrong. Attack by highway brigands I could have understood – though Mars knows that's bad enough – but –' she used one plump hand to fan herself – 'if the Druids are involved it's something else again.'

Trullius put out a warning hand, but she brushed him off.

'Don't interrupt me, Trullius! He will hear from others, if he doesn't hear from us. Anyone in town will tell him what's been happening.' She turned to me again. 'Perhaps, citizen, you don't know what these Druids can be like – unless you've heard the tales – but there's been a lot of trouble with them round here recently. Curse-tablets and spell-casting and Jove knows what. It's said that sheep and cattle are falling dead from it, and children born with crooked arms and legs, all because the Druid priests are looking for revenge.'

'Revenge?' This was a new idea. I was so surprised I swallowed the whole crust and had to wash it down with the last dregs of my sharp-tasting wine. I knew that there were odd bands of western rebels still hiding in the woods and that they often clung to the old religion as part of the protest against Rome. But generally their efforts were not of much account – a futile rearguard action against the conquerors, harrying military convoys or picking off solitary soldiers as they passed. So . . . ? 'Revenge?' I said again.

This time Trullius did exert himself. 'Silence, woman! You have already talked too much. I will tell him, if anybody does! I won't have you spreading rumours that there's no foundation for. I am still the master of this house.'

And so he was, of course, and I would need his help as well. I turned towards him with a deferential smile. 'I'd be glad of any information you can give.'

He was a little mollified. He cleared his throat – so like an orator on the forum steps that I half-expected him to strike a pose before he spoke. 'Then I will tell you what is certain – not stoop to rumours. The authorities found a nest of Druid rebels in the woods. They had been making their usual bloody sacrifice – several heads of murdered legionaries were hung up on the trees and it was decided that an example must be made. A trap was set against them, and instead of killing them, the military managed to bring a lot of them to trial.' He paused, to make sure I was following all this. 'You can imagine the result.'

'Of course! It is a capital offence simply to be a member of the sect – let alone murdering soldiers,' I replied.

He nodded. 'There have been public executions every day, as part of the civic *munus* – the five days of public games, leading up to and including the Imperial Birthday feast. Most of the prisoners were sentenced to the beasts – though one or two were fortunate enough to purchase poison and escape the worst of it. The last of them was executed only yesterday.'

His wife broke in again, clearly unable to hold her tongue for long. 'There were some more victims in the ring today, but they weren't dangerous, they were only followers of that Jewish carpenter – refusing to make a sacrifice to the Emperor, publicly saying that he is not a god, instead of keeping silent and going through the pretence, like anybody else. But of course they're funny folk. They even claim that they forgive their enemies. The Druids don't! They're quite the opposite! So that is why I ask. Do you suppose the Druids killed Audelia in revenge?'

I nodded thoughtfully. It was the likely explanation, given these events. There would be a risk, of course – penalties for laying sacrilegious hands on a Vestal Virgin are even more severe than being fed to beasts. But provided that the rebel perpetrators felt themselves secure . . . 'A Vestal Virgin would be a kind of symbol, I suppose,' I said slowly.

Priscilla looked impatient. 'More than just a symbol, citizen. Everyone knows the fate of Rome depends upon the sacred flame that they maintain in the Imperial capital. And it is the same with the Vestal temple in Britannia. Audelia was telling us about it yesterday: the altar flame was brought here in braziers as a "daughter fire", and if that goes out it's said the Empire will fall.'

I doubted that the Druids believed all this, in fact – they

had their own ways of trying to defeat the might of Rome –
but I could see how the ritual murder of a Vestal might affect
the public mind.

It was clear what the authorities had intended to achieve by
the recent executions in the ring: to punish the victims with
humiliating death and frighten off other would-be supporters
of the sect, and also to undermine the influence of the Druid
priests – whose skills at divination are supposed to be their
strength. It was equally clear why the rebels might have seized
and killed Audelia in revenge. What defeated me was how
they'd managed it.

Which did not mean they hadn't done it: quite the contrary!
It was just the kind of coup which would appeal to them,
designed to terrify the populace and taunt the conquerors by
proving that the sect had secret, magic powers and that its
members' deaths would not go unrevenged.

'I can understand the impulse to retaliate,' I said. 'I have
witnessed an execution *ad bestias* myself, in company with
my patron. It is a dreadful death.'

Even now the memory raised bile in my throat. First the
snarling and slavering of the wolves and bears (the favoured
animals in this northern outpost of the Empire, where more
exotic creatures are not easily obtained) as a taunting fragment
of raw meat was held in front of them, to demonstrate that
they had not been fed for days. Then the convicted criminal
dragged screaming to the ring, flogged so that the smell of
fresh blood would reach the starving beasts, before he was
tied naked to a post on a sort of chariot, and thrust into the
snarling cage to be torn apart for the entertainment of the
crowd. I pushed my plate away.

Trullius seemed reluctant to accept this train of thought,
perhaps because it had been suggested by his wife. 'What
makes you so certain it was Druids, anyway? I'm sure they've
not confessed. You must have a reason for thinking it was
them?'

There was nothing for it. I told them everything, including
a description of the mutilated corpse. There was a silence. The
woman turned a paler shade of white and I almost feared that
she would slump onto the floor again.

Trullius took one look at her and seized the empty jug,

hugging it to him as he took the lamp again. 'I'll get some more of this. My wife could do with something, by the look of it, and – frankly – so could I, though, not being Roman citizens, we're unaccustomed to drinking late at night. You, citizen, are welcome to have some if you wish. There won't be any charge.' He shambled off into the back part of the house.

I realized that Priscilla was looking desperately around. 'Searching for something?' I enquired.

She didn't answer, merely seized the wooden tray, knocked on it three times and spat onto the floor. I realized that she had been seeking to 'touch wood' and keep ill-luck away. A Druid superstition if I recalled aright – though everyone seemed to have adopted it these days.

When she spoke her voice was tremulous. 'The head chopped off and sprigs of mistletoe enclosed – it certainly sounds like Druid handiwork.' She rallied as a sudden thought seemed to occur to her. 'But if that's true, no blame can fall on us. If they murdered her, it must have been in Glevum, citizen. They did not do it here, and they could not possibly have done it on the way. There would have been a dreadful skirmish: it would have rocked the coach, and someone would have noticed, the raedarius or the maid. To say nothing of the mess it must have made.'

I toyed with the remaining breadcrumbs on the board. 'There wasn't any mess. That is one of the most interesting aspects of the whole event. And she was not killed in Glevum, there are witnesses to that. The coach was under observation all the time.'

I saw the look of horror slowly dawning in her eyes. 'So what are you suggesting? That she was dead and already in the box when she left here? Well, I can tell you certainly that she was not. With my own eyes I saw her get into the coach.'

'And you could swear to that? Did she not have a veil?'

That took her aback. 'Well, of course she did. So does any modest Roman matron, come to that. So did all the women, except the slaves, of course. But all the others were standing round while she got in, and they knew her well. They would have recognized her – from her voice, if nothing else – and realized if there was anything amiss. I was upstairs and looking down into the court and I heard her speak myself – and anyway, I would have known the cloak. Only a Vestal Virgin has a snow-white cape like that. In fact it had already attracted attention from the street – later I saw an ancient slave-woman still goggling at the gate. I actually had to wave at her to shoo her off.'

Something that she said had struck a chord with me. 'So Audelia was not only veiled, she had a hooded cape?' I frowned. Another mystery. There had been no cloak inside the raeda when we found the corpse.

Priscilla noticed my perplexity. 'Well you did not expect her to get wringing wet? Not on her wedding day?'

'Of course, it was raining! Ephibbius told me that!' I was annoyed, but only with myself. Why had I not seen the significance of that fact before? 'So not only did Audelia have a cloak and hood, the others had one too?'

Priscilla took my irritation for rebuke. 'Well naturally, citizen. The women anyway. What else would you suppose?' She got to her feet and started clearing the table noisily, banging the cup and plate onto the tray. 'But if you're suggesting what I think you are – that it might have been someone else who got into the coach – then, forgive me, citizen, but I think that you're insane. I saw her do it. Ask my husband if you doubt my word for it. He was in the courtyard near the raeda when she got into it. Wouldn't he have noticed if a stranger took her place?'

I had to admit that she had a valid point, but I was loath to abandon the only theory that I had. 'Then is it possible that someone was already hiding in the coach? Someone concealed beneath the seat, perhaps? Or in the box itself? Suppose the Druids had got to hear there was a Vestal here – it is not impossible to break into the house. If Lavinia could get out of it so easily, then someone could get in, find the box and hide away in it.' I was warming more and more to the idea.

She paused in her noisy clearing of the board. 'But Audelia and her cousin shared a room last night. No one could possibly have hidden in the box without their noticing. Besides, Audelia had me bring a tray to her before she left – some washing water and a little bread and milk – and I saw her with my own eyes, collecting her possessions and refolding them. She'd unpacked everything the night before to hunt for wedding-shoes. So no one could have hidden in her box overnight and jumped out in the coach.' She paused to look at me. 'You keep looking for logic, citizen. If this is Druid magic, there may be none to find. It may be the work of spells and sorcery. They have their secret methods of bringing things about.'

I had my methods too, and I was reluctant to abandon them. As with the street-magicians in Glevum earlier, I was sure that there was some logical explanation of the trick – even if the Druids had a hand in it. But how had it been done? Something, somewhere was not as it appeared. I mentally rehearsed the details of what I had been told. 'About those wedding slippers . . . ?'

Priscilla looked surprised. 'I suppose the horseman told you about that? He was sent to find them – I don't know if he did.' She had finished clearing up the remnants of my meal, and she rubbed down the tabletop with one sweep of her sleeve. 'Audelia was angry when they could not be found – quite unlike herself.'

'So angry that she wouldn't have her slave-girl sleeping in the room?'

Priscilla almost smiled through her nervousness. 'There was hardly room for that in any case, with her box and Lavinia taking up the floor. Generally we provide a sleeping mat and have the servant's bed down just outside the bedroom door. And that's exactly what happened yesterday. The nursemaid and Audelia's maid were both on guard up there, and – before you ask – the horseman and the raeda-driver slept beside the coach, so I don't see how anybody could have got in there unobserved.'

I shook my head. Another theory ruined.

She saw the gesture. 'I told you, citizen. This is Druid sorcery at work.'

I met her eyes. 'But how would Druids know there was a Vestal here? Her presence was not publicly announced, though you said that you had boasted about it to your acquaintances. Are there Druid followers among the people that you told?'

She hesitated. Not for very long, but before she found her tongue her husband had already spoken from the darkness of the door.

'None that we know of, citizen. Although, of course – as I
said before – since membership of the sect is officially a crime,
nobody is likely to admit to it.' His tone was so open and
hearty, suddenly, that I was convinced that he was attempting
to hide something from me. He came in and slapped the jug
down on the board, together with two extra cups that he'd
been carrying crooked into the elbow of his damaged arm.
'Here is the wine. Enough of your prattling, wife.' He poured
a little into the smaller cup and pushed it towards her. 'Have
a draught of this . . .' He paused. 'Before the Druids come
for you as well.'

That seemed to silence her. She took the cup and had a
small obedient sip. 'The citizen thinks there was a substitution
made – that it was not Audelia that got into the coach,' she
said, slowly. 'I have told him otherwise.'

He poured himself some wine, and – as an afterthought –
poured out some more for me. 'For once, citizen, the woman's
talking sense. I saw the Vestal climb into the seat myself. I
helped the raedarius hand her up the steps.'

'You heard her voice?' I said, remembering the veil.

He took a long and savouring sip of wine, and licked his
lips. 'I did. She even spoke to me. Thanked me for my help,
and slipped me a small coin – I forgot to tell you, wife. Then
I went and found the stable-slaves to carry down the box, and
supervised them while they put it in the coach. There was no
chance of a substitution, citizen. Everyone was clustered round
her making their farewells. Secunda was very nearly in the
coach herself, helping Audelia to put the shutters up. And
when it left here she was terribly upset – smothering her hands
with kisses and blowing them towards the coach. You'd never
think the family had insulted them, by refusing to invite them
to the wedding feast.'

Priscilla nodded. 'Not that the poor thing was really well
enough to go. She walks so badly and is generally so frail,
she was leaning on her husband all the time that she was here.
And so quiet and timid all the while. I don't believe I heard
her speak above a word – except to say goodbye and thank
you as they left.'

'Was that long after Audelia had gone?' I asked.

'They did not finally depart for at least another hour, but

they did go into town immediately she'd left. That had always been the plan. The slave-market opens shortly after dawn, and they wanted to be there as soon as possible – before the best were gone. There was one in particular that they had heard about – a female slave who had been injured in the throat and afterwards had lost the power of speech, and was no doubt offered at a bargain price. Damaged goods, of course. Who'd want a slave like that?' She seemed to be aiming this at Trullius, as if to point out that he was damaged too.

He said, with a certain patient dignity, 'They wanted to buy her for their daughter, I believe, thinking that another mute would make a bond with her and might even help her to understand the world. No doubt the slave was cheap, but I believe Paulinus would have paid any price at all, if he thought it would help his precious child in some way.'

She smiled, contemptuously. 'That is exactly the point I made to you before – yet you think my arguments are foolish ones. Of course he'll pay too much. He's already spent a fortune, which he could ill afford, on charms and cures for her – not that they have done any good at all. And of course, they'd lost the nursery-maid she was familiar with—'

'Enough of your gossip, woman,' Trullius broke in. 'Drink your wine and get yourself to bed, and I will assist this citizen to his.' He put his cup and jug down on the tray, which he deftly scooped up and balanced as before. He turned to me. 'You don't require a servant sleeping at your door? I could fetch the horseman and provide a sleeping-mat. Or put a stable-slave on duty for you, if you wish. I'll light another taper and accompany you upstairs.'

I did not need a candle to see what was afoot. A blind man might have seen. All this solicitation was a desperate attempt – and a clumsy one at that – to shut the woman up and hustle me away.

SIXTEEN

I was tired and shaken from my journey and would have gladly gone to bed, but it was so evident that there was something here Trullius was trying to hide, that I took a deliberate sip of my not-much-watered wine and slowly shook my head.

'In a little while, Trullius. I have not finished here.' The drink was sour and unpleasant – clearly inferior to the vintage they'd offered me before. I put the goblet down. 'There are some further questions I would like to ask your wife, since it seems you are not willing to tell me everything yourself.'

He was about to bluster, but I cut him off.

'What is it about Paulinus that you don't want me to hear?' I made a guess – it wasn't difficult. 'This is something connected with the Druids, isn't it?'

Priscilla put down her cup and took the tray from Trullius's hand. 'You tell him, husband, or I'll do it myself. And don't look at me like that. You were the one who insisted we should tell him everything, because he was sent here by Lavinia's family. Well, from what he's told us, this concerns Lavinia as well. You can't go on supposing – now – that she simply ran away?'

He said nothing.

'Oh, by all the gods! Audelia has been murdered and her hands and head cut off. Do you want the same thing happening to that little girl? Vain and self-important as she might have been, she was just a child. Spoiled by her parents and her nursemaid – that was obvious – but nothing to deserve a dreadful fate like that.' She slammed the tray down on the table. 'Tell him, Trullius! You can't escape it now. This household is already implicated in this mystery. It's obvious that the family will blame us when they know – and it won't help you to start concealing things.'

Trullius reached out and poured himself another cupful from the jug. His one good hand was trembling as he raised it to his mouth but he wiped his lips against his sleeve and said, with violence, 'Oh great Mars, woman, why did I listen to your pleas? Why did we ever have these people here? Of course we had no intimation at the time . . .' He took another gulp. 'It's like this, citizen. My wife is quite convinced – though it is only hearsay and supposition on her part . . .'

'Oh, get on with it,' the woman said. 'It's Paulinus and Secunda, citizen. Their servant was a Druid. And there's no supposition. They told me so themselves – although they claim they didn't know she was a member of the sect until she came to trial.'

I stared at her. '*She?* It was a maidservant?'

Priscilla pursed her lips. 'Well, not exactly that. They don't have what you and I would call a proper set of slaves. One or two labourers to run the farm, and some old crone who cleans the house for them, but otherwise they seem to do everything themselves, like common peasants. This was an outside wet nurse whom Paulinus employed.'

Trullius agreed. 'Used her to suckle that afflicted girl of his – because the mother was so frail she could not feed the child herself. This woman seemed ideal – she was healthy, clean and strong, lived not far away, and had just finished suckling children of her own. She took the foster-infant in to live with her, for a while at least.'

I nodded. This was not an unusual arrangement in a Roman family. Many Roman mothers farm their children out to some healthy female who has ample milk to spare, in return for a small income and the certainty of good nutritious food – which of course the parents are anxious to provide, since their own offspring will benefit from it. Only the wealthy have a slave-nurse come to live with them, as Lavinia's family had evidently done. 'But this wet nurse proved to be a follower of the Druids?'

Priscilla laughed harshly. 'Not just the wet nurse. The whole household was involved – the very house where the infant had been kept. The husband went off to the woods each day – supposedly collecting firewood to sell – but actually fighting on the rebel side and supplying them with food and informa-tion all the time.'

'Though, whatever anyone may tell you to the contrary,'

Trullius said, 'I am sure Paulinus had no idea of that. He was only anxious that his daughter should be fed, especially since the mother was getting feebler all the time – until, of course, eventually she died.'

His wife was making impatient noises now. 'Well, tell him everything. Don't stop the story now. Tell him how Paulinus kept up the arrangement for three years or more, until the child was weaned – though by that time it was clear that the thing was deaf and mute and there was no chance of it ever having a proper life. Couldn't even sensibly be offered as a slave.'

I could feel some sympathy with Paulinus over this. A deaf person is regarded as a 'hopeless maniac' under Roman law – meaning that education is impossible – and therefore the person has no legal rights at all and cannot get married or inherit property. I said aloud, 'It must have been difficult for Paulinus.'

Priscilla laughed again. 'Indeed it was. He spent a fortune which he didn't have, trying to find some sort of cure for it. And now tell me he wouldn't be glad to earn some gold, spying for the Romans, if he got the chance. Though I for one would not blame him if he did. After what the Druids have been doing with their curses around here, they deserve their punishment.'

'You think that he betrayed the wet nurse to the authorities?' I said. If so, it opened up a whole new avenue of thought.

Trullius shook his head. 'I'm quite certain he did nothing of the kind. I don't believe he had it in him to be cruel to anyone. And Secunda is the same.'

Priscilla looked at him sharply. 'She's his second wife, of course, and they've not been married long. She's very dutiful. Of course she would support him in anything he did. But Paulinus would do anything to save his child from threat, including betraying his grandmother, let alone the nurse. Though admittedly he kept her on in his employ right up to the night when they arrested her.'

'The wet nurse was still with them?' I was surprised at that. 'Surely it is not the custom to retain the nurse, after the child has been weaned and gone back home again?'

Priscilla sighed, as if explaining to a simpleton. 'But the child was deaf, of course. It could not be left, and no ordinary slave could cope with it, poor things. And Paulinus refused to do the obvious and have the child put down – she was the only reminder of his beloved wife, I heard him say. So he paid the former wet nurse to come in every day and take care of the girl.' She glanced at Trullius. 'My husband will not have it, but there must have been a cost, and everybody knows that household wasn't rich. Yet now he's suddenly got money in his purse, and is talking about buying a pair of live-in slaves. Don't you think that is significant?'

Trullius was pouring yet another cup of wine. 'Don't listen to her, citizen. There's nothing odd at all. Secunda brought him a small dowry when they wed, no doubt part of that was used to cover the expense. And it was sensible. The child had known the wet nurse all her life and was fond of her. They even managed to communicate, after a fashion – so Paulinus said – waving their hands about and drawing on a slate. I simply don't believe that he'd betray the wet nurse to the law, whatever the reward. Especially since he knew what punishment they would inflict on her.'

I was appalled. 'They threw her to the beasts?'

The two householders exchanged a glance at this, but it was Trullius who spoke. 'It didn't come to that. Paulinus did his best for them, I heard Audelia say. Bribed the guard to give them hemlock they could drink and die with dignity – both the wet nurse and her child and husband too.' He rounded on his wife. 'Would he have done that, woman, if he'd betrayed them first? It isn't in his character. You say yourself he is a gentle man. And yet you think he'd do a thing like that? It makes no kind of sense.'

She tossed her head. 'Even a good man knows his duty when it comes to Druids – and serve them right, I say. I don't believe he'd let them suffer, if he could save them that, but after the atrocities that took place in the wood, he might have felt obliged to name them to the authorities. After all, he is a citizen, and related to an important family, even if he isn't a wealthy man himself. And that is just the point. Here are the authorities offering a reward, and suddenly the wet nurse is arrested and arraigned, and those two, who never had a proper establishment before, are suddenly in the market for not one slave, but two.'

'One who is mute, and the other a mere child. An untrained one at that, from what I glimpsed of him. Cheap bargains, both of them.' He gulped down the contents of his cup. 'Don't be so stupid, wife! Secunda's dowry would have paid for slaves like that a thousand times.'

I cut across the bickering. 'Did you say they had not been married long?'

Trullius shook his head, and said, now with the careful diction of the slightly drunk, 'Not very long at all, I understand. A month or so at most. I'm not sure exactly when. Paulinus told me he'd been looking for a wife to help him raise the girl, but most women would not take on such a burden all their lives. Then he met Secunda, who was longing for a child, and didn't care what defects it might have. Not a wealthy marriage, but it has worked out very well. He is clearly fond of her, and she is fond of him.'

The woman snorted. 'They were lucky then.' She sobered suddenly. 'Or perhaps he's not. His first wife died and now Secunda clearly isn't well.'

'Yet she went to the slave-market?' I said, thinking of the markets I have known myself – both as a purchaser and as a slave for sale. They are unpleasant places: the buyers prodding muscles and assessing teeth, the menfolk leering and pinching the females on display, amid the nauseating smell of fear and unwashed flesh. 'Hardly a place for anybody frail.'

'Wanted to see what her husband bought, I suppose,' Trullius replied. He'd begun to wave the wine-cup in an emphatic way. 'And when they'd finished shopping they didn't have to walk. They had their cart to take them home again. They didn't leave it here – I could hardly have a farm-cart in the court with Vestal Virgins here – Paulinus took it to a hiring-stables at the gate where they look after passing horses overnight. And before my wife has theories about that, I'm sure Audelia gave them money so they could pay for it! I know she'd slipped Secunda some jewels before she left, and I suspect she let her have a purse as well. Certainly there was some kind of parting gift and it would be like Audelia to be generous.'

'Did you see the party after they came back from town?' I asked.

He nodded. 'Of course. They came for their possessions, citizen. They had some luggage which they left here while they shopped – another travelling box: much rougher than Audelia's, of course, and a lid that didn't fit. They'd brought a lot of stuff with them in fact. There was a present for Audelia, I know – I saw Secunda hand it to her in the coach – and they'd brought goods to trade in town while they were here: several amphorae from the weight of it, most likely full of produce from the farm. They clearly sold a lot of it, as well. I saw Paulinus take a clanking sack of something into town but all I saw him carrying when he came back again was a woven rug that he said Secunda chose.' The wine was making him rather garrulous.

'You see?' Priscilla said, triumphantly to me. 'Buying not only slaves, but luxuries. And they can't have bartered all the goods they'd brought – the box was still quite heavy when they brought it down.'

Trullius waved his cup at her. 'But, woman, since the Vestal had given them her purse they didn't need to barter everything. And there wasn't that much left. The box was not too heavy for one man to lift. Paulinus lifted it onto the cart himself.'

That rather puzzled me. 'Yet they had slaves by then? You would have expected them to bring the baggage down.'

Priscilla answered that. 'They would have been no use. A skinny woman – who in any case stayed attending Secunda in the cart – and a scruffy little lad who looked too thin and weak to carry anything. Unprepossessing creatures, both of them. Personally, I wouldn't have them in the house. Whatever Paulinus paid for them, it was a lot too much. And that won't be the end of the expense. They'll both want new tunics, by the looks of it – the one the boy was wearing was scarcely more than rags.'

Trullius shook his head. 'You always have a theory about everything! Make up your mind which one you think is true. One moment Paulinus is taking Roman gold, and the next he can't afford a decent slave. Anyway, I don't know how you saw enough to know. They looked all right to me.' He turned to me. 'And that is all we can tell you, citizen. If you want more information you should ask the slave trader – he'll be in the market for another day. You can see him in the morning, if you are quick enough.' He seized the lamp again. 'Though you will have to rise betimes. So if you would like to follow me upstairs . . . ?'

Priscilla had leapt up to her feet at once. 'Husband, don't be so ridiculous! Of course he doesn't want to go to bed. There's someone he must see.'

'Can't it wait till morning?' he grumbled. 'It's far too late to see anyone tonight.'

'It's not too late for this! Can't you see what's clearer than the candle on that wall? Look at what's happened. When Lavinia disappeared, we didn't think of Druids. We had no idea that they might be involved. But now it seems certain that they had a hand in this. This citizen is right. Someone in this household must have dealings with the sect – someone told them who was coming here, someone who let them in. And it must have been someone who was in the house today – there have been no visitors, till this citizen arrived.'

'Except the temple messenger,' Trullius pointed out, putting down the lamp and fumbling to pour the last few drops of wine.

She treated this with the disdain that it deserved. 'Even you, Trullius, don't believe that it was him. But someone was clearly in contact with the Druids. It wasn't you and me. It certainly wasn't Audelia herself. It wasn't the raedarius or the horse-rider, they both left here when Audelia was alive. Paulinus and Secunda may have had unwitting dealings with a Druid, but they're hardly followers, and anyway they were gone before Lavinia disappeared. So unless one of our own servants is involved – which I don't believe – there is only one person left that it could be.'

The metal cup dropped from Trullius's good hand and bounced sharply on the floor, hard enough to make a big dent in the rim. He stood mouth open, looking at his wife. 'You mean . . . ? You can't mean . . . ? Not Lavinia's nurse?'

Priscilla smiled triumphantly. 'Well done, husband. I was sure you'd work it out. Now aren't you glad you let me lock her up?' She took the lamp and motioned me to rise. 'Follow me, citizen. I'll take you there at once.'

SEVENTEEN

I followed Priscilla through a musty painted passage, out into a sort of courtyard where – by the smell – the kitchen and the stables were. But the kitchen fire was evidently doused again by now and it was cold and dark out there, so that even with the oil-lamp it was hard to see. A quiet whinnying from a building close nearby suggested where the horses and the horsemen had been housed. There was no light from there either – even the slaves were clearly all abed, as I was beginning to wish I was, myself.

I stumbled on a cobblestone, bruising my big toe. 'You've got her in the stable?' I said, as my mishap brought the party to a halt.

Priscilla laughed. 'We've got her over there.' She gestured to a squat little circular building on the right, which I had not noticed up till now. It was hardly taller than my shoulder and an arms-width round, with a low entrance at the front and a sort of open chimney at the top. 'It used to be the kiln, though the roof's part-ruined now. But it's got solid walls, apart from the fire-hole in front, and we block that up at night. We use this now as a punishment-cell for disobedient slaves.' She bent down to roll a large stone from the entrance as she spoke, and I found myself peering into a tiny clay-lined space, cold and damp and disagreeable.

There was a woman in there, blinking in the light. She was no longer young. Her plump flesh was sagging and her reddish hair – pulled back from her face into a coiled plait – was streaked with grey. She was huddled in the centre, knees pulled to her chin, and shivering in the draught from the chimney-space. In the glow of the oil-lamp I could see that her hands and feet were loosely bound with rope, and her thin tunic was the orange-colour of the livery worn by the servants in Lavinius's country house.

She squinted up at us. 'What do you want now? You've no right to keep me here. I've told you all I know. I'll answer to my mistress, if to anyone. She knows I would have guarded Lavinia with my life! Send me back to her.' Her voice was harsh, almost defiant, but she spoke Latin well. Then she noticed me. 'Who is the citizen in the toga?' she enquired. 'Has he come to harry me as well?'

'He will ask the questions!' Priscilla snapped, but she answered anyway. 'His name's Libertus, and he's been sent here by Lavinia's family to find out what happened and what you know of it.'

It was not quite the truth and I was on the point of setting matters straight but the prisoner forestalled me. Something that might have been a spark of hope flashed into her eyes. 'Cyra sent you?' she said, eagerly.

'She knew that I was coming,' I agreed. 'But really I am here at Publius's behest to find news of his bride. But then I learned that Lavinia had disappeared as well, and I am bound to investigate that matter too, of course.'

The hope – if that was what it was – had died. She looked away and stared dully at the floor. 'Then I really cannot help you, citizen. As I told these householders, I can't imagine what would make Lavinia run away. She seemed so happy with her cousin yesterday.'

Her voice had softened, and she spoke with such concern that I was moved to murmur, 'You were fond of your young charge?'

She raised her eyes. They sparkled in the darkness like a wolf's. 'It is no secret, citizen. I adored that little girl. Loved her like I would have loved my own, if it had lived. I swear to you, citizen, I would lay down my life rather than have any harm come to that child. So can you imagine what a shock it was, when I went into the room and found she wasn't there? When I'd been on guard outside the door all day, as well? I was asked, you know, to fetch a tray for her and when I went back, it was to find she wasn't there – almost as if I'd been sent deliberately away. It almost breaks my heart – just ask that woman there!'

It was clear that she was speaking with completely sincerity. Yet something was stirring in the cobwebs of my brain. There was something about this account that did not quite make sense, but I could not for the life of me work out what it was.

I searched my memory. Surely this version of events tallied exactly with what I'd heard before? Yet I still felt that some important detail was eluding me. I was still puzzling over it when Trullius spoke up.

'Well, slave, it seems that Lavinia did not run away at all.'

'What?' the nursemaid queried sharply.

Trullius raised his hand. 'It seems more likely, now, that Druids captured her and simply made it look as if she'd made her own escape. What do you say to that?'

'Druids?' The nursemaid looked incredulous. 'How could Druids get into the house? Or get out again? Someone would have seen. I would have seen myself! I was on guard all day outside the door.'

My hostess thrust the lamp in to look more closely at her captive's face. 'Not if they climbed up the cloth-rope to the window, when no one was about. That must be what it was! And you must have helped them plan it. I'll wager you sent a signal that you had come downstairs and the room was unguarded while you fetched the tray and kept me busy in the kitchen area! Come to think of it, I saw you at the time, carrying something out into the alleyway beside the house. I thought it was a chamber pot for the midden-pile. But it was a signal, wasn't it? Admit it now, and make it quicker for us all.'

Trullius was right about her having theories, I thought – this one almost sounded plausible. I was about to say so, when she spoke again.

'Though Minerva knows why you'd agree to help them in that way, if you are as fond of Lavinia as you seem to be. More magic, I suppose. If the Druids put a spell on you so that you couldn't help yourself, then say so straight away. It might go easier for you when it comes to punishment.'

She was offering the slave-woman a convenient excuse, and one which might have stood up at a legal trial, but the nurse disdained it. 'I've never knowingly spoken to a Druid in my life. Why should you think they'd want to . . . ?' She broke off suddenly, and looked at me again. 'Is this to do with Audelia, citizen?'

I nodded. 'We think the Druids murdered her, as well.'

'As well?' The voice was sharp with shock, but I quickly

realized it was not concern for poor Audelia's fate. Her only interest was in Lavinia. 'You mean the child is dead?' She strained forward and would have struggled to her feet, but her bonds prevented her. Bright tears were glistening in her eyes. 'Dear Juno! Not Lavinia! Tell me it isn't true.'

I shook my head. 'We haven't found Lavinia, alive or dead,' I said. 'But if the Druid rebels have her, I worry for her fate. They are not noted for their mercy, even for small girls.'

She sank back, forlornly, but obviously relieved. 'You are right, of course. We can only pray she's safe.' She nodded towards the owners of the house. 'Make them let me out of here tomorrow, citizen, and I will help you search. I know the sort of places she would go to hide.'

Trullius's wife, who had been stooping forward with the lamp, made an exasperated little noise. 'What? Let her out, when she has been so clearly negligent? She must think me simple, citizen.'

I motioned her to silence and took the lamp myself. I wanted co-operation, not defiance from the nurse. Besides I had identified what had been troubling me. 'You don't think she's dead, do you?' I murmured to the prisoner in the kiln. 'You are not grieving, you are talking about places she might hide. What makes you think that she is still alive?'

She shook her head. 'I can't explain it, citizen. I'm foolish, I suppose. But . . . if she were dead, I'm sure I would have known – felt it somehow in my blood and bones.' The tears were brimming over now, and coursing down her face unchecked. She could not move her hands to wipe her cheeks. 'I can believe she might have run away, if she thought she was in danger – especially if she could not find me when she looked for me. But when you mentioned Druids and said they'd murdered her "as well" . . .' She broke off, shuddering. 'What did you mean, if not that she was dead?'

'I meant it seems possible they are involved in this, as well as playing a part in poor Audelia's death. And – before you ask – we're fairly sure of that. They deliberately left symbolic tokens with the corpse.'

'Poor creature,' the nurse said, soberly. 'She will be greatly mourned.' She tried to wipe her wet cheek on her tunic-shoulder, but it would not reach.

'You knew Audelia?'

'Not well. I met her for the first time yesterday. I liked her very much. I thought her very kind and beautiful. And surprisingly clever and intelligent, as well, quite capable of signing contracts and understanding them. Just like her young cousin would have been, I suppose, if Lavinia had ever had the opportunity of training at the shrine.' She gave a bitter smile. 'But now she never will. And poor Audelia's dead, you say, and on her wedding day. I hope they build a fitting tomb for her.'

'This is getting nowhere,' Trullius's wife exclaimed. She nudged me in the side. 'Do you wish me to wake the stable-slaves and have her flogged a bit? That might persuade her to tell us what she knows. My husband would do it for us but he only has one arm these days, and he finds it hard to hold the victim down.'

I shook my head. 'I don't think it would help. If this slave cares for Lavinia as much as it appears, she'll help us all she can without the use of whips. I'm interested in her assessment of the child.' I turned back to the nurse. 'Can you think of any way she might be bribed to leave – tempted by an offer, or lured to run away?'

A stubborn shake of the head. 'Nothing like that, citizen. Lavinia was obedient to a fault.'

That wasn't altogether the picture I had gleaned, but the nurse could clearly see no defects in her beloved charge. I leaned closer still, and murmured, in a gentler tone, 'I am not suggesting this is Lavinia's fault. If someone gave her orders which she could not ignore – purporting to be from her family, perhaps, or from the Vestal shrine – wouldn't she obey them, if she is as dutiful as you say?'

There was a longish silence while the nurse considered this, staring at a creeping damp patch on the wall. Then she turned an ashen face to me – even in the dim light I could see that she'd turned pale. 'Now that you say that, citizen, there is one possibility that occurs to me . . .'

'Well, tell him, for Mars sake!' Priscilla, behind me, was exasperated now. 'And then perhaps we can all get to our beds. Don't contradict me, Trullius,' she went on, as her husband made a noise as though he would protest. 'You said yourself, it's too late to do anything tonight.'

I turned back to the nursemaid. 'You were going to say . . . ?'

She shook her head. 'It's only an idea, and I'm not quite sure of it. I need time to think it out. It will make no difference for an hour or two – even my captors both agree we can't do anything further tonight. I'll tell you in the morning, supposing I'm alive.' She gave me a wan smile. 'I have had nothing to eat or drink all day, and a damp kiln is not kind to aging bones. But, citizen, to find out if I am right in what I think, I'll need to see the things that Lavinia left behind – the clothes that were made into a shape inside the bed. Provided that nobody has moved them up to now?'

Trullius stepped forward. 'We haven't moved a thing. We wanted to have proof of how we found the room – something to show the family and the authorities. But if you want the garments that were left inside the bed, that's easily arranged. I'll have them brought to you.'

She shook her head again, more violently. 'It's most important that they are not touched!' She looked at me. 'I'm sorry, citizen, I don't know why I didn't think of this before – only at that stage there was no talk of Druids. It simply looked as if she'd run away. But now . . .' Her voice was cracked with tears, and it was a moment before she gained control. 'We had a secret, Lavinia and I. A private way of doing things her father didn't know. He was very prone to punish – and severely, too – if he thought that she'd done the slightest thing amiss, though sometimes I could talk him out of blaming her. So we had a little game. If there was any chance of trouble she would leave certain things arranged . . .' She trailed off again.

'You mean she may have left a message? In the way she piled the clothes?' I was incredulous.

'It sounds ridiculous, I know. But she's too young to read and write, and it isn't always possible to talk when there are slaves about – at least without it reaching the master in the end. I always told her . . .' She turned to me again. 'Citizen, there may be nothing there to find. Certainly there won't be anything to tell us where she's gone. But if she thought she was in danger, she would try to let me know. I don't suppose . . . ?'

Trullius's woman made that snorting sound again. 'Surely she's not proposing that I should let her go and look?'

I looked at Trullius. He shrugged. 'Why not? Her hands and feet are bound. We could loosen them a bit and take her upstairs to the room. She couldn't get away. In fact, I think we could leave her there to sleep. If she's tied up, she can't climb out of the window-space – especially in the dark.'

'And you were offering a slave on guard, I think.' I said. I saw him hesitate. 'If there is an extra charge for this,' I added, 'I'm sure Publius will pay.'

I wasn't sure of this at all, in fact, but the suggestion did the trick. 'I'll go and wake a stable-slave, then,' he muttered in my ear, and we heard him scuffling to the stable in the dark, and – a minute later – rapping loudly on the door.

His wife was clearly furious with me. 'You will be asking me to feed this wretched slave, next, I suppose?' Then, when she saw my nod, she added, 'Are you sure that you don't want me to give up my bed for her?'

The nursemaid turned her head to look at me. 'I beg you, citizen. Take me to the room. Starve me if you like. But let me spend this night there, where my darling was. Bind my feet by all means, or chain me to the bed. Though I have to warn you, I may need my hands, if I am to find what I am looking for. It may not be obvious to the casual glance . . .'

'Tell us what it is, and we will search for it.' The voice was sharp, but Priscilla had seized the woman by her two bound arms and was jerking her forward and out into the night.

'You wouldn't know what you were looking for. I hardly know myself. But I'll know it when I see it.' The nurse was on her feet now, and stood there tottering. 'I may have to wait for daylight to find it, anyway. Though, even then – you understand – I make no promises. If she was abducted, it is a different thing. If anyone but Lavinia made the model in the bed or knotted the cloths to make the rope, then obviously there will be nothing there to find.' She managed half a shrug. 'Our best hope, in that case, is that she managed to throw some garment down, in a way that did not alert her kidnappers.'

She was surprisingly tiny now she was upright, no higher than my chest-clasp as she looked up at me, but there was nothing little about the anguish in her eyes. 'Believe me, citizen. I am as anxious for her safety as you are yourselves. I swear by all the gods – on my own life and Lavinia's if you wish – that I won't try to run away.'

'You will not have the chance. You'll be guarded anyway.' There was a muffled commotion in the stable, as I spoke. The door creaked open and a shadowy form appeared, a blacker shape against the darkness of the night. Trullius said something and the figure disappeared again, to return a moment later with a sleeping-mat and what proved to be an unlit taper in its hand.

When Trullius brought the stable-slave over to the light, I got a look at him. He was a young man, tousled and more than half-asleep, but from the look of the brawny muscles in his arms – as he straightened the outer tunic which he'd hurriedly pulled on – he was more than a match for the tiny aging nurse. Even a Druid might think twice before attacking him, I thought, as he pulled out a knife and cut the ropes around the nurse's legs.

I surrendered the oil-lamp to the lady of the house. She allowed her husband to light the taper from the flame, and she set off towards the kitchen-block, while we filed back through the painted passage and the dining-space into the entrance-way where I'd first been received. This time, however, I was ushered up the stairs.

'This was Lavinia's bedroom,' Trullius said, stopping at the first door on the landing, and hustling the nursemaid roughly into the room beyond. I followed them and had a look around.

There were two beds in there. I should not have been surprised – I'd heard that Audelia and her cousin had shared the room – but I somehow had supposed that they had shared a bed, as people in a guest house generally do. But these were individual, proper sleeping frames, with goatskin mattresses and woven blankets too – though on the bed beside the window-space these had been thrown back to reveal a pile of clothing carefully arranged to look at first glance like a sleeping form. A travelling box, in which the clothes had evidently been packed, was standing empty by the window-space.

The nursemaid saw my glance. 'That was Lavinia's, of course.

It held her dowry too – though it seems that it has disappeared as well. Through there, do you suppose?'

She nodded to the window-space. The covers from the other bed had been deftly knotted into a sort of rope, secured firmly around the bed-frame at one end, the rest of it still snaking downward towards the inner court.

I walked across to get a better look. The knotted rope extended almost to the ground, but it was not strong enough to take a lot of weight. A supple climber, or a child, might manage to descend. I shook my head and glanced around the room. I wondered anyone would want to run away from here.

There was a handmade carpet on the floor and a wooden chair nearby, with a large pot under it, complete with lid and fresh water in a jug, Whatever the dining arrangements downstairs, this was luxury. No wonder that Cyra and Lavinius had thought it suitable.

Trullius had joined me at the window-space and seemed about to pull the rope inside, but the nursemaid stopped him. 'Tie my feet again – do anything you like – but let me pull the rope in, so I can see the knots.'

He looked at me. I nodded and we two stepped aside. The slave-boy set the taper down and drew the knife again, cutting the rope-bonds which still bound her wrists. She flexed her hands a moment, and then came across and pulled in the twisted cloth, lingering over every knot as it appeared. As she undid the last of them she shook her head at me. 'Nothing of interest in that, citizen. I'll have to look elsewhere. But I'll see better when the daylight comes.' She turned to Trullius. 'If I may use the far bed, you can tie my legs again and seal the shutters if you wish. Not that I could climb out of the window in the dark.'

'I'll tie you up all right!' It was Trullius's wife appearing in the doorway with the lighted lamp, a hunk of dry bread and a heavy length of chain. 'You think I'm going to leave you virtually free, after what has happened in this house?' She thumped the bread down on the chair-seat as she spoke. She turned towards the slave and motioned to the chain. 'The nursemaid wears a slave-collar with her name on it. Attach this to the back of it and chain her to the bed. Make sure that the screw-link at the end is out of reach. Give her enough slack to reach the pot, of course – I don't want staining on my mattresses – and she can eat and drink this if she can find it in the dark. If that arrangement meets with your approval, citizen?' she added in my direction with a sneer.

It was hardly what I would have chosen, but I did not object. Far better to be chained up in a comfortable dry room, with food and drink – however minimal – than to spend a freezing night starving in a draughty ruined kiln. 'I'll come back in the morning, then,' I murmured to the nurse. 'And hope that you have something to report.'

The slave-woman, who was submitting to the chain, gave me a rueful smile. 'If I have nothing to tell you in the morning, citizen, do as you wish with me. I will have nothing left to live for, anyway, if my darling's lost. But I swear by all the gods that I'll do all I can.'

I nodded. 'Goodnight then.' I followed Trullius. He led me into the other attic-room, as the stable-slave spread out his sleeping-mat outside the nursemaid's door.

I looked around my attic. So this was where Secunda and her husband slept. Priscilla had said that this was her room as a rule, and certainly the accommodation was much less lavish than next door. There was no chair or table, no covering on the floor, and only a crude bolt to latch the door. The bed provided was far more primitive, simple wooden slats and a stuffed straw palliasse, but it was still much more luxurious than my pile of reeds at home. Besides, I was so tired I would have slept on cobblestones. I paused just long enough to unwind my travel-stained toga and pull my sandals off, then – without even waiting to crawl beneath the woven covers on the bed – I lay down on the pillows and was instantly asleep.

EIGHTEEN

I woke from a confused dream in which a man in Druid robes was cooking headless corpses in a kiln, while a giant in yellow wedding slippers kicked the chimney down.

I forced my eyes open, uncertain for a moment as to where I was, and peered around until I recognized the room. Dawn light was streaming through the shuttered window-space, my shoes and toga were where I'd put them down and I was still lying on the covers. It was obvious that I had hardly stirred all night. But the noisy kicking of my nightmare seemed still to be going on.

I struggled to sit up but the banging didn't stop. Sleepily I realized that it was not a dream at all, but somebody knocking loudly on the door. And the landlord's voice was hollering my name. 'Citizen Libertus, I can't unlatch the door. Are you all right in there?'

I swung my feet down, shambled to the door and pulled back the bolt. I had scarcely time to do so before Trullius burst in. He was still in his under-tunic, without even a blanket to hide his ruined arm, but he made no excuse. 'Oh, citizen! Thank Mars you are all right. I had begun to worry when you didn't answer me. I suppose you were asleep. I'm sorry to wake you but you'd better come at once.'

I grovelled for my sandals, but he shook his head.

'There isn't time to dress. I don't know what to do. My wife went in there when she first got up and . . .' He shook his head. 'You'd better come and see.' He was already hustling out of the door again.

I followed stupidly, still more than half-asleep. What was the panic? Surely Lavinia had not unexpectedly returned? I shook my head. That was unlikely. If that had happened Trullius would have told me so at once. More probable that the nursemaid had found her promised secret sign. I was encouraged in this hope when I saw where Trullius was leading me.

He kicked aside the sleeping-mat which still lay outside the nursemaid's door, though there was no sign of the servant who'd been left on guard, and motioned me to go inside the room. 'There!' he said, and gestured.

The slave-woman was slumped half-lying on the floor, held to the bed-frame only by the chain – in a way which would have choked her if she had not already been so evidently dead. She had arched against her collar in some final spasm: there were cruel marks visible on her neck and chin even from this distance, and her bloodless face was tinged with purpish-blue as though she had found it difficult to breath. Death had not been painless. I prayed it had been quick.

'That's how we found her,' Trullius went on. He would have wrung his hands if he'd been able to. 'It must have been those dreadful Druids at their work again. Though how they got in unobserved I cannot think. My wife is right, it must be sorcery. Oh, dear Mercury, what will Lavinius say?' He shook his head, from side to side, like a wet dog in despair.

I could think of nothing intelligent to say, so I simply moved past him to look more closely at the corpse. She had not been dead for long. The body had not begun to stiffen very much. There was no wound or sign of other damage to the corpse, except the bruising round her neck and that – though quite extensive – seemed more the result of violent movement than the cause of death: there was none of the protruding tongue that is produced by strangling. This looked more like a poisoning to me.

But what had done it? There was no cup or phial in evidence. I glanced around the room. The dried morsel of loaf had not been touched at all, but some of the water in the jug had disappeared. Could that have been the source? I dipped a little finger into the liquid in the jug and – daringly but idiotically – placed it on my tongue. To my relief there was none of the burning or numbness which I half-feared to feel, only the faint stale taste of water from a city well. (My wife Gwellia was furious with me later, when she learned of this, and I admit that she was right. It was a particularly foolish thing to do – perhaps the product of not being properly awake – but I reasoned that my tiny sample was too small to cause me harm.)

So, if it was not the water, what had killed the nurse? Was it possible that, despite the guard, someone had come in during the night and forced some potion down her throat? I am not generally a believer in sorcery, but even I was beginning to wonder if there was something supernatural and sinister afoot.

Trullius had more practical concerns and was wittering in distress. 'We shall be ruined, citizen. Who else will come here now? Even supposing that Lavinius does not have us dragged before the courts and sent into exile with nothing to our names.' He stopped and looked at me. 'My wife has taken the stable-slave and locked him in the kiln. He swears that he heard nothing except a muffled thud. But something must have happened. You think he was the one who was working with the Druids? Perhaps he heard us talking yesterday and – once he heard that Lavinia might have left a sign – he feared the nurse was going to discover that he was involved.'

'And so he killed her, having fortuitously brought some poison with him when you roused him from his sleep?' I shook my head. 'I doubt it very much. But just in case Lavinia did contrive to leave a sign, I'll have a look myself – although I've no idea what I am looking for.'

There was nothing at all of interest in the luggage-box, except a wisp or two of long red curly hair, which – from the description that I had received – were presumably Lavinia's own, so I moved to examine the pile of clothes, still on the other bed. They were no longer piled into a human shape, but scattered as though the nurse – as she promised – had made a search of them. But if there was a signal, I could not fathom it. There seemed to be nothing of much consequence, at a casual glance – mostly girlish stoles and tunics such as you would expect Lavinia to have.

Except . . . ? If a girl was on her way to join the Vestal house, why would she take with her all the clothes that she possessed? She was never going to wear them any more. Even the youngest novices at the shrine are given special robes as soon as they arrive – just as a boy puts off his *toga praetexta* when he becomes a man, or a bride abandons her childish garments when she weds. Besides, not all of these garments were Lavinia's, when I looked more closely at the pile.

There was an adult's cloak, for instance, made of woven plaid: and when I rummaged further, I found a woman's pale-brown tunic which had been much repaired and a well-worn drawstring purse of the same coarse material. Who did these belong to? Not the nursemaid, most assuredly – one glance at the body was enough to tell you that. These peasant clothes were much too big for her, and clearly far too large to fit a six-year-old. Besides, they were of inferior quality, thick cloth and roughly sewn – not the sort of thing Lavinius would have permitted in his house. So where had they come from? Was this somehow the sign the nursemaid had been looking for?

I picked up the empty purse. It was a useless thing (only the poorest do not have a leather money-pouch) and this one was stained yellowish and had a hole in it, so that any small coin would have instantly gone through. It smelt of carrots, too. I put it down again. Who would want to hoard a purse like that, which was no use at all except to hold a . . .

'Wait just a heartbeat!' I exclaimed aloud. Yellowish stains and carrots? I knelt down and began to scrabble on the floor beneath the bed, but there was nothing there except dust and a few cobwebs where the broom-bunch had not reached.

Trullius came over and stood staring down at me. 'Shouldn't we go down now and question the slave-boy, citizen? What are you searching for?'

'Something that isn't here!' I looked up to answer and saw him silhouetted against the open window-space. I clambered to my feet. 'The window-space, of course! Let me get my shoes on and I'll come downstairs with you. We'll decide what to do with this body afterwards.'

He looked completely mystified as I rushed into my own room and pulled my sandals on, but he didn't question me and when I clattered down the dimly lit staircase he followed close behind. His wife was waiting at the bottom of the stairs, still dressed in an under-tunic as though she'd just got out of bed – with her legs exposed and only a cloak around her top for dignity.

'Jove save us, citizen,' she wailed. 'Another death. This is some Druid curse and we shall all be murd—'

I cut off her lamentations without courtesy. 'Which way to the courtyard?' I demanded. She must have judged my mood of urgency, because she stood back without protest and indicated the direction I should take, though she joined in the procession as soon as I had passed.

'I've locked the stable slave-boy in the kiln,' she was saying, at my heels. 'I'll take you to h—'

But I brushed all this aside. 'Stay where you are. Don't step on anything. I'm sure there's something here. It is already broken, almost certainly, and may be hard to find. One misplaced foot, and if it's made of glass the whole thing will be crushed beyond all hope of learning anything. I trust I'm not too late.' I began to pace the courtyard, searching every inch.

She hovered at the doorway, with Trullius at her back. 'Tell us what it is you're looking for. We'll help you search for it.'

I shook my head. 'I'm not sure myself.'

'You're worse than that nursemaid,' the wife said in disgust. 'Dead bodies everywhere and people keep searching for things they won't describe! I'll leave you to it, then. I've got real jobs to do, if others haven't.' And she turned away, muttering as she did so, just loud enough to hear. 'Watch him, Trullius. I know he says he had a letter from Audelia's bridegroom, but I'm not sure that I'm convinced. He might be the one who is working with the Druids.'

Trullius shuffled forward. 'I'm sorry, citizen. She has no right to speak like that. She's worried, that is all, and perhaps that's no surprise. She forgets that you're a citizen, deserving of respect, even without your toga. I'll go and tell the slaves they're not to come out here until you've finished searching underfoot. And I'll make sure that I don't stand on anything myself.'

I did not stop to answer, just continued with my systematic search. It was not an easy one. No doubt the courtyard was occasionally swept, but between the cobbles there were oddments and fragments of all kinds – scraps of wood and old material, wisps of hay and rusty nails – as well as mud and tufts of grass and the inevitable evidence that horses walked that way. In one corner by the kiln, I found a pile of greening, dusty, broken pots, presumably a remnant of the previous business here. But nothing that matched what I was looking for. I had worked my way right to the inner wall before Trullius returned.

He came across to me. 'I see you've not succeeded in your search. What did you hope to find?'

'This!' I swooped on something which I'd just spotted on the ground. I picked it up and held it triumphantly aloft.

It was a little silver bottle, smaller than my hand, bruised and badly dented where it had hit the ground and bounced – indeed, one side was split – but, being metal, otherwise intact. It was shaped like an amphora (or it had been once) with a handsome corkwood stopper still attached by a length of woven cord around the damaged neck. It was quite empty now, but clearly fashioned to hold medicine of some kind. Threaded through the handles was a slender chain, of the kind which – on little potion-flasks like this – holds a little silver disc on which a reminder of the contents and dosage can be etched. This one had obviously been designed to hold a sleeping draught: the label had been most delicately and expertly inscribed, though the disc was no bigger than my thumbnail and had been bent against the body of the flagon in the fall.

'There you are! A pretty object and no doubt a costly one, clearly made by a master-craftsman for a woman of some rank,' I said to Trullius. 'And there's the proof.' As I turned the stopper over I could see that the silver top was marked with a device etched into it – a device I recognized. It was the same pattern as the seal-stamp I'd seen on Cyra's desk. 'In fact it carries Lavinia's family seal,' I said to Trullius.

He nodded. 'No doubt it was given to the nurse. She mentioned to Secunda that she had a sleeping draught. Offered it to her in case she found it hard to sleep.' He stretched out his one good hand to take the flask, and I was about to pass it up to him, when I noticed something else which made me hold it back.

The corkwood stopper had a slightly yellow tinge – very much the colour of the stain I'd noticed on the drawstring bag upstairs. I raised the stopper to my nose. It smelt faintly of carrots, as I feared it would. 'Someone clearly has tampered with it since,' I said, wondering who was responsible for this. 'Poison hemlock, by the look of it.' I handed him the flask.

Trullius took it from me and moved away into the centre of the courtyard where there was stronger light, and he carefully examined the wording on the disc. 'Poison hemlock, clearly. You are quite right, citizen. You think it was the Druids?'

I was about to tell him about my theory – that the poison had been brought here in the drawstring purse and decanted later to the flask, from a different phial which was doubtless somewhere in a rubbish-heap by now – when an uncomfortable suspicion flashed into my head. There was something odd about the way that Trullius had made a point of taking the label to the light. He'd done the same with Publius's letter when I gave that to him. Yet both things were clearly written and Trullius showed no other symptoms of short-sightedness. A wild hypothesis was forming in my mind.

I gestured to the label. 'I wonder if we're right. Have a look again. The third word, Trullius. Can you make it out?'

He looked disconcerted but he lifted up the flask and repeated the performance of examining the words. I watched him as he frowned at the inscription for a time, balancing the jug against his withered arm and holding the chained label close up to his eyes. After a long pause he turned to me again. I was still crouching on the cobbles by the wall. 'Oh hemlock, hemlock. It's hard to make it out, but I am quite sure you're right.'

I took the flagon from him and laid it on the ground. 'Trullius,' I said gently. 'The inscription's very clear. It says "Poppy-juice for sleeping – take no more than half a phial". It doesn't mention hemlock anywhere. You can't read it, can you? Are you having some sort of problem with your eyes?'

A silence, and then he shook his head at me and muttered sheepishly, 'The truth is, citizen, I never learned to read. There's a few words I recognize. I can read my name. And I can tell all the numbers, for the bills and things.'

The enormity of this revelation had just begun to dawn. 'But you said Audelia wrote to you, asking if Paulinus and his wife could have a room. How did you know that, if you couldn't read the words?'

No answer.

'Your wife, perhaps?' I asked.

He shook his head again. 'Priscilla can't read either. Not as much as me. When we were dealing with the pots, it didn't matter much. Mostly people came and simply picked one out. And even now it doesn't often create a hindrance. Most people send a slave to see the place – just as Cyra and Lavinius did – or if they've stayed before, they send a messenger to book a bed with us, usually with a down-payment to secure the room. So almost all the arrangements are made verbally.'

'But if you do get a letter, as you sometimes must?'

He shrugged. 'The same as we have always done. We take it to an amanuensis in the forum, and have it read to us. If it needs a written answer, he'll do that for us as well. He makes a charge, of course, but if it means another client it is well worth the expense.'

'So how do you keep a record of who is coming when?' I was trying to imagine running a lodging-house without the written word.

I think it was the first time I saw Trullius smile. 'My wife worked out a system,' he said. 'She's good at things like that. I've got a special board that shows the phases of the moon, and we mark it so that we can see what day our guests are coming and how many to expect. I can manage numbers, as I said before. I'll show you if you like.' He gestured to the house. 'It works out very well. Though we don't tell the customers – there's no need for them to know, and when they are coming to a private place like this, people like to think they have an educated host.'

I scrambled to my feet, narrowly avoiding treading on the flask. 'Trullius,' I said. 'Can't you see the implications of what you're telling me? You say you took Audelia's letter to the town to have it read aloud. So whoever read it knew, not only that she would come herself, but also that she had asked you for a second room for her humble relatives as well.'

Trullius looked flustered 'Well, now you mention it, I suppose that's true. It was a new amanuensis, too, not the one I've used before. You mean he might have given information to the Druids?'

'Worse than that,' I said. 'He might be one himself. Or anyone in the forum might have overheard. Think, Trullius, when he'd written out the answer saying they could come, how did you send it to Paulinus and his wife? Did you use the same messenger who brought Audelia's note to you?'

He shook his head. 'He had already gone. He'd told us that Audelia was expecting a reply as to whether or not we could make the arrangements she required, and Priscilla – like an idiot – assured him that we could, and that he could take that verbal message back to her at once.'

'Though you didn't at that stage know what you'd agreed to do?'

He shrugged. 'We thought it would be something about arrangements for her stay – fresh water or special food or something of that kind: she was a retiring Vestal Virgin after all and priestesses are liable to have peculiar needs. But we would have provided anything she wished. It was good for business to have her here – or so my wife believed.'

'Of course it was good business,' a sharp voice put in, and I turned to see Priscilla standing by the door. She was dressed in a full-length day-tunic by now, and holding an empty cooking-vessel in her hand, but she made no move towards the kitchen-block or the store-jars next to it. I wondered how long she had been standing there behind us listening in. 'What have you told him, Trullius? I warned you to beware.'

Her husband rounded on her. 'I haven't told him anything. He's worked it out himself. And don't start imagining that he's involved with Druids. That nursemaid was poisoned in her sleeping draught. He's found the little flask, it must have been thrown down through the window-space, I suppose.' He gestured to where it had been lying on the ground.

I frowned at him. Once again there was something in his words I couldn't place – some deduction that I knew I should have made, and which had escaped me. I must be getting old.

Trullius had misinterpreted my frown. 'I'm afraid he's also worked out that we cannot read, and now he is worried about Audelia's note: whether someone in the forum might have overheard, and learned that there was likely to be a Vestal Virgin here.'

'Do you still have that letter, by the way?' I said. 'I'd like to look at it, if only to make sure it did say what the amanuensis said it did.'

'Of course we haven't got it!' The woman gave me a look, quite as poisonous as the sleeping draught had been. 'It was Audelia's writing-block. We gave it back to her while she was here.' She crossed to one of the amphorae set into the ground, raised the lid and began to ladle olive oil into the cooking-bowl. 'Anyway,' she added, straightening up again, 'it didn't have her message on it any more. We let the amanuensis scratch it out and use the wax again, to write the letter to Paulinus – who of course returned it when he confirmed that he would come. So we gave it to its owner when we had the chance. What else would you expect?' She moved as if to go back into the dwelling-rooms.

I stood between her and the doorway so that she couldn't pass. She had come back of her own volition, but now that she was here I wanted her to help. 'So how was it delivered to Paulinus and his wife? If you didn't use Audelia's mounted messenger?'

Priscilla shrugged. 'A boy with a donkey in the forum who was looking for a job. We had the directions to the house, Audelia gave us those . . .'

'Or rather, the amanuensis told you that she had?' I corrected.

She ignored the interruption. 'And the boy rode out with it. What else could we do? We don't have a private messenger, and with such important people coming there was no house-slave to spare. Anyway, what difference did it make? Paulinus obviously got it – since he not only replied, but came the day that we had settled on.'

I looked at her steadily. 'Are you quite sure of that?'

She still had not seen what I was driving at. 'Of course he came here – I don't know what you mean. Now if you'll excuse—'

I cut her off again. 'But how can you be certain it was him at all? Suppose your letter was delivered somewhere else – for example to the rebels in the wood – you would not know the difference. You can't even be certain what message it contained. The amanuensis might have written anything he liked, and addressed it to anyone at all – saying, for instance, that the Vestal's relatives were due to stay with you and inviting the rebels to come and take their place. Had either of you ever seen Paulinus in your life before?'

Trullius shook his head, quite stupefied at this. 'Of course we hadn't, citizen.'

'But Audelia had,' his wife put in, triumphantly. 'Paulinus

and his wife had visited the shrine to pray about their child. I told you that, before.'

Even then I had to spell it out to them. 'Supposing that it was really Audelia who arrived? Who in this household would have known her face? You and your wife had not set eyes on her before, neither had Lavinia or her nurse, or even the raedarius who was to drive her back.'

Priscilla had suddenly seen the force of this and had turned deathly pale. 'So she might have been an impostor too?' She put her cooking-bowl down on a stool beside the door. 'But what about the driver of the temple-coach in which she came to us? He would have known her, wouldn't he?'

It was Trullius himself who saw the flaw in that. 'That might depend on when he saw her last. Obviously the true Audelia set off from the shrine, but she wore a cape and veil when she was travelling and I presume he always did as he did here – drop her where she was staying, together with her guard, and go to the temple to find a bed for himself. So if a false Audelia got into the coach one day, he might not notice until she spoke to him – and from what we witnessed she did not generally do that. The changeover might easily have taken place somewhere.'

'But surely . . .' his wife began.

He shook his head. 'Provided the substitute was roughly the same build, the coach-driver would see what he expected to, and what he had seen every other day. Why should he start to doubt? All you would need is a second set of robes – or something sufficiently similar to pass a casual glance. That would not be impossible to arrange. No one is going to go up close and start to scrutinize a Vestal Virgin's clothes.'

'You mean the murder might have taken place before they got to us at all?' All at once the woman's voice was bright with hope. 'And the real Audelia's headless body was already in the box?' Her face fell suddenly. 'But what about that giant horseman who was riding guard? He would have noticed if someone took her place. He'd been with her from the outset and he is not a fool.'

'But he didn't see Audelia after they got here!' Trullius sounded quite excited now. 'She was veiled when she arrived and didn't stop to speak to anyone. You showed her to her room. He went off to the stable, just as he did tonight – and when she found the shoes were missing, she did not come down herself to tell him to go and find them the next day. She sent a message down, by that maidservant of hers.'

'That's right! The maidservant! What's become of her? The one who overlooked the slippers when she packed the box? Puella, was she called?' The landlady looked at me enquiringly. 'She had been with Audelia all the way. She would have known if someone was impersonating her.'

I had to confess how Puella had mysteriously disappeared, and had last been seen riding in a farmer's cart towards Corinium – and that I had chosen not to search for her. A farmer, I thought, rather guiltily. Paulinus was supposed to have a farm not very far from here. Was that significant?

Priscilla was not concerned with that. Her face was quite aglow. 'You see? That maidservant was obviously a party to the plot. She left the wedding-shoes behind deliberately – on purpose so that the rider could be sent for them. And of course she made quite certain that he set off at first light, before the imitation Vestal had come down herself. So when the impostor got into the coach he wasn't there, and . . . Dear Mars and Venus! We brought it down ourselves! The real Audelia was already murdered and headless in the box that you, husband, packed in next to her.'

Trullius was frowning. 'Another of your theories! What was the impostor going to do? Jump out of the raeda when it was going along?'

Priscilla looked snubbed, but she said, with dignity, 'Perhaps the first intention was that she should ride all the way and make her disappearance when they got to Glevum gate, but the citizen has just told us that the raeda stopped outside that basket-stall to let the troops go past – it's obvious she seized the opportunity to slip out and escape.'

'Dressed as a Vestal?' Trullius put in.

She was not deflected from her argument. 'If she took off that long white cloak, she needn't have been wearing Vestal garments underneath. Especially if she had a wig with her, to hide the bridal plaits – false hair would draw no attention, even out of town. Wigs are becoming very fashionable these days: even poor Secunda had one, if I am any judge. Or perhaps the Vestal hairdo was a clever wig itself! Either way the impostor could quickly change her looks. There would be other people waiting to let the soldiers pass. She could simply have disappeared unnoticed into the crowd and made her way back to the rebels in the wood.' She turned to me. 'You've solved it, citizen.'

NINETEEN

Of course, I had done nothing of the kind. This theory – which in any case was hers and not my own – was hardly more than guesswork, though I was forced to grant that there were elements of it which did seem plausible.

'It's a clever explanation,' I agreed, putting the silver flask carefully into the pouch-purse at my waist. 'And you may well be right. But remember, at the moment we are lacking any proof. In fact, at present, that line of reasoning raises problems of its own.'

Now that she had found a version of events which satisfied her, though, she was unwilling to admit that there might be flaws in it. She leant back against the limewashed wall, her hands defiantly upon her hips. 'Such as?'

There were so many unanswered questions that I couldn't voice them all. I seized on some at random. 'Such as who put the poison in the flask, and what became of the original sleeping draught? To say nothing of whether Paulinus and his wife were really who they seemed and – above all – whether Lavinia is safe and how she disappeared. We are still only guessing that the rebel Druids had a hand in that.'

The woman shook her head impatiently. 'These are mere details, citizen. You have solved the central mystery, the one that you were sent here to investigate. You've managed to explain, and rationally too, how Audelia could appear to leave here in good health, ride to Glevum on a public road and end up beheaded in a box without anyone apparently noticing a thing. What's more, you have lifted a big weight from my mind: you have shown me that this household was most likely not involved and you have demonstrated that it could all have been achieved without the use of sorcery. I shall sleep a great deal better for knowing that tonight. You have made such a good beginning, and in so little time, I'm sure you'll find the answers to your other questions soon.' She picked up the cooking-bowl of oil and held it balanced against one ample hip. 'I'll take you to the market in the forum if you like, and locate the donkey-boy. He'll take you to the farmstead where he took the writing-block and you can check if it is really the home of Audelia's relatives.'

I nodded. 'That would be excellent. Perhaps, if I am quick about it, I can find the slave trader as well. He may have useful information to impart.' If Paulinus knew about the mute maid-servant in advance, I thought, it would indicate that he'd had previous dealings with the man. 'But before we do that . . .'

Priscilla had decided that I was now a friend. She gave a half-flirtatious little gasp. 'I forget my duties, citizen. I do apologize. Of course, we must first arrange a meal for you. I was on my way to do so when I first got up, but I delayed to look in on the nurse.' She was already leading the way back into the house, her buttocks waggling like rounded grinding stones under the tight blue fabric of her gown.

Breakfast had been the last thing on my mind, but I was obliged to follow her. 'I was about to say that before I leave the house, I would like to interview the slaves – including the one that you have locked up in the kiln,' I called to her retreating form.

'I'll go and let him out,' said a lugubrious voice behind me. It was Trullius, bringing up the rear. 'I told her that the stable-boy had no part in what happened to the nurse – why would he stay there, if he'd poisoned her? – but my wife would not listen. She likes to have her way. And with your permission, citizen, I will instruct the other slaves that they may now continue with their early-morning chores. I ordered them to stay indoors and out of sight while you were out there searching in the court.'

I nodded my assent. 'By all means, provided I can speak to each of them.' I realized that Priscilla had paused ahead of me and was now waiting in the passageway, poised like an actor depicting 'patience' on the stage. 'Perhaps your wife will indicate a place where I can conduct my questioning.'

'Use the dining-alcove,' the woman said at once. 'And if you start by talking to the kitchen-slave, you and your servants in the stable will be more quickly fed. Settle yourself, I'll go and show her in.'

I sat down at the table, and a few moments later the kitchen-maid arrived. She was small and skinny – not more than ten years old – and smelt of cooking-smoke. She was clearly terrified but desperate to help, though it seemed she genuinely knew nothing of any consequence and I soon let her go. It was the same with the other house-slaves and the stable-lads as well, all of whom the landlady had lined up at the door and who were officiously brought to me in turn.

'I don't know what you hope to learn from this,' Priscilla muttered archly, showing in the final slave. 'My servants don't have any connection with the Druids. I would soon have them punished if I thought they did. However, this is the last of them – the boy who was supposed to guard the nurse last night. When you have finished, I'll have your breakfast brought.' She pushed him forward and swayed off herself.

The stable boy was sullen and uncooperative, not at all grateful for my having had him freed – indeed he seemed to blame my presence for the whole affair. But his account of yesterday, when I extracted it from him, was much the same as I had heard from everybody else. Paulinus and Secunda were the first ones to arrive, and went straight to their room, because the lady wasn't well, and they did not come down again until Audelia drove in, in the temple carriage which then drove off again. Then they came down to meet her – and it was very evident that they had met before.

'And that's all I can tell you, citizen. The household was excited that the Vestal Virgin came, but we did not have a lot to do with her, because she was always attended by her slave. I had to help to take the boxes up, that's all – and jolly heavy they turned out to be.'

'And later the raeda came from Glevum bringing Lavinia and her nurse?'

A nod. 'More confounded boxes that I had to carry up. Then I went back to the horses and don't know any more.'

'But naturally you heard what happened in the house? Servants always gossip.'

He sighed, reluctantly. 'They had a meal – all except the sick lady who couldn't face the food – and afterwards they all went straight upstairs. The cousins shared a room and got on very well, from what I understand. There was a light in that window for a long time, anyway, and you could hear them whispering and laughing from the court. Then all of a sudden there was shouting from inside, and next thing there was a message to the stable-block, saying that the wedding slippers had been left behind and that the horseman was to set off at first light to try to get them back and take them to Glevum before the wedding-feast.'

'And who brought down that message?' It was vital that I checked.

'Audelia's personal slave. Crying like a waterfall, fearing she'd be whipped.' Then he said, with sudden spirit, 'Owners are all the same. Blame you for everything. The maid swore by all the gods that she had packed the shoes. Pretty little thing. I wish I'd had the chance to talk to her, but of course I didn't, because she slept indoors – the very place where I was set to sleep last night. But I can sympathize. My mistress tried to blame me for what happened to the nurse, though I was no more guilty than a fly . . .'

I cut off his protests. 'You were telling me about Audelia's maidservant. When the shoes were missing she seemed genuinely surprised?'

He shrugged. 'Surprised? She was aghast and terrified. She was still upset next morning when the coach set off. I helped her get up with the driver at the front. She was more than pleased to be there, because her mistress was still furious with her. But I couldn't stop to chat because I had to go and help them to bring down Audelia's box – and dreadfully heavy it turned out to be. No wonder if the driver's story turns out to be true, and it had a headless body in it at the time! We were told that there were extra gifts inside, and of course we didn't doubt it. Vestals never lie.'

He paused, evidently hoping that I'd confirm the tale, but I hadn't finished extracting his account. 'And then all the other guests came down to see the bride-to-be, and crowded round the raeda until the time it left?'

'Everyone except that girl, Lavinia. Someone said that she was already at her prayers – though I thought I saw her at the window looking down to wave.' He saw my startled look. 'Is it important?'

If true, it might be pivotal, but I didn't tell him that. What if Lavinia had seen something significant in the court? Something which meant she must be hustled off – or permanently silenced – before she talked too much? Yet what could she have seen? The landlady had also been looking from above and she had clearly seen nothing whatever untoward. 'I don't know,' I answered, truthfully, 'but thank you anyway. This is at least a detail that I hadn't heard before.'

He looked at me slyly. 'Worth an *as* or two?'

But I had no tip to give him and he was scowling again as he stomped out of the room, almost colliding with the little kitchen-maid who was hovering at the doorway to bring in my breakfast tray. She brought it at my signal and began to set the contents on the tabletop: two pears, a pot of strong-smelling cheese-curds, and a hunk of bread, with a small dish of salt and olive oil to dip it in. Quite a little feast. This was going to cost Publius a few sestertii.

'The mistress wants to know if you want watered wine as well, or if you'd rather just have water from the well?' She gave a timid smile. 'And she's very sorry that it is baker's bread – we'd made our own loaf freshly yesterday, but you and your servants ate the last of it last night and we'd raked out the fire that heats the clay-oven, so there was no chance to bake another batch in time.'

I waved all these domestic apologies away and indicated that fresh water would suit me very well. I did not add that I would much have preferred a couple of hot oatcakes from a street-vendor to any of the Roman dainties set in front of me. I picked up a piece of fruit. 'I am not very hungry, anyway, but there's one thing that I've heard which I would like to check with you. Did you see Lavinia at the window-space when the raeda left?'

The slave-girl paused in the act of taking out the tray. 'I didn't, citizen. We house-slaves were busy with our duties by that time. Audelia had us carrying cushions to and fro, but I didn't see her leave – or any of the other guests for that matter. We aren't allowed to stop and watch visitors depart.' She flashed that timid smile. 'Although, I would not be surprised if Lavinia did look out and wave. I know that she wanted to come down and say goodbye.'

'Then why didn't she? I thought Lavinia generally got her wish?'

'That was Audelia's doing, citizen.' She smiled at my surprise. 'I heard them talking when I took the child's washing-water up. The girl was begging to be allowed to come downstairs and wave, but her cousin told her that it wasn't fitting for a Vestal candidate. "Much better that you stay here in the dry", I heard her say. "Fast and pray and purify yourself, ready for the wonderful new life which lies ahea . . .",' She broke off as her mistress came into the room, dressed now for outdoors in a handsome cloak.

Priscilla rounded on the kitchen-slave at once. 'What are you doing loitering in here? Get back to work at once. And bring the citizen a drink as you were told to do.' Then, as the servant hastened to obey, she turned to me. 'I'm sorry, citizen. The girl has no business to interrupt your meal.'

She had caught me in the middle of a mouthful of ripe pear. 'On the contrary,' I murmured, when I'd swallowed it. 'She was answering my questions – and being quite a help.'

Priscilla snorted. 'Well, I'm glad she's good for something. But I've come to say, if you wish to find the donkey-boy, we should leave fairly soon. Otherwise he'll have found a different job to do – a message or a parcel to deliver out of town – and he won't be able to lead you to the farm where he took the letter. And weren't you hoping to see the slave trader as well?'

I nodded, finishing the remnants of my pear.

'Then when you've finished here, I will accompany you to town. Do you wish to take the horseman too – or the raeda-driver, perhaps – since you have no other servant to attend on you?'

I shook my head. 'I think that the raeda should take the nursemaid back to her owners,' I said, dipping a little of the bread-crust in the oil. 'Ephibbius will have to purify the coach, in any case, before another paying customer will dare to ride in it. Another body will not make much difference at this stage. Shroud it in something for the trip and treat it decently.'

She nodded. 'If you think that Lavinius will meet the cost of it, I'll get the undertaker's women to lay out the corpse. I think I've got some funeral herbs around the house – we had a slave-boy recently who died. That will purify the room as well so we can let it out again – supposing we ever get another guest when news of this gets out! And what about the clothes

Lavinia left behind? Should I box them up and send them
back as well?'

I nodded. 'Keep back the adult clothes and drawstring purse.
I would like to look at them again. Ascus had better ride back
to Lavinia's family and break the news to them – not just
about the nurse's death but the fact we haven't found the girl.
He can also tell Publius where I'm going and why, and say
that I'll report in person in a day or two.' I risked a smile. 'I
take it I can stay here for another night? It will be too late for
me to walk back home today, whatever I discover at the farm.'
Poor Gwellia! I was already planning that, whatever news he
took to Publius, Ascus could carry a reassuring message to
her on the way.

Priscilla nodded. 'Then, there's a lot to organize. I'll go and
make a start. Meanwhile here's that useless slave-girl with a
drink for you. I hope you've brought the citizen a proper metal
cup and not one of those beakers that we use ourselves?' And
she stalked out of the room.

The slave-girl hadn't brought a metal cup, of course, but I
indicated that she should pour me some water nonetheless. As
she raised the jug she looked timidly at me. 'Permission to
ask you something, citizen?'

I nodded. The water was clear and cool, but not as good as
that we get from Glevum's public well.

'Then . . .' She hesitated for a moment, then said in a rush,
'There is a rumour in the slave-quarters, that you don't think
that the woman who came here yesterday was really the Vestal
Virgin Audelia at all. Is that true, citizen?'

'Who told you that?' I spluttered, taken by surprise.

She shook her head. 'Something that the mistress mentioned,
that is all. She came into the kitchen, saying that you'd proved
Audelia was dead before she reached Corinium, and that was
a blessing because it means the household could not be to
blame. But – do you really think that, citizen?'

Something in her manner made me put down the cup. 'You
don't believe that theory?'

She shook a doubtful head. 'I might be wrong, of course –
I'd never seen Audelia before. The woman who came here might
have been anyone at all. But there is one thing you should know.
Whoever she was, she certainly knew a lot about the Vestal

shrine: what they did with all the newcomers, how they shaved their heads and what the rituals were, and everything that her young cousin could expect. She talked of little else all through the meal last night – saying how revered Vestal Virgins are, with the right to pardon prisoners who crossed their paths – and you could see that young Lavinia was thrilled. And she also made the offering at the household shrine, like someone who had done it all her life, when the master suggested that she should.' She paused and looked at me. 'If that was not a Vestal Virgin, citizen, how could she know all that?' She glanced around. 'But here's the mistress, don't say I questioned it.' She seized the jug and beaker and scuttled off with them.

Priscilla was already speaking as she came into the room. 'I've left my orders with the household now. So, when you are ready, citizen? You will need to dress, I suppose?'

I could take a hint. I left my breakfast, went upstairs and wrestled with my toga as I tried to put it on – not an easy business with no attendant slave – but finally I managed and came downstairs again.

Priscilla was already waiting by the door. 'Ah, citizen! If you'd like to follow me,' she said, and led the way out into the street.

TWENTY

Corinium is primarily a market town, of course, not a colonia like Glevum – no streets of retired legionaries or heavy garrison – and at this time of the morning it was abuzz with trade and noise. Even the small street outside the house, which had seemed so quiet and secluded last night in the dark, was now full of street-sellers and people plying wares outside their homes. A man and his four children sat outside their door, weaving osiers into eel-traps, and an enterprising cobbler who had set up a small last, paused in his hammering to hail me as we passed.

He spat out the hobnails he was holding in his teeth. 'New sandals, citizen? A special price for you. I'll take an outline now and have them finished by tonight?' He indicated the leather where I should put my foot so he could scratch a pattern from my sole. 'Guaranteed best quality.' He clutched at my toga but I eluded him. 'Make it two pairs, citizen, and I'll add spare laces, free.'

I was about to refuse and say I had no purse with me, but Priscilla took my elbow and steered me straight ahead. 'Pay no attention, citizen. You stop and talk to one of them, they'll all be after you. You come along with me!' And she strode purposefully on.

She was quite right, of course. I was dressed in a toga and a stranger to the place, and every dealer tried to wheedle me to buy. There was much to tempt a purchaser: the stalls and shops sold almost everything from fine imported silver to mended copper pans; in every doorway there were trays of leather belts, used clothes, brass ornaments, and pots of eye-ointment, heaped up on trestle tables and spilling out into the street while the hawkers invited me to 'come and look inside'.

Even the pedestrians had dubious offerings: boys with handcarts hawked firewood, turnips, reed mats and cabbages; pie-sellers and bakers' slaves came jostling by, balancing trays of steaming food upon their heads, and a man with a pair of yoked pails around his neck accosted me, offering a drink of milk or fermented whey from a battered metal cup he carried on a chain. Priscilla waved them all imperiously aside.

As we neared the forum, though, I paused and tugged her arm. I could see an amanuensis sitting by the wall, among the moneylenders who were busy at their trade. 'Is that . . . ?' I shouted, doubting she would hear over the general hubbub of the town.

She shook her head. 'That's not the one we used the other day. It was a young man we hadn't seen before. Now – you go down there, and find the slave-market, and I'll go and see if I can locate the donkey-boy for you.' She gestured in the direction I should take and turned away.

I followed her instructions and was soon in the square behind the forum, where the butchers had their stalls. It was also the area where the livestock market was, where all kinds of domestic animals, including slaves, were sold. The noise and smell was indescribable. I declined an offer to purchase fresh fish from a pool or make a choice from buckets full of squirming eels and, edging round a ragged urchin with a pail (who was scavenging manure from the road to sell), I spotted the slave trader at the far end of the square.

He was a swarthy fellow – probably a Greek – and clearly prosperous. His coloured tunic was of many hues, his cloak was of expensive scarlet wool and the clasp on his heavy leather belt appeared to be of gold. When I approached he was already offering the last lot of the day, a pair of dusky females chained together by the feet; either he'd had a busy morning or he'd not had much to sell. He saw me coming over and he called to me at once.

'What do you bid me for this pair of slaves? Guaranteed disease-free and no rotting teeth. Direct from the Province in North Africa. Not virgins, but they have years of service left. Come on, citizen, you know you can't resist.'

I could resist quite easily; I shook my head at him.

He turned his attention back to the small crowd of spectators. 'Well, what am I offered, gentlemen?' But there was no response. I could imagine why. Both girls were plain and scrawny, unwashed and sullen-faced, although I could hardly blame them for their scowls. I have been offered at a slave-market myself, and I know the degradation of being just a 'thing', to be handled and inspected by prospective customers who want to feel your muscles and inspect your teeth. And for females, of course, it was a great deal worse.

There was a balding, greasy, paunchy fellow in a toga now, stepping forward and demanding to 'see the merchandise'. The girls were stripped naked, and made to turn around while he examined and prodded every part of them.

'They will do, I suppose.' He took the straw that he was chewing from between his teeth, and made an offer so low it made me gasp.

The trader shook his head. 'Cost me more than that for each of them!'

'Then you were cheated. Half as much again, and that's my final offer.'

There were no other bids forthcoming, it appeared, and after a little more haggling the females had changed hands. Their new master seemed reluctant to allow them to be clothed, but they were put back in their tunics and led away, still chained, while he casually pinched and fondled any part that he could reach. I almost wished I had a purse so I could have rescued them from this, but I had no money and certainly I did not need two extra mouths to feed.

The small crowd that had gathered began to drift away, now that there was nothing more to see. The slave trader slipped his takings into his leather pouch and sauntered over to speak to me.

'You wanted something, citizen? You were too late, I fear. I had quite a good selection a little earlier. Next moon, perhaps, when I'm this way again. Were you looking for something in particular?'

'I believe you know a certain Paulinus, who has a farm a little way from here? You sold him a mute slave-woman to tend his child, I think?'

He leaned back on his heels and gave me a strange leer. 'It will cost you extra if you have special tastes. It's very hard to find a slave that doesn't speak. Why would you want one anyway? Different for that Paulinus, he has a deaf-mute child. If you want a girl that can't protest, just put a gag on her. Now, if you want something special, I shall have a girl next week—'

I cut him off before he imagined any worse of me. 'I do not want a girl of any kind. I have all the slaves I want. I am interested in information about Paulinus, that's all.'

The leer transmuted to a crafty look. 'With respect, citizen, why should I give you that? I deal in slaves, not information about my customers. Unless of course . . .' He rubbed his thumb against his first two fingers in the time-honoured signal that he wanted to be paid.

I shook my head. 'I haven't any money that I can offer you. It is on my patron's orders that I am asking you.' That was true, in a circuitous sort of way. 'Marcus Aurelius Septimus. Perhaps you know the name?' Marcus, of course, had a substantial residence in this town. I could be cunning, in my fashion, too.

It worked. The slave trader's expression changed like quicksilver. 'Why did you not say so when you first arrived? Of course I have had dealings with His Excellence. I've sold him several slaves – though he often prefers to have the more expensive ones the specialists bring in. So, how can I help you? What is it about Paulinus that you want to know?'

'Have you known him long?'

He seemed to contemplate. 'Eight years or so, I suppose. We first met when I found him a house-slave when he married first, but when his wife died he sold that servant on. Wanted to use the money to help that girl of his, but how he managed in the house without a slave I don't know. So when I heard about the mute I sent him word at once and he sent back agreeing to the price, and saying he would pick her up as soon as possible.'

'And that is what he did?'

He nodded. 'He seems to be extremely pleased with her – and she could hardly believe her own good luck. After she'd had that injury and lost the power of speech, her owners didn't want her, they thought she was a freak. They were going to cast her out – they actually approached me to find a substitute, but I thought of Paulinus and purchased her myself. The moment that he bought her, she bent and kissed his feet – she had feared that she would end up as a beggar at the tombs. So everyone was happy. I made a profit, too.'

'So you've known Paulinus for some little time?' I said.

He frowned at me. 'Have I not just said so, citizen?'

'And you can confirm it was the same man that came here yesterday?'

'Of course I can. You could not mistake him, he is very tall and thin, gentle, anxious-looking, with an air of mild bewilderment at fate. I don't know why it is important, citizen, but it was definitely Paulinus in the market yesterday – though of course, I hadn't seen that brand-new wife of his before. Not that I had very much to do with her. She was buying something from the garment stall. It was Paulinus who came to talk about the mute.'

'And he also bought a little page from you? Though not a very trained one, from what I hear of it.'

He shook his head. 'Not me, citizen. I don't deal in children very much. More trouble than they're worth. You have to feed and train them before they're fit to sell, and even then you can be undercut by amateurs – peasants wanting to sell one child so they can afford to feed the rest. If Paulinus bought a pageboy yesterday, then it was not from me. More likely from one of those peasant families. In fact I think I saw him talk to one of them. You'll find them over there – in the corner by the fish-market.'

'I'll go and ask,' I said. 'I would like to talk to the family of that lad.'

He stuck his fat thumbs into his leather belt. 'I shouldn't bother, citizen. You won't find that family now. These paupers only ever bring a single child to sell – and that reluctantly. Once they've got the money they go back home again and try to scratch a living for another year – until they end up starving, and have to sell another one. It's usually a boy, they bring a better price. Sometimes, especially if the winter's bad, children are the only saleable asset that they have.'

I tried to envisage how my adopted son would feel if he was forced to sell his own beloved child to keep the rest of the family alive, but my imagination failed me. I shook my head. 'Then I will try to find Paulinus at his farm and see if he can tell what I want to know. You have been most helpful. Thank you very much.'

He gave me that sideways look again. 'Perhaps you'll tell your patron if I have been of use? But you look as if my information was not quite what you had hoped.'

I gave a rueful smile. 'It seems to disprove a theory that I had, that's all. There is a mystery surrounding his family yesterday and now I'll have to find another explanation of events.'

'Is this about that Vestal Virgin who was here? She was some relation, wasn't she?' He caught sight of my face. 'It is no "mystery" how I came to know that, citizen – he was so proud of it, he told me she was coming the last time that we met.'

So there was yet another way in which the Druids could have learned the news! I sighed. 'Well, there's nothing else to do but go out to the farm and try and talk to Paulinus himself. He and his family might have noticed something, I suppose.' I glanced up and saw Priscilla striding through the square, accompanied by an urchin with a donkey on a string. 'And here, I hope, is someone who is going to guide me there.'

The slave trader flashed his pointed teeth at me. 'Well, remember, citizen, I'm here three days each moon. If you ever need a slave-girl or a manservant – indoors or outdoors – I always have a range.' He winked. 'And – in future – since you're the protégé of His Excellence, I'm sure I can manage a special rate for you.'

I thanked him and turned away to greet Priscilla and the boy.

TWENTY-ONE

Priscilla came breathlessly up to me at once. 'Did you discover anything?'

I shook my head. This was not the time or place to tell her that the information I'd received only served to make me more bemused. 'Only that I need to go out to the farm and speak to Paulinus as soon as possible.'

She smirked triumphantly. 'That won't be difficult. I've found the donkey-boy for you. He remembers exactly where he took the writing-block and he will take you there, although it's quite a walk, he says – several miles at least.'

I nodded, though not without an inward sigh. I am quite used to walking from my roundhouse into Glevum town, and that is a walk of several miles as well, but this was different. I couldn't take my time. Two females were already dead and another one was missing without trace: I wanted to ask more questions as soon as possible.

The urchin tugged my toga. 'You could come up on my donkey, citizen, if you don't mind sitting at the back and hanging on. Long Ears is used to carrying panniers so he'll bear you easily, though he can be a stubborn old creature when he tries. I may have to give you a branch-switch to help to urge him on.' His grimy face split in a mocking grin. 'Might not be very dignified, but it would get you there – a little bit quicker than walking anyway, there are a lot of hills and valleys between here and the farm. Or I could lead Long Ears and walk along beside, though that would obviously be slower and cost a little more.'

I was about to protest my complete lack of ready cash, but Priscilla said at once, 'I've told him, citizen, that we will put it on your bill, and pay him what is owed when Publius pays us.' She saw my look and added urgently, 'I had to promise something or he wouldn't have agreed. The boy has to make a living, after all – and he can't be doing other errands if he's guiding you.'

I was obliged to see the force of this and I agreed the terms, wondering what Publius was going to say to this. No one had mentioned hiring donkey-boys.

Priscilla smiled. 'I will leave you to it, then, and go back to the house and see if the undertakers' women have finished dealing with the nurse's corpse. If so the raedarius can take it back to Lavinius again, as you sensibly suggested, citizen.'

'You will send news back with them, and warn the family what has happened, I suppose?'

She looked pityingly at me, as though I were foolish to have asked. 'I'll do more than that. I'll send the horseman off at once to tell them to expect her body later in the day, then they can make arrangements for a pyre. No doubt they'll know if she was a member of the funeral-guild.'

I nodded. It was probable. Most slaves in wealthy families belonged to such a guild, which – for a small subscription – ensured a decent send-off after death. Some masters, like Marcus, paid the fee themselves, it saved them having to arrange a private pyre.

I said, 'If not, I suppose Cyra and Lavinius will do something for their slave.'

'Then, with your permission,' Priscilla said, 'I'll send that flask back too, since clearly at one time it belonged to them. The household would expect to have it back, I'm sure. It is still a valuable object and if it can't be repaired, at least the metal could be used again. Though whether Cyra will want to use it in any form at all, when she hears that it was used to murder that poor nurse, only Juno knows. Perhaps they'll use it as a grave-offering for the corpse.' She looked from left to right as though we might be overheard, then added in a whisper, 'Should I get Ascus to tell her that we think it was tampered with by Druids?'

I remembered the courtyard and the finding of the flask. What was it about the scene that still faintly troubled me? The little jug had been exactly where it would have bounced if it had been thrown out of the window-space above . . . Of course! I was a threefold idiot! I took a sharp breath and turned to Trullius's wife. 'Better perhaps, for Ascus just to say that the nursemaid drank a poisoned sleeping draught. It's—'

She was sharp-witted enough to see the point of this at once.

She looked from left to right, then held me by the arm and tugged me to one side. 'You don't think it was the rebels, after all? Then who . . . ?' She looked into my face. 'You're not suggesting that she drank it knowingly?'

I said slowly, feeling for the truth, 'It occurs to me that it is possible. That flask may be the so-called "sign" that she was looking for. It would explain why she begged us to let her back into the room, and why she wanted to have her two hands free, although she seemed perfectly happy to be chained.'

Priscilla took a moment to consider this. 'I said that we should never have allowed her back upstairs!' She sidestepped a ribbon-vendor who was proffering his tray and dropped her voice again. 'But surely it's more likely that a murderer exchanged the poison for her sleeping draught and she drank it by accident? The same person who kidnapped Lavinia earlier – and perhaps, who then climbed out of the room down that knotted cloth-rope which we thought the child had made?'

'In that case,' I said, 'why throw the flask away?' Now that I had realized the unlikelihood of that, I wondered why it had taken me so long to question it. 'Yet she must have done. No one else could have got into the room last night: there was a slave outside the door, and Trullius and I watched with our own eyes as she pulled up the cloth-rope and undid the knots – making a pretence of examining each one – so there was no chance of anyone gaining access from the court. Besides, if a murderer had got into the room and forced the nurse to drink the poison he had brought, he wouldn't have thrown a valuable jug away – especially where it was possible that it would be found, Surely he would have taken it with him when he went?'

The ribbon-man bobbed up beside us, offering his wares, but she waved him off as though he were a flea. She turned to me. 'I see your reasoning. Rebels are always robbing people on the road to get hold of valuable things that they can sell.' She frowned. 'But what about the nurse?'

'You don't believe that she would kill herself?'

'I can see she might want to do that!' she replied. 'Especially if – as now seems likely – she was party to the plot, either against the Vestal or against Lavinia. If her owners found that she was guilty of anything like that they'd have her put to death in ways that would make the poison seem an easy route. I can understand all that. But even if she took the potion willingly, the problem still remains: why throw the flask away?'

I had been asking the same question of myself. 'Perhaps to make it look like sorcery,' I said. 'She was unlucky there. I have had dealings with an infusion of crushed hemlock once before. Otherwise I wouldn't have recognized the stain on the drawstring of that purse – or identified the smell.'

'And we'd have gone on thinking this was a Druid spell?'

'Well, wouldn't you?' I asked.

She nodded thoughtfully and seemed about to speak, but the hopeful ribbon-man was back, bobbing up between us with his tray again. 'Best ribbons, lady. All hand-dyed and woven by my wife.'

She turned on him. 'I'll hand-weave you, if you don't move along!' and he sidled off to hustle someone else. She gave me a knowing look. 'And you had better move along with your donkey-boy as well, before some other customer appears who offers ready cash. But after what we've said, I think that I agree. I'll simply send the message that the nurse is dead. If there are other explanations you can make them when you get back to Lavinius yourself.' She made a wry face. 'Perhaps it's just as well. This way the nurse can have her funeral – if only with the guild – before her owners know that she was working for the Druids. Otherwise they might simply throw her body to the dogs, and then who knows what trouble we might have with her ghost. So I'll go back and send that horseman with the message straight away, unless there is anything else you need me for?'

'There is one thing that you can do for me, when you get back to the house. I think you said the nursemaid took Lavinia's pot outside to empty on the midden-pile? Yesterday noontime, when she came down for the tray?'

'That's right.' She looked surprised.

'Then will you have your house-slaves search the rubbish pile for me? They're looking for anything resembling a phial, or some container to put poison in. I still believe the hemlock mixture was carried into the bedroom in that pouch, and almost certainly not in that silver flask. If your slaves find anything unusual, have it put aside for me.'

'With pleasure, citizen.' Priscilla smiled. It struck me that – though she talked too much – she had a lively mind and now that her household was no longer under threat she was actually delighted to be asked to help. She beckoned to the donkey-boy, who had been lingering nearby. He came across at once. 'Now see that you take this citizen the shortest way,' she said to him. 'If I find you've been taking detours, just to raise the fee, I'll tell the magistrates – and I warn you this citizen has a wealthy patron, too, who knows how to make your life a misery. You understand?'

The boy looked sheepish but he said stubbornly, 'I wasn't going to cheat him. I'll go the quickest way. But if he wants to get there for the fee that we arranged, we ought to go at once – give me a chance to earn some food today. I know you've promised to pay me later on – quite handsomely, I grant – but that's all very well. I still need to eat and you can't buy bread without real money in your hand. The baker doesn't trade in promises. So, if you are quite ready, citizen?'

I signalled that I was and he set off at once, tugging his reluctant animal. There was nothing for it but to follow them. The donkey was a melancholy-looking specimen, all skin and ribs, and I feared it had the mange, so I consoled myself that perhaps it was as well that I was not to get my ride. But when we reached the eastern gateway to the town the urchin paused beside a mounting stone, and indicated that I should climb onto the creature's back.

The only saddle was a patched and tattered rug, tied underneath the belly with a piece of hempen string. I climbed up, graceless and rather hesitant. I was accustomed to owning horses in my youth, but I scarcely went near one when I was a slave and it is many years since I have ridden anywhere.

This donkey was bony and bouncy compared to my fine steeds of long ago, and distinctly slow. But it was not displeasing to be on its back and although my toga billowed out and threatened to unwind, I very quickly got the hang of it. The donkey-boy was even more surprised than I was at my skill.

'He seems to like you, citizen. Sit tight, and I'll squeeze in ahead of you.'

I was certain that the donkey would refuse – it seemed

recalcitrant in any case – but to my surprise it answered to the switch and we found ourselves swaying precariously along, not very quickly, but faster than on foot.

We must have presented a strange spectacle: a scruffy boy and a Celtic citizen with his toga half-undone, squashed together on a skinny donkey's back. Certainly we did not go unremarked. Cart-drivers and riders who passed us on the way grinned and raised their whips in mock-salute and various land-labourers turned their heads to look.

The track – we had long ago turned off the Roman roads – swung uphill and down the valleys as the boy had said. In places it was barely wide enough to take a cart, but wheel-tracks in the mud were evidence that a wagon had indeed lurched past this way, and fairly recently. The presumed Paulinus and his wife were said to have a farm-cart, I recalled, and certainly the homesteads here were agricultural.

I began to wonder if my mission was a waste of time and this farmer and his family were not impostors, lured by the reading of the letter – as I'd thought – but exactly who they claimed to be, in which case all my careful reasoning fell apart and I had no other theory to advance. I would have liked to ask the donkey-boy about his previous mission to the farm, but he would have had to turn his head to catch my words, and such was the concentration required to stay on – particularly here, where the road was rough and steep – that there was really no opportunity for that.

At last the lad urged the creature to a stop, close to a clearing where there were several homesteads scratching a living from the land. 'Here you are, citizen. This is the very place.' He gestured with his switch.

I looked where he was pointing. Paulinus was a Roman citizen, from a patrician family and, although I had several times been told that he was not a wealthy man, I had expected something more like Lavinius's estate, though on a smaller scale. This was a humble farm. The house was square and made of stone, as Roman dwellings generally are, and there was a land-slave working in the grounds outside, but there all resemblance to a normal villa ceased. There was no handsome court, no separate slave-quarters, no gatekeeper on watch inside imposing walls, just an enclosure made of piled-up stones, a single dwelling with a stable to the side and rows of turnips and cabbages behind, and a tiny orchard with chickens pecking free. There was a pig-byre just beyond the house, sharing a scruffy pasture with a cow and several piebald goats, while the entrance to the whole was guarded by a large dog on a chain. This was more on the scale of my own abode than anything more grand.

The donkey-boy was looking impatiently at me. 'This is where I brought the letter, citizen, following the directions that were given me. Are you not getting down? I thought I was to leave you here, when I'd delivered you?'

I swung off my makeshift saddle, which swivelled under me and almost deposited me head-downwards on the ground. However, I managed to keep my balance and maintain my dignity, though I discovered that I ached in every limb. 'And the man who lives here is called Paulinus?' I said, with as much gravitas as I could muster.

He looked at me as though I were the donkey here. 'That's right, citizen. Or that's what I was told. The letter was addressed to someone of that name, and when I brought it here, the slave I spoke to went and got him from the house and he came out personally and took it from my hands. Seemed very pleased to get it, from what I saw of him. Gave me a piece of bread and cheese for bringing it. Not the sort of greeting I usually expect, especially from proper citizens: generally they keep you waiting for an hour and then send a servant out to deal with you.'

'So you'll remember what he looks like?' I said eagerly, glad to be making progress of a kind. If the description did not match what I had been told this morning by the slave trader, then the man who took the letter was not Paulinus.

'Naturally, I do.' The donkey-boy looked doubtfully at me. 'You want me to describe him? It won't be very flattering. He's not a handsome man.'

I reassured him that he would not be punished for his words.

'Well . . .' The urchin dropped his voice, because the land-slave in the tattered tunic had come over to the pig and was feeding it something from a wooden pail, and it was possible that we could be overheard. 'Tall and rather stooping, with a skinny face. Just a little balding, with protruding teeth. But he's got a kindly smile, when he uses it. Took him a minute. Quiet voice as well. I thought he might be shy – if that's not a silly thing to say about a Roman citizen.'

I was dumbfounded. The description matched exactly what I had already heard. 'That is very helpful,' I said untruthfully. 'I'll . . .' But before I could complete the sentence the land-slave had looked up from his task and was calling out to us.

'You have business with my master?' He put down the pail and came over to the boundary wall, if you could call it that. The pile of stones at this point came no higher than his waist. His skin was tanned and wind-burned to an even darker brown than his coarse tunic and his leather boots, except where mud and grime had turned him to the greyish-black colour of his tousled hair.

'I am looking for a man called Paulinus,' I said. 'I believe he was in Corinium yesterday.'

'That will be my owner,' he said cheerfully. 'You've come to the right place. He went to Corinium all right – took some goods to sell and went to the slave-market while he was in town. What do you want with him? We don't very often get visitors round here. Is there some trouble with a bargain that he struck?'

I shook my head. 'There have been a couple of mysterious deaths,' I said, choosing my words carefully. 'Someone that he knew was set upon and killed, and a slave was found dead this morning at the very lodging-house where your master stayed. I'm hoping he can help me with my enquiries.'

The land-slave rubbed his filthy hands across his filthy hair. 'I don't mean any disrespect but, who are you, exactly, citizen?'

'My patron is Marcus Aurelius Septimus,' I said, but his expression told me that the name meant nothing here. I tried again. 'I am sent here by the bridegroom of one Audelia, who was a Vestal Virgin until recently, and by her uncle who is called Lavinius.'

He grinned. His remaining teeth were crooked, but only one was black. 'Oh, I see. We know all about Lavinius – he's quite famous around here. Refused to help my master when he applied to him for aid. Wanted to take the child to a healing shrine. You know about the daughter of the house . . . ?' He saw my nod and went on, more soberly, 'Fortunately this new wife has got a kinder heart.'

'And I suppose that your master was offended, too, by the fact that Lavinius did not ask him to the wedding feast?'

That jagged smile again. 'On the contrary. Quite relieved, I think. My master never liked Lavinius very much and now that he has married for the second time, this household is too busy with its own affairs to spend the time and money that would be involved in travelling all the way to Glevum for a feast. In fact it is as well you came today. Another day or two and you would be too late. He and his wife are leaving here to take the child to Gaul – there is said to be a healing spring there, which they want to try. Not that I suppose it will do any good – nothing else has ever helped her in the least – but Secunda's brought a dowry with her, so they can manage it, and if he wants to use her money in this way, I say good luck to them. Anyway, you never know, the spring might do the trick.'

I looked around. 'And what about this farm, the slaves and everything? Surely they will not just abandon it?'

'They've found a fellow down the road who will look after it in return for a half-share of the crops, till they get back again. Or, if they do decide to stay in Gaul, he'll buy it as it stands – but I think they only mean to be away for a half a year. I hope so. I have worked here since a child, and you couldn't ask for better owners. Both this wife and the first. I would hate to see a change. But if you want Paulinus – that's him coming now.'

He gestured to where a tall, thin, stooping man – slightly balding and with protruding teeth – was hurrying towards us across the pasture-field.

TWENTY-TWO

'That's him, citizen!' a voice behind me said. 'Exactly as I told you. Now that you've seen him, am I free to go?'

I had been so busy with the land-slave, I'd forgotten all about the donkey-boy. I dismissed him hastily and turned to meet the owner of the house, who was by this time at the gate. He muttered something to his land-worker, who picked up his pail and scuttled off with it. The master turned to me enquiringly.

'You are Paulinus?' I said foolishly. Short of a portrait or a statue, I could not have had a better picture of the man than the one that I'd been given. He was not dressed in a toga but in a stained green tunic belted at the waist, but otherwise he was exactly as I'd envisaged him, down to the furrowed brow and slightly anxious expression of surprise.

'Paulinus Atronius Marinus, at your service, citizen. I am the owner of this smallholding. How can I be of help?' His voice was soft and cultured and his Latin quite impeccable. The quiet insistence on his full three Roman names was a way of telling me he was himself a citizen, despite his working dress.

I answered him in kind. 'Longinus Flavius Libertus,' I replied, wondering why this commonplace exchange was sending me inward signals of alarm. 'I have bad news for you. You are a friend and relative of Audelia, I think?'

He stiffened very slightly. 'You bring us news of her?' A tiny pause. 'I trust her marriage was a great success?'

'She never reached her marriage,' I said solemnly. I told him briefly what we had discovered in the coach.

'Beheaded! Dreadful!' he said, with a shudder that could hardly have been forced. He closed his eyes as though he could not bear to think of it. 'Poor girl – the gods know she did not deserve a fate like that. What will they do with her? I suppose the family will cremate the corpse?' He peered anxiously at me. 'I imagine that they'll have to, although it's incomplete?'

It seemed an odd question to a Celt like me: even those of us who are not actually Druids revere the head as more or less the dwelling of the soul. But of course the Romans have a different attitude. They see things the other way about – a headless body might create a restless ghost, stalking the world until it found the missing parts. 'I'm sure her family will give it proper rites, and do their best to see that her spirit is at rest,' I said, aware of sounding oddly sanctimonious.

'I hope so, citizen.' He gave the famous smile and I saw at once what the donkey-boy had meant. It quite transfigured him. 'Perhaps you didn't realize that I know Audelia well – did know her, I suppose that I shall have to learn to say. My wife and I went to the Vestal temple many times when she was serving at the shrine.'

'You and your first wife, that was?' I was still double-checking details in my mind.

'Indeed.' He raised an eyebrow, as if he were surprised. 'You must have heard that I have lately wed again? Did they tell you how fortunate I am? I have found an angel not just to care for me but to look after my poor mute daughter too. I am a lucky man. But I forget my manners. You have come all this way to bring me this distressing news about my relative. Please come inside and have some food and drink before you leave. We don't have dates and Rhenish wine, I fear, but we can offer you some home-made bread and cheese and water from the well.' He smiled at me, the perfect picture of a Roman host. 'Indeed I have already sent the land-slave in ahead of us to warn the household you are here and thus ensure a light refreshment is arranged for you. I am afraid you find us in a little disarray.'

'I hear you are preparing to go overseas,' I said, as he dragged the snarling dog away and tied it to a post.

He came back to hold the gate ajar for me. 'How did you learn that?' His look of astonishment was almost comical.

I explained about the land-slave and he smiled again. 'Well, citizen, what my farm-servant says is true. We plan to leave as soon as possible.' He escorted me up the stony path towards the doorway of the house, skirting piles of kindling wood and avoiding the wet garments, clearly washed and dyed, which were draped over bushes in the wind to dry. When we reached the threshold – no more than a single piece of stone placed where people would walk in and out on it – he stepped ahead of me and called in through the door. 'Are we prepared? Our visitor is here.'

A woman-slave came hastening out at once, rubbing her hands against her tunic-skirt as if they had been damp. She was a tallish, unattractive female of advancing years. Her wan face was worn and mottled, cobwebbed with fine lines, and she had the doubtful darting eyes of someone who has learned – by hard experience – to distrust the world. Her curly hair, which she wore severely short, was dull and mousy grey and her mouth was clamped into a tight, suspicious line. However, her sharp expression softened when Paulinus talked to her and the look she gave her owner was an adoring one.

'This is Libertus, Muta,' she was told. 'He is a citizen and will be our guest. Kindly show him in. I will change out of my dirty working clothes and join you very soon.' He turned away towards the rear part of the house.

Muta bobbed me a stiff curtsy and led the way inside, through a narrow passage into a sort of waiting-room. Her form was generally sinewy and thin, but the swollen ankles which I glimpsed beneath the tunic-hem suggested a reason for her awkward gait. I could see exactly what Priscilla meant – this servant was no bargain, whatever price he'd paid.

The room was as bare as my own roundhouse at home: only a large wooden table and a brazier, a little household shrine set into a niche and – beneath a lone high shelf which held the household cups and bowls – a small amphora leaning on the wall and a few jars and storage-pitchers standing on the floor. The servant gestured to a small three-legged stool beside the table, where a bowl of curd-cheese and a crust of new bread had been set for me.

I sat down, rather awkwardly, while Muta picked up a brass water-pitcher from the floor and poured some into a handsome metal cup. She handed it to me without a word, and made a signal that I should start to eat.

'Is your new mistress home?' I ventured. I had hoped to meet Secunda and hear from her own lips that she was happy for her dowry to be squandered in this way. Besides, this silence was beginning to unsettle me.

The woman didn't answer, just made a gesture to the inner door. Of course, I remembered, the poor thing couldn't speak! I recalled that this was why she had been chosen for this house but that – unlike the daughter she was bought to serve – the woman could still hear.

I tried again, hoping to obtain at least a fleeting smile. 'I hope that you are learning to be happy in your work? You will be a comfort to the daughter I am sure.'

'It is no good talking to her, citizen. She cannot answer you.'

I turned to see the owner of the voice, and caught my breath. The woman at the inner door was singularly pale and far from young, but she was beautiful – one of the most beautiful women I have ever seen. She wore no trace of kohl or lamp-black round her eyes and there was no stain of wine-lees on her lips or cheeks but, despite her pallor, she did not need any. Her skin was soft and flawless, like a piece of kidskin cloth, and her hair, which hung in tight ringlets from a central band (in a fashion favoured by an Empress long ago, but long since out of style), was palest faded gold. She wore a simple floor-length lilac shift and as she walked towards me, holding out her hands, I thought that I had never seen a person more ethereal and serene.

'I am Secunda, the wife of Paulinus.' The tone was soft and very musical. 'I am sorry that I was not here to welcome you. I was in need of rest. We are in train of packing, as I believe you know, and I am not accustomed to such activity.'

'Pray do not mention it.' This household's slight formality and old-fashioned speech was infecting mine. I tried to fight this and conspicuously failed. 'I had already heard that you were indisposed – not in the best of health.' Now that I had seen her I could understand – already she seemed closer to the next world than to this.

She smiled rather sadly, revealing a set of almost perfect teeth. If I were a single man, I thought, I could have lost my heart. It was doubly tragic knowing that she was frail. I had heard that the gods take their best-beloved first, and now I could believe it. She was speaking, in that gentle voice of hers, and there was real emotion in her words. 'You bring us dreadful news about Audelia. I am most distressed to hear that you found the body in that mutilated state. It must have been a dreadfully upsetting shock for you.'

It was the first time – almost in my life – that anyone outside my family had ever shown the least concern for me, and what my feelings were when confronted with a death. I could have kissed her feet. Instead I put my hands together in the greeting pose, bowed my head and introduced myself. 'I fear,' I said – and for once that common form of words meant something genuine – 'that is not the only piece of bad news that I bring.'

'Then I will sit down and wait until my husband comes before I hear the rest. I should not like to make an exhibition of myself by fainting on the floor.' She turned to the slave-woman and murmured with a smile, 'A seat for me, perhaps?'

Muta made a signal of assent and left the room.

While she was gone I tried to turn the conversation to more cheerful things. 'You are pleased with your acquisitions at the market yesterday?'

Secunda looked bemused. 'I am not sure I follow . . . ?'

'That slave-woman. You bought her yesterday, I think? Together with a page?'

'Ah, of course.' A blush of soft confusion suffused the lovely face. 'I cannot think of slaves as acquisitions, citizen. I thought you were referring to this gown I bought. I wondered how you knew. Indeed, we are delighted with the slave. She is so good with Paulina, my husband's child, you know.' She smiled her rueful smile. 'He will be here shortly. In the meantime, do refresh yourself!'

Thus encouraged, I did try the bread and cheese. They were extremely good. Simple but excellent. Somehow, in this household, I was not surprised. All at once, I wished I hadn't come. I was here to find the answer to a gruesome tragedy – a nasty murder and a kidnapping plus an explanation for the nurse's suicide. I had been convinced that I would find the answer in this house, but if these people were involved I didn't want to know. I desperately wanted to believe them innocent.

I shook my head. This was ridiculous. Murder is still murder, whoever does the deed – and some of the cruellest emperors were famous for their charm. What was I thinking of? I could

guess what Priscilla would have said if she had known – that
I was the victim of some Druid spell. I do not generally believe
in the efficacy of love-potions and the like but I put down the
cup of liquid, just in case, and assumed my most severe expression as I said, 'Secunda – the matter of your dowry . . .'

She beamed, the happiest expression I had so far seen. 'Ah
yes, citizen. Was that not fortunate? I had never married, so I
brought my parents' whole inheritance with me. I am so happy
that Paulinus can have the use of it. Typical that his first care
should be for the child. My husband is so generous and
thoughtful, citizen.'

No question then of any rancour or mystery on that score,
and Priscilla's doubts about a Roman bribe appeared quite
baseless too. The only question was the obvious. 'You never
married earlier?' It seemed impossible. 'A woman of such
charm and elegance?'

She turned that charming pink again and dropped her eyes,
to stare at the floor with unforced modesty. (It was tiled, but
very roughly, with poor quality materials and no attempt at
pattern even round the edge. If I had been the workman, and
not done a better job, I should have been embarrassed to be
paid.) 'I had household duties to perform, so for a long time
I could not be spared . . .' She broke off as her husband and
the slave appeared.

The servant put down the stool she had been carrying, and
Secunda sank gracefully down onto the seat. Her husband
came and stood beside her, saying tenderly, 'Wife, be careful.
You should not be here. Don't put yourself to unnecessary
strain. You never . . .' Now in his toga, Paulinus paused as he
looked down at her with affection.

Secunda looked back up at him with such an expression on
her face that I was almost jealous of their tranquil happiness.
'It is all right, husband. I can manage well enough – and I
should be here to learn what Libertus has to say. Apparently
he has more items of alarming news for us.'

Her husband looked at me, furrowing his face in anxiety
again. 'You didn't mention this.'

'I scarcely had the chance. Besides your wife thought it
was better that we should wait for you.'

The couple exchanged glances, then Secunda said, 'Whatever

news you bring us, citizen, it cannot well be worse than what
we know already. Tell us what it is.'

'Lavinia is missing.' I put the fact as baldly as I could. 'At
first sight it seemed that she had run away.' Secunda turned
so pale that I forgot my fear of potions and swallowed the
remainder of my drink.

But her voice was steady. 'Run away?' She gave a pretty
little frown. 'That hardly seems like her, she was very keen
on taking up her role.'

'It is possible she did not go willingly.' I wished I did not
have to tell them this since it would cause them grief but if
they were to help me there was no alternative. 'It seems more
than possible that Druids were involved.'

'Druids!' they exclaimed, in unison. I saw the startled look
that passed between the pair.

'Could it have been a vendetta against the family? I understand that this household has had dealings with the sect,' I
muttered, apologetically.

Secunda answered in an altered voice, as though she were
struggling with emotion inwardly, 'In other circumstances,
citizen, we might have helped you there. There was a servant
in this household who proved to be a Druid, but she and her
whole family were sentenced to the beasts – so if there was
any information to be gleaned from them, I fear it is too late.'

'My dear . . . !' It was unusual for Romans to express
affection in this public way, but Paulinus did not seem to care
for such conventions. He even touched her shoulder as if
warning her. 'These things are best forgotten.'

She smiled up at him. 'There is nothing to be feared from
telling him the truth. He seems to think the Druids may have
harmed Lavinia and we should assure him that the sect is not
an enemy of ours. The fact is, citizen – though Paulinus seems
to wish me to obscure the fact – he was very good to them.
He could not bear to think of that little family – who had been
so helpful to our Paulina – torn to pieces for the entertainment
of the crowd. You know the way that the officials at the games
will lure a child into the arena first, so that the mother will
willingly run in after it – I understand the spectacle is very
popular. He could not stand for that. Paulinus bribed the guard
and managed to get poison in for them and even made

arrangements for disposal afterwards – to ensure as far as possible that they got proper Druid rites.'

Paulinus, who had been looking more and more embarrassed and bemused, now ran his hand through his receding hair and broke in awkwardly, 'Well, be that as it may, it does not help us now. Have you been searching for Lavinia, citizen? Perhaps she went to the temple by herself? Have you been to look for her?'

I had to admit that I'd not been there myself, although I assumed that Trullius had done. 'The news of her disappearance came to Glevum from a temple messenger,' I added, 'which does seem to indicate that she did not go there.'

'When did they find that she was missing?' Paulinus enquired.

I explained about the nursemaid and Priscilla and the tray. 'And that is not the end of it,' I said. 'This morning, at the guest house, the nursemaid was found dead. Poisoned, by the look of it. I think by her own hand.'

'Dear gods!' There was no mistaking Paulinus's sharp astonishment. 'Dead! But . . . she was so happy for Lavinia . . . why should she . . . ?' He looked helplessly towards his wife.

She reached up slowly and took his hand in hers, as if she could pass on some of her own serenity through the gentle pressure of her fingertips. 'It must have been a gesture for Lavinia's sake,' she said. 'It was clear to everyone how much she loved that child. I wonder if she smuggled her away some-where and killed herself to keep the secret safe.' She looked at me. 'Perhaps we'll never know. But thank you, citizen, for bringing us the news. We must send a message to Glevum with our condolences. My aunt and uncle will doubtless be distraught.'

I was touched by her thoughtfulness again. And then I saw the implication of her words. 'Your uncle?' I said, sharply. 'You mean Lavinius?'

The pale face coloured prettily again and she gave a laugh. 'My half-uncle by marriage I suppose that I should say. He is related to Paulinus, of course – as I presume you know.'

I did, if I had only stopped to think of it. 'I should have realized that.'

She twinkled. 'I suppose that you could say he is a relative of mine as well – though only through his wife.'

'Which makes you a distant kinswoman of your husband?'

She saw my face and twinkled even more. 'Does that surprise you, citizen? It is not uncommon for people of patrician lineage to marry others in the clan who are not direct blood-relatives of theirs.' The grey eyes sparkled slyly up at me from under downcast lids. 'Often it's to keep the fortune in the family. In my case, it is the only reason that we ever met. A woman in my situation – bound to house and hearth – does not in general encounter many men.'

She was quite right of course. Indeed, now that she told me she was a kinswoman I could see a slight resemblance to Lavinius's wife. Cyra was a good deal uglier – her face was harder and her features sharp, and of course her hair was dark – but there was something about the shape of her face which was not unalike. Secunda was almost what Cyra might have been, given different colouring and a happier life.

However, I could hardly say so, with Paulinus there, so I made a rather unfortunate remark. 'You were never sent to be a Vestal Virgin then? It seems to be traditional, in your family.'

She dropped her eyes again. 'I managed to escape that, citizen.' She spoke with such embarrassment that for the first time it occurred to me to question whether she was quite the innocent that she appeared to be. There was more than one reason why a girl might be turned down for acceptance at the Vestal shrine – and more than one reason why a family might keep a single daughter under lock and key at home. I wondered suddenly if there was something in her past, even, possibly, without her full consent? Some importunate, wealthy visitor perhaps? I tried to force the unpleasant picture from my mind.

My unhappy thoughts were interrupted by a strange noise at the inner door, which instantly flew open and a stumpy girl came in. She was not very old – no more than five or six – and might have been quite pretty, if her little face had not been flushed and screwed into a frown. She stumped across the room, ignoring all of us, and stood with arms folded in front of Paulinus.

'!!!! !??!!!' She stamped her foot and gestured angrily towards the inner door, moving her mouth although no sound came out. Another of my private theories turned to smoke at once.

It had occurred to me to wonder, before I'd reached the house, whether this so-called deaf-mute might be Lavinia in disguise – but now that I had seen her I was practically certain she was not. This girl seemed genuinely deaf and dumb. However, there was only one way to be completely sure. I waited until she had her back to me, and then mock-accidentally knocked the metal cup and sent it flying against the great brass pitcher on the floor.

It bounced against the jug with an alarming crash. I muttered an apology, 'So clumsy. Pardon me! Lucky it was empty.' But I had learned what I had hoped for. Everyone had jumped and whirled around – except the girl. It was quite evident that she had not heard a thing.

My excuses were mercifully cut short by the sudden arrival at the inner door of a breathless, rather scruffy little slave – clearly the purchase that I'd heard about. He was skinny as a sparrow, though clearly in fair health and cleaner than I'd expected him to be from the description which I'd had before. Someone had obviously bathed him in the stream. His face and hands were noticeably scrubbed, and so were the skinny legs beneath the tunic-hem, although there were still dark marks in the creases of his ears, and his scalp and spiky hair were streaked with grimy black. He paused at the doorway and gazed around the room, his eyes widening with alarm as he caught sight of me.

'This is the new page that you brought home yesterday? Brave of you to take a child who is quite untrained, though no doubt the parents were grateful for the money,' I said to Paulinus.

He did his haunted look. 'How do you know that?'

'I asked in the market,' I told him, with a grin. 'And you were seen at the guest house with him afterwards.'

Secunda had risen serenely to her feet. 'But of course we were. Come here, Servus. You need not be afraid.' The urchin came obediently across and stood in front of her. She turned him round to face me. 'Now bow to our visitor as we showed you how. Don't alarm him, citizen, he is very shy and has trouble finding words. You are right about the training. He has much to learn and at present he is very frightened, as you see.' She was quite right. The child was trembling.

'We are hoping that he might become a companion-help to poor Paulina,' she went on. 'Now that we have lost the wet nurse, as you know. But it is too early to expect a friendship there, I suppose. Servus was supposed to be guarding her while we were here with you – we do not commonly introduce her to our visitors – but evidently that has not been a success.' She bent down to the slave. 'Now then, Servus, bow politely to our guest, then take that jug and go and fill it at the spring – up in the field where I showed you earlier.' She turned to the slave-woman who had been waiting by the wall. 'And Muta, I think you'd better take Paulina back into her room and fetch her slate for her. She likes making pictures, citizen,' she added, for my benefit, as the slave-woman nodded and took the daughter's hand.

The child trotted off with her contentedly enough, and Paulinus watched them go with as much paternal pride as if this were a son. I was struck again by the unusual affection in this unlikely house.

The paterfamilias turned to me. 'Is there anything further that we can do for you? I would offer you a cart to take you into town, but we have none to spare. And it is a long trek back to Corinium, I fear.'

I shook my head. 'If I set off at once, I'll be there before dark. I think I know the way.' It was not difficult in fact, if I kept to the track and did not deviate to either side, I would eventually meet up with the proper Roman road. A long, demanding walk, but not impossible. The prospect made me sigh. If only I had kept the donkey-boy with me!

It was my own fault, I told myself. I had been so convinced that the solution to the mystery was somehow in this house – yet everything had proved to be exactly what it seemed. 'Thank you for the food and drink,' I said, and meant it, too. Another outcome of my stubbornness. It was unlikely that I'd get another meal before tonight. I smiled at Paulinus. 'And for allowing me to meet your family.'

'Then,' he said, 'I will escort you to the gate. I'll have to get back to checking fodder for the beasts. We don't have

many land-slaves, as you can observe, and there is much to
see to if we're to go to Gaul. Thank you for coming all this
way to bring us news.'

And there I would have left it, almost certainly, had the
maidservant, Muta, not come back into the room and started
beckoning her master urgently.

TWENTY-THREE

Paulinus turned his attention to the slave. 'What is it?' he enquired.

She mimed at him, pretending to be a driver of a carriage urging on the horse. Even I could understand the message she was trying to convey.

'I do believe there's someone at the gate,' I said, wondering whether the raeda had been sent to fetch me after all. If so there must be news. Perhaps Lavinia had turned up again? I was about to voice this happy possibility but my words were interrupted by a loud imperious rapping at the door.

I saw the look which flashed between the owner and his wife – a look of total apprehension and surprise. Paulinus closed his eyes. 'I forgot to let the guard-dog loose again,' he muttered, in evident distress. 'Somebody's managed to come directly up the path.'

Secunda had turned even paler than she'd been before but she said calmly, 'Then we'd better answer it. Go yourself, Paulinus. It isn't fair to Muta otherwise. Strangers ask her questions and she can't explain. Much better if she goes back and looks after Paulina.'

He nodded and went out into the little passageway towards the outer door, from whence the hammering was getting louder all the time. Muta disappeared to tend her charge again, while Secunda and I stood – as if by mutual consent – in silence, listening.

We heard Paulinus saying, 'I am the householder. Can I be of help?' And then his startled, sharp intake of breath. 'Dear Mars! To what do we owe this?'

'I am looking for a citizen named Libertus,' said a voice I recognized. 'I understand he may be calling at the house. I am sent here to inform him that – since Audelia is dead – he is to discontinue his enquiries and return to Glevum with us instantly. The gig is waiting for him at the gate.'

I was already in the passage by this time. I did not need to see the scarlet tunic and the fur-edged cape, to know the visitor's identity. 'Fiscus!' I exclaimed. 'What are you doing here?'

He looked at me with that expression of disdain. 'I am sent here to inform you that . . .' he began again, with elaborate patience, but I cut him off.

'I heard that! What I mean is, how did you find me at this farm? And how do you come to be here at this time of day? You must have left Glevum shortly after dawn.'

'We did!' The eyes took in the two Roman togas with contempt: mine, which was even more dishevelled and travel-stained by now and the old (though cleaner) one which Paulinus wore. Fiscus's own attire was immaculate. 'Publius was for sending us after you last night, as soon as Audelia's body was brought home, but Cyra and Lavinius said it was too late to travel then and we would never get to Corinium safely before dark. So, instead, they sent us at first light. We called at the lodging-house and they told us where you were. We would have been here rather sooner, in fact, but earlier in the day the sky was overcast and we had no sun and shadows to judge direction from. Several times we had to stop and ask the way.'

Paulinus had been listening to all this with interest. 'You are Lavinius's servant?' he asked, and then – aside to me – 'I did not think my kinsman kept menservants like this! But evidently you two have met before?'

'This slave belonged to Publius, originally,' I explained. 'He made a gift of him to my patron, who then lent him to me, just for a few hours when I had no servant of my own to travel with.'

'I imagine that's why I was selected for this task,' Fiscus said, with evident distaste. 'Riding and jolting all this way in a gig. And jammed in with a slave-girl all the way!'

'A slave-girl?' I was mystified. 'Whatever did they send a slave-girl with you for?'

'To ride back in the raeda and guard the nurse, of course – though naturally the prisoner would have ridden back in chains. Lavinius was going to send her to the torturers, to see if something could be extorted out of her about the disappearance of his daughter. Obviously at that time we did not know the nurse was dead.'

'They told you about that at the lodging-house, I suppose?'

It was a rather fatuous question and he treated it with the disdain that it deserved. 'They could hardly hope to keep it a secret, citizen!' he said, with a façade of politeness that was more humiliating than open rudeness would have been. 'But in fact we met that horseman on the way. That giant fellow. He recognized the gig and waved us down. He warned us what had happened, so by the time we reached the lodging-house we knew what we would find. Obviously, in the circumstances, we didn't linger there.'

'But I want to go back there before I leave Corinium,' I said. 'I need to speak to the landlady again. There are some clothes I want to look at, and something that her slaves were going to try to find for me.'

He looked at me coldly. 'That will not be necessary now. Your involvement in the matter is to cease at once. I am instructed to make that absolutely clear. Audelia is dead, and being cremated as we speak. Since there is no question of a Vestal marriage now, Publius has no further interest in the case. Clearly feels the match was ill-omened from the start. As for Lavinia, since she has run away, her father has formally washed his hands of her in front of witnesses and her parents would disown her if she ever did return. Certainly they do not wish to waste more money seeking her.'

'I would still like to call in at the lodging-house,' I said stubbornly, wondering whether Trullius would ever now be paid.

He raised a supercilious brow at me. 'In that case, citizen, you are fortunate. We will have to stop there on the journey back. The undertaker's women hadn't finished with the nurse and the slave-girl didn't want to stay in the same house with the dead, so we brought her here with us. It seems she's superstitious about accompanying the corpse and wants to appeal to you about the necessity of riding back with it.'

He seemed so irritated by this appeal to my authority that I was instinctively in favour of the plaintive in the case. I peered towards the gig. A skinny figure in the back seat waved a timid hand at me. 'Is that Modesta?' I said, incredulous.

Fiscus made his self-important face. 'It may be, citizen. I didn't ask her name. Anyway, we shall take her back as soon as possible and she will have to do her duty and ride home with the corpse – on the front seat of the raeda, if she must, since there won't be room inside. I don't suppose she'll like it very much but those are my instructions, so perhaps you will be good enough to see that she obeys? She's a slave-girl after all and her master put me in charge of her today. I wasn't consulted about bringing her out here – that was the landlord's doing, I believe, or I would never have agreed to that. It's the sort of concession to the foibles of a slave that may be frequent here, but would not for a moment be condoned in Rome.'

His condescension made me furious and I was suddenly determined to impede him if I could. For instance I would not be hurried into driving back with him. I turned to Paulinus. 'These poor slaves have driven all the way from Glevum ever since first light, and I doubt they have been offered rest or any food and drink. I myself am not quite ready to depart . . .'

The householder made a little deprecating gesture with his hand. 'We really have no slave-quarters that we can offer them. Only the nursemaid has a room inside the house and she shares that with Paulina, to keep an eye on her . . .'

'And the little page?' I asked.

'Has been sleeping on a pile of rushes at the door,' he said. 'We have not made permanent arrangements, since we're due to leave for Gaul . . .'

He broke off as Secunda came out from the house. It was evident at once that she had overheard. 'Paulinus, these are servants sent from your kinsman's house. Of course we must provide refreshment as the citizen suggests. It would seem remarkable to do otherwise.' She smiled at Fiscus and I saw him melt. It was magic. Who needed Druid spells when Secunda's smile could charm a man like that? 'We'll bring it to the barn. There's clean hay there where they can sit and eat. Perhaps they would also like to make use of the latrine? It's a long way to Glevum.'

I wouldn't have minded using the latrine myself and I murmured something of the kind to Paulinus. He nodded. 'Then I'll show them to the barn and take you there myself. In the meantime, I'll put the dog on guard. We can't have just anyone coming to the door!' He left us in the entrance and went back to the gate. He summoned the two slaves from the gig and moved the dog back to its earlier position where it stood bristling and growling at the gig-driver and had to be restrained from leaping at his throat as he went past. At Modesta, for some reason, it only bared its teeth and barked.

I was directed to the small latrine and by the time I had emerged from it, the three slaves from Glevum were already in the barn and Muta was crossing the yard towards it with a tray, on which I could see another hunk of bread, more of the curd-cheese which had been offered me and three wooden drinking bowls.

'I'll send some water when the page comes back with it.' Secunda's unexpected voice at my shoulder made me whirl around. 'Meanwhile would you care to come back into the house? I think you said you were not wholly ready to depart? Is there something else you wished to ask of us?'

'Not really,' I said wryly, and when she looked surprised, I confessed why I had said it. 'Fiscus is so arrogant and pompous, for a slave,' I finished, and rejoiced to see her smile.

'He values himself higher than his slave-price, doesn't he? I suppose it is his training,' she said, with humorous sympathy. 'I think you said that he was Publius's slave? No doubt he's spent his whole life in the capital and, because his master is a very wealthy man, he feels that deference should be shown to him. I expect he gets it, for the most part, too – and that is how he calculates his worth.' She gave that lovely smile. 'I'm very glad I'm not obliged to go and live in Rome. I think that I should hate it in those circles, citizen.'

I looked around this simple, happy home and I could only nod. I would not have swapped my roundhouse, with all its smoke and draughts, for the underfloor heating and marble colonnades of a great house in the Imperial city, either – to be spied upon and taxed, obliged to spend one's days currying favour from the Emperor's latest favourite, and being forced to feign support even for Commodus's more outlandish fads. Of course, I was too careful to voice this thought aloud. Fiscus was about. Even here, such criticism might be dangerous.

I was still smiling hopelessly at my beautiful hostess when a small scruffy figure tottered through the gateway at the back, struggling with the pitcher which was now evidently full. It was clear that Servus was not used to this: he put the jug down more than once or twice as if it were too heavy and he couldn't manage it.

Secunda stepped towards him and I thought that she was going to send him to the barn with it, but instead she stooped and picked the pitcher up herself. 'Get into the house at once,' she muttered urgently. 'Don't stop and stand about. Go inside and play with Paulina – see that you look after her this time. And don't come out until I call for you. You understand?'

Servus stared and nodded, rather doubtfully.

Secunda turned to me. 'Perhaps, citizen, you would be kind enough to go with h—' She broke off as Muta came out from the barn, carrying the tray, with Modesta trailing after her and earnestly attempting to converse.

Servus took one look at them and bolted for the house, while Secunda murmured, 'I'm sorry, citizen, to have spoken so sharply to the child – and before a guest as well – but I could hardly let Servus go into the barn. That poor creature is too nervous to say a word to me! Imagine how Fiscus would have frightened him! We should have had this water spilt all over the new hay! And what stories Fiscus could have taken to Lavinius about us!' She paused to look at Muta, who had crossed to us by now and was making irritated signals with her hand, pointing at Modesta – who came up close to me as though for protection.

I looked down at the slave-girl and she gave a little bob. 'I'm sorry, citizen. I don't know why this slave-woman is so upset with me. I was only asking if there was any watered wine. Fiscus said there should be, since we were offered cups, but when I approached this slave she wouldn't answer me.'

I shook my head and said, as gently as I could, 'That is because she cannot speak at all. The poor thing is a mute. You must be kind to her.' I found that I was trying to model my reply on what I thought Secunda might have said. 'Anyway,' I went on, 'there isn't any wine, not even for visiting citizens like me. But there is water, and very good it is – the slave-boy has just brought some from the well.'

Modesta gave her timid sideways smile. 'Is that the little fellow that I saw scurrying inside?'

'Exactly. He is very new and does not understand his duties yet. But here is the water that he brought,' Secunda intervened, proffering the jug. 'Now, if you have everything that you require, there are matters in my household to which I must attend. Paulina – my husband's daughter – has been alone too long, though I think her father may be taking care of her. I will relieve him of that woman's chore. I know he wants to go and tend his beasts again. Join us when you are ready, citizen.' And attended by her ancient maidservant she went into the house.

Modesta watched them go, clutching the pitcher against her skinny chest. 'What a lovely lady. Shame about her slave.' She giggled. 'And what a funny little page they seem to have. You would think he'd never carried water in his life.'

'Quite possibly he hasn't,' I told her, with a smile. Talking to Secunda made me feel benevolent. 'They only got him from the market yesterday. Sold by his parents to buy food, I understand.'

'No wonder he hardly knows where to begin!' Suddenly she creased her brow at me. 'I wonder if they tried to sell him in Glevum market once before? I've got the oddest feeling that I've seen that boy somewhere – though for the life of me I couldn't tell you where. Perhaps it is simply that he looks like someone else. That must be what it is! You would not forget that haircut and those knobbly white knees!'

I found that I was standing very still. 'Who is it that the slave reminds you of?' I said, almost fearing what she might reply. 'It wasn't the mistress of this house, by any chance?' That at least, would make a kind of sense – and explain the mystery of Secunda's past. I added, 'I can see no such resemblance myself.'

To my relief the slave-girl only laughed. 'That lovely lady? Not a bit of it. Someone in our household, or in Glevum, I am sure,' she said. 'And not my master or the lady Cyra, certainly. Perhaps the chief steward or possibly the nurse, or maybe even . . .,' She broke off, laughing, 'I don't know why I'm bothering to tell you all of this. It's nonsense, anyway. How could a pauper from Corinium have anything to do with my master's slaves at home? Anyway, it was just a brief impression, I only got a glimpse.' She glanced towards the barn. 'But now, forgive me, citizen – I must take this water back. Fiscus will be angry and I'm more afraid of him than

I've ever been of any of the usual stewards at my master's house.'

'Tell him that it's my fault because I kept you here,' I said, although I did not have much conviction that it would help her cause. 'In the meantime, I should go myself and conclude my business in the house.' I looked up at the sky. How long would it take those slaves to eat some bread and cheese? I made a calculation. 'When the shadow of that oak tree meets that flagstone there, I shall be ready. Come and get me then. In the meantime, enjoy your little meal.'

She nodded and went hastening back into the barn, carrying the brimming pitcher on her head. There was no doubt that she was used to doing it.

I was feeling very thoughtful as I went back to the house. Muta was waiting and she let me in, and when I reached the central room I found Paulina there, scribbling a picture on a piece of slate, while Servus crouched down on a stool and watched her work.

He sprang up when he saw me and murmured, 'Citizen!' It was the first time that I'd heard him utter any word at all and I realized that my unspoken theory had been wrong again. This child had no impediment of speech, beyond the terror that was clearly in his eyes and which was evident by the tremor in the syllables. Like all such young pageboys he had a fluting tone, but there was no stutter and he spoke quite well.

He saw me looking and he backed away from me until he stood with his back against the wall. I wondered where he had learned that defensive strategy. I said, quite kindly, 'Will you go and find your mistress and tell her I am here?' He looked panicked and bewildered and he did not move. I tried again. 'Find Secunda for me. Tell her I am here. Or Paulinus if that is easier.' It had not occurred to me, until I said the words aloud, that I should – of course – have asked first for the master of the house.

This time he nodded and edged slowly to the door although he didn't for a moment take his eyes from me. Meanwhile Paulina scratched away with her chunk of chalk-stone, happily oblivious to the pair of us. Once or twice she even put it in her mouth.

I did not feel that the pageboy kept a proper watch on her,

certainly he hadn't since I was in the room. I decided I would have to mention it to his mistress when she came. It was just as Modesta said about the water-jug – it was evident that Servus had a lot to learn. At the moment he had no idea at all of what was expected of a household slave.

I looked at him again. What else was it that Modesta said? That he had reminded her of someone she had seen before. And then, like a mosaic, all the little fragments settled into place. It was hardly credible. But it must be the solution. How could I find out? As he turned away to lift the latch and push open the door he had his back to me.

'Lavinia!' I called softly, and Servus whirled around.

'What is it, citizen?' And then I knew for sure.

TWENTY-FOUR

She realized immediately that she'd betrayed herself. Without another word she flung open the door and launched herself – not into the interior of the house, as she had meant, but into the arms of Secunda who was in the act of entering the room.

'What is it little one?' she murmured soothingly.

The child looked up at her beseechingly. 'He knows! He's found us out. He called me by my name.'

I saw the look of sorrow cross the lovely brow. 'Very well. You take Paulina and go in there to play. I will deal with this. I promise faithfully no harm will come to you.'

The look the child gave her was an adoring one. Paulina was not delighted to be made to stop her scribbling on the slate, and at first she sat protesting in her silent way – kicking her feet and refusing to be dragged – but Secunda called the maid and the child was led away, still looking furious but no longer struggling. I found myself again alone with the lady of the house.

'I might have guessed that you would work it out,' she said, giving me the rueful smile that tore my heart. 'That is Lavinia, of course. What gave us away?'

'I asked myself why you should be so keen to keep your slave from meeting servants from the Glevum house,' I said. 'Especially when Modesta said that there was something slightly familiar about the page. It occurred to me that there is little difference between a boy and girl, except the clothes and haircut, when they are as young as that. What one mostly sees is just the hairstyle and the differing tunic length. But of course it's possible to shorten both these things. Once I'd had the wit to question it . . .' I left the words unfinished, quite ashamed of how long it had taken me to question anything.

Secunda nodded, still remarkably unruffled. 'The hair was a problem, it was a striking red and of course she had always worn it long. We cut it off as short as possible, and tried to colour it.'

'With lampblack?' I said, understanding as I spoke. 'I noticed that the scalp seemed very stained.' I should have seen the significance of that – I had been told the colour of Lavinia's hair.

'Lampblack and writing ink. We rubbed some on the hands and knees as well – although she hated that – and dressed her in a tattered tunic that we purchased yesterday. It was enough to delude the casual eye and the land-slaves here and very shortly we were going to go to Gaul where it was unlikely that anyone would come and hunt for us. But it seems we did not manage to disguise the truth from you.' Her cool grey eyes met mine and I saw great sadness in them. 'I do not expect you to condone what we have done, but at least you know no harm has come to her.'

'Except that her father will disown her now. She has dishonoured him and she can't go home again.'

There was little furniture in here beyond the stools but Secunda signalled that I should sit on one, while she sank down on the other with her accustomed grace. 'You call that misfortune, citizen? I fear Lavinia might think otherwise. Her paterfamilias has never been particularly kind. How do you think he would treat her after this?'

I thought of the way the so-called slave had backed against the wall, and how the nurse had claimed they had a private code for moments when Lavinius threatened punishment. How many whippings had she endured in Lavinia's stead, I asked myself – and did not care to answer. Whipping-slaves were commonplace in many Roman homes, though more usually they were reserved for sons. Lavinius, however, had no son to whip. I said, 'But what will become of her, now she has no home?'

'She had a home here, citizen, until you came along. We would have cared for her. So it is up to you. Will you betray us to Lavinius, or not?'

'But what about her mother? She will be ill with grief!'

'If you are referring to Cyra, citizen – who was it, do you think, who made this possible? Who pressed and pleaded that Lavinia should spend the night in Corinium with her cousin – and at a lodging-house – and not at the chief priest's residence as one might expect?'

It had occurred to me before that this arrangement was a bit unusual, but since all the parties had seemed entirely content, I thought no more of it. 'So with Cyra's collusion, Audelia arranged that you two should also spend the night at the same place and take the girl away?'

She looked embarrassed but said steadily, 'That is effectively the case.'

'But why? Surely the Vestal Virgin's life would have been excellent? It would have removed her from Lavinius's power: she would have been cared for all her life and indeed, retired with a pension and a dowry to her name. Why would Cyra interfere with that? Wouldn't any mother want that for her child?'

Secunda dropped her eyes. 'Not every mother's child would qualify.'

I stared at her. What did she mean by that? But Secunda merely fiddled with her stola-folds and said nothing further. I searched my brain. Cyra had explained the criteria to me: two living parents, both of patrician birth and physical and mental perfection of all kinds – all of which Lavinia had been judged to have, as well as a useful dowry which had avoided the entrance lottery. So what was I missing? Then I recalled Secunda's words when I mentioned Lavinia's mother. 'If you are referring to Cyra . . .' she had said. Was it possible?

'Cyra was not Lavinia's mother after all? Or was Lavinius not her father?'

She raised her eyes and smiled. 'Neither of those things. Poor Cyra's infant turned out to be a son – and boy-children in our family never seem to live. My father and my grandfather were both of them convinced that it was some sort of curse on us, and that it could only be removed by offering the girls to be Vestal Virgins, if they qualified.'

'As you did not,' I countered, but she did not rise to that.

'As Cyra didn't, citizen. And when she gave birth to yet another son, and it began to show the signs that all the others had – swelling up and screaming when he got a bruise, or if they got the slightest cut they almost bled to death – she knew at once that it would not survive. And what's more, that since she'd failed again, she was likely to be instantly divorced and thrown onto the mercy of her distant relatives. Not a pleasant prospect when you're no longer young – and she had very little money of her own, scarcely a dowry that was worthy of the name. So she found a stratagem. Lavinius of course had not been near her since the birth, so when the child was brought to him for him to pick it up – and thereby officially accept it as his own . . .'

'She substituted someone else's child?' I finished. And then: 'It was the nurse's? Of course – the hair was red!'

'Naturally, citizen? Who else could it have been? The wet nurse who was acting as attendant at the birth had very recently had a child herself – I think it was arranged between them in advance. If Cyra's child had been a living girl, then well and good, it would be presented to Lavinius and all would be exactly as it appeared to be . . .'

'If, however, it proved to be a son and sickly – as it was very like to be – then the promised substitution would be made? Especially since you tell me that he actually died. But why would the nursemaid agree to such a thing?'

'Cyra had promised her a comfortable home and her infant the best upbringing that money could provide – and since the woman was a widow with no money of her own, naturally it seemed a wonderful exchange. What was there for her precious child otherwise? This way she would even have the chance to tend the child and watch it all its life . . .'

'Until Lavinius decided that his daughter should join the Vestal house?' I said.

'Exactly, citizen. You can imagine what a turmoil that decision caused. You know how strict the rules for choosing Vestals are – and what the consequence would be if anyone infringed them knowingly. The omens would be simply terrible. And whatever Lavinius might or might not know, one cannot keep this kind of secret from the gods.'

I looked at her but she was clearly not in jest. 'You believe in such a curse?'

'Remember, citizen, our family history – the boy-children who always die in agony. What else is it but a kind of punishment? My grandfather was right. To defy the goddess by offering a girl who did not begin to meet the foremost rule was almost begging for a further curse. The nurse was terrified and Cyra even more, because she feared that if Lavinia was sent off to the shrine the slave would tell her master and the truth would be revealed. After all the child had the colouring of a Silurian slave, rather than a patrician Roman family, though it seems that Lavinius never thought to question that. So between them, they got in touch with me – Cyra writes a good deal better than her husband knows and always managed to find a public courier in town who would deliver her messages to me – and we hatched this little—'

Whatever she was going to say, the words died on her lips as Muta came stumbling frantically from the inner room, making painful strangled noises in her throat. She grasped her mistress by the stola and tugged at her, in a way that no normal household slave would ever dare to do. It was evident that she wanted her to come, and urgently.

'What is it, Muta?' Secunda was already following, and – since there was clearly some emergency – I came along as well, through a little anteroom, which led out to the rear and where querns and bowls and sweeping-brooms were stored, into a little sleeping room beyond.

It was a small room by any standards and it seemed smaller still for the Roman bed in it: a simple wooden bed-frame with a palliasse, not unlike the one in which I had spent the night before. Beside it on the floor was another smaller mattress, clearly made of straw, where I imagined Muta slept herself. On it sat Paulina, happily engaged in drawing patterns on her piece of slate and not even glancing up as we approached. It all seemed very tranquil but Muta was clearly very agitated still.

'What is it, Muta?' Secunda said again.

The slave-woman pointed to the window-space. The shutter, if there was one, had not been put in place and the room looked out onto the grounds. I went across to see. To one side was the gate, and on the other the pasture-field and the wood beyond. Nothing was moving out there except a tranquil cow. I shook my head. I didn't understand.

Muta held one hand out at the level of her waist and made a motion as if running on the spot. We frowned at her, and then understood her at the same instant. I cried out, 'Lavinia! She should have been in here. What has happened to her?'

just as Secunda said, 'She must have recognized that slave-girl from the gig and taken fright.'

More pointing at the window.

'She ran away through there?'

Emphatic nodding.

Secunda looked at me. 'We shall have to find her, citizen – whether those slaves from Glevum learn of it or not. If she gets in the forest, the gods know how she'll fare. She's not used to walking anywhere alone and there are bears and wolves about. And Paulinus has just gone out to feed the beasts, he isn't here to help. Oh, Vesta and all the household gods preserve the girl! We cannot even be sure which way she might have gone. Did you see her, Muta?'

Muta shook her head. She pointed from herself to the inter-vening room and made a motion as of sweeping up. I had noticed that there was a bundle of tied brooms in there.

Secunda looked frantic. It was the first time I had seen her other than serene. 'Then it must have been the window. I don't know where to start. If only Paulina could tell us what she knows.'

Muta squatted down beside the deaf girl, leaning very close. She pointed to her eyes and then the window-space and made that running motion that she'd made before. Paulina beamed. She took the slate and smudged it with her sleeve, half erasing what she'd drawn on it. She took the chalk and started drawing something else.

'It's no good,' Secunda said. 'She doesn't understand . . .'

But Muta had held up a warning hand. She pointed to the slate. It was a childish drawing but unmistakeable. It was a little building with a sort of doorway at the front. Secunda was about to turn away again and start the search, but Muta seized the chalk. She drew a sketchy picture of a cow.

Paulina rubbed it out and drew what looked like a long fat table on two spindly legs. She stared at it a moment, as if dissatisfied, then drew a spiral at one end of it.

I frowned at it a moment and then had an idea. Very gently, I took the chalk-stone from the child and gave the thing a head. I looked at Paulina, who smiled delightedly. I tried a pair of ears, and then a flattened nose – and the 'table' had transformed itself into a pig.

Paulina was grinning as though her face would burst. She took my arm and dragged me to the window-space where I could see the byre. It was not much like the picture she had drawn, but she pointed to the slate and then to it and then made the running motion which she'd seen Muta make. There was no doubt at all what she was telling us.

'Lavinia's hiding in the pig-byre,' I announced, but the others had already worked it out.

'Muta, go and find her. Better still, go and find the master and get him to come here. He can go and tell her that we know where she is, but that she can stay there until the gig has gone. You'd better warn him that the land-slaves mustn't move the pig back to the byre. That sow's a heavy beast. If it turns on Lavinia, she will certainly get hurt.'

Muta nodded and disappeared at once in search of her master. Secunda turned to me. 'So I ask you once again, are you going to betray her, citizen?'

I could not answer her. 'Do I not have duties, lady?' I said, thoughtfully. 'I am being paid.'

'Duties to whom, exactly, citizen? You know now that the girl that we have taken in is not the child of Cyra and Lavinius, but of a Silurian widow who entrusted her to us.' She held out those lovely pale white hands to me. 'Libertus, you are a man of some intelligence. You will see that there is little to be gained by returning a girl – whatever her legal status may have been – to a cruel man who has in any case announced that he has rejected her. If she were dragged back there she would find herself at best obliged to sell herself to slavery – or at worst, reduced to being a beggar or a fugitive. I cannot believe that you'd connive at that – or even that you would tell Lavinius the truth about her parentage. Think what would happen to Cyra, in that case. It would serve no purpose, human or divine. Better that he simply believes the girl has run away.'

I have heard lawyers argue with less force. I looked at her with even greater admiration than before. 'You have a point, of course,' I said, slowly. 'Lavinius has no natural claim upon the girl and he has publicly renounced his legal one. And as you say, her mothers – if I may use the phrase – were both content that she should stay with you.'

She could see that I was weakening and she sealed it with a smile.

I found myself saying, by way of self-excuse, 'Besides, I was not actually required to find Lavinia at all – it was simply that I chose to do so while I had the chance.'

'Then you will not betray us?'

'That might depend,' I said untruthfully, 'on what you tell me next.'

TWENTY-FIVE

Secunda had recovered something of her tranquillity. She sat down on the bedframe and – watching Paulina who was busy with her drawing, as if nothing had occurred – said soberly, 'We owe you a proper explanation, I suppose. What do you want to know?'

I looked round for a seat where I could sit, myself, but there was nothing in the room except a little clothes-chest with an oil-lamp on top and the straw mattress where Paulina was. I leaned against the wall. 'Tell me how Lavinia escaped the lodging-house. Did she really climb through the window-space, as she just did here? When I first realized that she hadn't run away, I thought the cloth-rope through the window was a ruse, intended to mislead.'

Secunda gave the smile that would excuse her anything. 'You are quite right, citizen. The nursemaid made it and put it there (having made sure that there was no one watching in the court, of course) but not until her daughter had safely gone. We had taken Lavinia with us – she was hidden in the travelling box, asleep.'

I frowned. 'But I thought you had your so-called slave-boy with you when you went? Several people mentioned seeing him – though nobody recognized him as the Lavinia they knew.'

'That was not Lavinia, of course. That was a pauper's child that we had hired for just an hour or two. His parents were delighted when we wanted him. We kept him with us till we were out of town, then let him go again and sent him home. He could not believe his luck. But by that time Lavinia was beginning to wake up.'

'But how . . . ?' I was about to say, and then I understood. 'She had been given the sleeping-potion in the phial. Of course!' I have never had a child, but I can imagine that it would be hard to keep Lavinia quiet and still if she had been awake. 'Cyra provided the potion for you, I suppose? I noticed her seal-mark on the wax seal of the flask. Though at that time I was more interested in the hemlock that the jug had obviously contained.'

'Hemlock? In the flask?' She sounded quite surprised. 'Then the nursemaid must have put it there. Certainly there was no hemlock in it earlier.'

'But there was hemlock somewhere. That's what killed Lavinia's mother and she drank it from the flask.' I stopped lounging on the wall and pushed myself upright. Paulina glanced up at me and gave me a huge smile, then moved a little and patted the space that she had made.

I squatted down beside her, thinking how bizarre it was to be talking of such things, while this child was totally oblivious of all the tragedy. She was engrossed in drawing something now, something with sticks which might have been a tree. I looked up at Secunda, not unhappy to be sitting at her feet.

'There was some hemlock left from what my husband gave the Druid girl,' she was saying, thoughtfully. 'It was still with her effects. The nursemaid asked to keep it, "just in case of an emergency", she said, though at the time we hoped that everything was going to go to plan. She gave the sleeping potion to Lavinia and it worked beautifully.'

I was still trying to get a picture of events. 'It must have been a strong one.'

'Very strong indeed. Cyra warned us not to use the whole of it. I think the mother only used a half, but even that much had a fast effect, because when Paulinus and I got back from the slave-market, the child was sound asleep. Her mother had cut her hair off, while she slept, and put her in the half-empty box that we had left behind.'

'I found a hair or two,' I said. 'I didn't find a razor or a knife.'

'We put it in the box beside Lavinia, together with the hair. We had thought of selling it to a wig-maker – hair of that length and colour would fetch a handsome price – but we decided it might cause remark. So we put that in there too. We covered her loosely with a rug that we had brought, and pulled the lid down – Paulinus had deliberately chosen one that didn't fit, so that it stayed a little bit ajar – and he personally carried down the box and put it on the cart. And

we drove off with it. It went off more smoothly than we
dared to hope.'

I was aware of something tugging at my sleeve. I looked
down. It was Paulina wanting to show me what she'd scratched
onto the slate. A big head and fingers had sprouted on the tree
– I realized it was meant to be a person. Was it me? I pointed
to myself and she nodded gleefully, then took it from me and
went back to work, blissfully unaware of the amazing story
that was unfolding here.

I looked at Secunda. 'So all that time the nurse was apparently on guard outside the room, Lavinia wasn't there at all?'

'Of course not citizen, that was the whole idea. The nurse
was to wait until she heard the noonday trumpet sound, then
go down for the tray – as if Lavinia had just requested it.
There were deliberately quite a lot of items to be brought
upstairs, so many that she could not carry up the tray alone.
That way someone from the lodging-house would be a witness
when she knocked the door, and – when there was no answer
– help her to burst in and so raise the alarm. Though Lavinia
had been gone for hours by then, of course.'

I was marvelling at the beautiful simplicity of this. 'And
she even took the poison afterwards to put us off the scent?'

Secunda shook her head. 'That was not originally part of
the plan at all. The idea was for the nurse to go out into the
town – allegedly searching for the missing girl – and, following
our directions, find her way out here. But she did not come.
By this morning we were anxious, as you may suppose. When
you arrived we thought it might be to bring us news of her.
Which in a way you did.' She sighed. 'Something must have
gone dreadfully amiss.'

'It did,' I told her. 'The landlady at the lodging house was
naturally afraid that she and her household would be held
responsible for Lavinia's escape. She decided (quite correctly
as it now appears) that the nursemaid must have had a hand
in it, so she had her locked up in the kiln-house in the yard
– I think you know the place – and sent word to Lavinius to
come and take her home and beat the truth from her.'

'As no doubt he would have done,' Secunda murmured. 'I
wish we'd thought of the possibility of suspicion falling on
the nurse – I think we all believed that she loved the girl so

much that nobody could possibly have thought she was involved. But from what you say it's clear now why she chose to kill herself. She obviously feared that she would not be strong enough to withstand questioning without betraying us. Lavinius can be ruthless. He'd have tortured the poor creature horribly if he thought that she knew anything at all.'

'Even though by that time he'd disowned the girl?'

'It is evident that you don't know Lavinius, citizen. Anyone who caused dishonour to his precious family name would be punished without mercy – you can take that from me. No wonder the poor woman chose to drink the hemlock-juice and die an easy death. There may have been some of the sleeping-potion in the phial as well, which would have eased it further. I only hope there was. I'm glad that she had the foresight to take it to the kiln.'

I shook my head, remembering the look of hope that crossed the nurse's face when she thought that I had come from Cyra, not from Publius. I knew now that she was hoping that this might be a subterfuge and that I had come to help her to escape. Poor creature, she was disappointed there. 'That was my doing, inadvertently. She persuaded us that there was something in the room that might help her to discover where Lavinia was. Only of course there was no clue at all. It was the poison that she wanted. She almost told me so.' (I remembered suddenly the last thing that the nurse had said to me, 'If I can tell you nothing in the morning, citizen, do as you like with me.' Those words had taken on another meaning now.) 'After she'd drunk the hemlock she threw the flask away – I think in one last attempt to create a mystery and persuade us that Druids were involved in that event as well.'

I had hardly finished speaking when the bedroom door burst open and Paulinus rushed in – now dressed in his faded tunic and his working-boots again. His face was ashen and his air of gentle bafflement had given way to something more like terror and despair.

'Wife!' he murmured, swaying on the spot. 'So everything is lost! I've spoken to Lavinia and she says the secret's out and Lavinius's servants are waiting in the barn. What are we to do?'

She was on her feet in an instant and rushing to his side. If she had not supported him by giving him her arm, I believe that he would have crumpled to the floor. I too had scrambled to my feet by now and I went over to assist her. Between us we held him upright by the door while Paulina gazed up at us in astonishment, chewing at her chalk.

How long we might have stood there I cannot say, but then Muta came hobbling into the ante-room from the yard outside – obviously her master had rushed ahead of her, and with her limping gait she had not kept up with him. She came to take my place supporting Paulinus but Secunda signalled her to stay there with the child. Muta looked doubtful, but nodded dutifully.

We left the maid admiring the portrait of the tree, while – between us – we led Paulinus next door to a stool and helped him to lower his body onto it.

He sat there for a moment, his head between his hands. After a little he looked up at me and I saw to my embarrassment that his lids were fringed with tears. It is a rare thing to see a Roman adult cry, even women tend to save their tears for funerals and for a male to weep in public is regarded as disgrace.

It was evident that Paulinus did not care a sugared fig for any such convention. He said to me in a voice which had lost all trace of joy, 'So it is all over. You have found us out. Why did you come here? Life could have been so good! Does it give you satisfaction to have ruined it? And why? Just to satisfy your curiosity?'

I found myself pacing up and down the room, not knowing how on earth to answer this. I stopped before the household altar in the wall, seeing the simple sacrifices that had been offered there to the household spirits and the goddess of the hearth. I felt a sudden fury with these Roman deities. Why had they not ensured that I had left the house before Modesta and the other slaves arrived?

I turned to Paulinus. 'I have decided that I need not tell anyone about Lavinia,' I said.

To my surprise this did not seem to comfort him.

It was Secunda who broke the awkward silence first. 'Husband, the citizen deserves more courtesy. I have told him the whole truth about Lavinia's parentage – he had very largely worked it out in any case. Don't you think that we should thank him for not betraying her?' Her voice was entirely serene, but I thought I detected a warning tone in it.

Paulinus seemed to sense it too. He raised his head again. 'Of course, but what about the rest of it? I couldn't bear to be without you, after all we've been through and everything we've planned.' He looked from her to me and his face took on that faintly puzzled air. 'Or hasn't he discovered the whole truth of it?'

She put an arm around his shoulder, gently, rather as a mother might console a child. 'Not until this moment, husband, I don't think. And none of it from me.'

I was frankly baffled for a moment, though I should not have been. Of course there was still a mystery to solve. Publius had employed me to try to find his bride, but then we had found her body in the box and I'd come on to Corinium to investigate. I still had no idea how that had come about. But I had been so occupied with the discovery of the truth about Lavinia that I had not turned my mind to the other matter recently.

Now though, as a result of what Paulinus said, I was forced to think again. It was becoming obvious that these two were involved in that grisly business with the corpse. My heart rebelled against the notion, but my brain refused to let the matter rest.

I turned to Paulinus, who was on his feet by now and staring at his wife with a look of dawning horror on his face. 'You were involved in putting that body in the box?'

He looked at Secunda as if for some support, but she shook her head at him. 'Tell him, Paulinus. There's no help for it. If he asked the question, we shall have to tell the truth. But since he's shown compassion for Lavinia, perhaps we can persuade him to do the same for us.'

I was about to insist upon his answering but he was too quick for me. He spoke before I had time to formulate my thoughts. 'Will you promise, citizen? Can we rely on that? You will not betray us either?' He reached out and slowly interlaced his fingers with his wife's – or rather . . . ?

I must have been baffled by her loveliness, or the obvious solution would have dawned on me before.

'Great Mars!' I said, hardly able to believe the words myself. 'You are not his wife at all!'

TWENTY-SIX

The ferocity of her reaction startled me. 'What makes you say that, citizen? Of course I am his wife.' She squeezed his hand and looked affectionately at him. 'True we did not have an expensive wedding feast, or a *conferratus* ceremony with witnesses and cakes, but when we reached here yesterday we summoned all the slaves and in front of everyone we lit the household shrine and made the proper vows before the gods.'

'Where you are Gaius I am Gaia,' Paulinus put in. 'And I swore the same.'

'But she isn't Gaia. She is Audelia.' Why had I not seen the possibility before?

'All the same I am as much his wife as anyone could be. I even had a bridal costume, more or less – although I lacked the proper shoes and veil – and my hair was plaited in the proper way. In fact –' she shook her faded golden ringlets with a laugh – 'it has been plaited in that way so long that even when – at last – I let it out, the tight curls still remain. My hair was absolutely straight when I first went to the shrine!' She laughed again, then said with dignity, 'Many people, citizen, are much less wed than that. And then, last evening, my husband came to me. I have become, in every sense, his wife. Even Lavinius's famous law courts would agree to that.'

'So what happened to the real Secunda?' I enquired, struck by a dreadful thought. 'Was it her body that we discovered in the box?'

'Of course not, citizen,' she said. 'I am the only Secunda that there ever was. And it really is my name. Audelia Secunda my father called me, at my naming day, because an earlier daughter called Audelia did not live for long. Another affliction for my family, though my sister died of fever, as many children do, not of that dreadful curse that carried off the boys.'

'The father was called Audelius and both girls were named

for him,' her husband said. 'I knew the family slightly when I was a boy – they were relatives, of course. I grew fond of Secunda, as we called her, even then.'

The woman nodded. 'To my mother I was always Secunda till the day I went away, though of course they called me Audelia at the shrine. But now I have retired. Besides –' she looked up at Paulinus lovingly – 'I am a second wife. It seemed appropriate to use the name again.'

'So who was the beheaded person in the box?' I broke off as the realization dawned. 'Oh, of course! It wasn't murder as we all supposed. It was a suicide. That was the wet nurse who was rescued from the beasts?'

'The body was released to Paulinus. It seemed the simple way. If my uncle found a body they would not look for me.'

'So you cut the head and hands off?' I saw Paulinus flinch.

'It was the vilest thing that I have ever done. But it was not done with malice. Druids attach extreme importance to the head – they think that it is where the spirit dwells. I gave it to her family for proper burial, in the sacred grove or whatever place they chose.'

'Besides,' I said, heartlessly, 'without a face, no one could be sure that the body was not Audelia?'

He nodded, with a kind of dignity. 'That's also true, of course. Don't suppose I didn't think of that. Otherwise I do not think I could have done the task.' He swallowed hard, his voice-box bobbing visibly up and down. 'But the woman's family agreed to take the head and asked no questions about the rest of her. They were actually grateful, that was the dreadful thing.'

'And what about the hands? I wondered at the time if they were calloused and would give the game away. I saw that the legs were strong and muscular.'

'Much worse than work-worn, citizen.' This time it was Secunda who replied. 'The woman had a birthmark right across her hand and two of her fingers had been joined since birth. Defects like that would have prevented anyone from being accepted as a Vestal at the shrine. When Paulinus realized, he removed them too. It was not intended as an act of violence, citizen. The poor woman was already dead, and it was simply to allow me to escape.'

'So you, Paulinus, cut off the missing portions before you left this house and put her in the box that you were travelling with – though, of course, the corpse was wearing her own garments at the time?' I had understood this now. A coarse plaid cloak and tunic with a drawstring purse. 'And when you reached Corinium you dressed her as a bride – or a Vestal Virgin, which is largely the same thing?'

Secunda – I could not think of her by any other name – laughed softly. 'Exactly citizen, except I kept my cloak. Fortunately the girl was very much my size. Except for my white slippers which did not really fit. Then we put her in the box. Along with the wedding veil that I did not intend to wear.'

'And the wedding slippers? You left them behind on purpose, I assume? To be rid of Ascus for an hour or two?'

A nod. 'If I'd had an escort I could never have escaped.'

'And then, I think, you blamed your little maid for it?'

She looked apologetic. 'I raised my voice, it's true. I told her that they had been left behind and that she had not packed them – which was strictly accurate. Poor Puella! She was so upset, but I dared not entrust her with our secret, naturally.' She gave her shyest smile. 'I did the best I could: warned her to leave the coach at Glevum, the instant it arrived – on pain of the severest penalty – and go back to her former owner near the shrine. I gave her a letter and her slave-price to ensure that she was freed, and could not be arrested on the way.'

'You did not think she might be blamed for what was in the box?'

Secunda shook her head. 'How could that be, citizen? She was sitting in the front with the raedarius – I made sure of that, so she had witnesses to her presence all the way. By the time the door was opened and it was found that I had gone, I knew that she was likely to have disappeared. If not, there was the letter to fall back upon. I hoped she would not witness the discovery of the corpse.'

'Ah yes, the unfortunate Druid wet nurse!' I exclaimed.

'We thought that Lavinius would build a pyre for her and give her Roman rites, so at least she would obtain a proper funeral. We were anxious to show as much respect to her as possible,' Audelia-Secunda told me earnestly. 'I even pinned a spray of mistletoe and oak onto the bridal veil I left with her, so that tokens of her own religion were attached to her. We should have guessed what someone might construe from that.' The gentle lips were almost twitching in a smile as she added softly, 'Though it was hard to answer, citizen, when you asked outright whether the Druids might have been involved. As a Vestal I am bound to always tell the truth – anything else would be a violation of my vows.'

'Yet you signed a contract, didn't you? Agreeing to marriage with a certain Publius? Surely breaking that was a violation, too?' It sounded quite severe, but I had put it mildly. It was much worse than that. A Vestal Virgin may not break her legal bond on pain of the most dreadful punishment, since if she does so she is seen to be endangering the state.

For the first time I saw a flash of anger in her eyes. 'Indeed I signed a contract. It is not a pleasant story. Sit down, citizen, and I will explain. We have no wine to offer, as we said before, but I think there is some apple-beer somewhere that Muta made last year from fermented windfalls. We had some yesterday when we got to the house.'

'I will go and fetch it,' Paulinus volunteered. 'This story is better coming from my wife. I blurt things out too much – look at the trouble I've already caused!' He got to his feet and went out in the direction of the ante-room.

But it was not his blurtings which detained me now. 'Muta made the apple-beer?' I said. 'But I understood you only bought her yesterday?'

She came across and stood very close to me. 'I thought better of your powers of deduction, citizen. Does Muta look like a brand-new servant in this house?'

Of course she didn't, now I came to think of it. For one thing she had clearly won Paulina's confidence, and learned to communicate in some way with the girl. I shook my head.

Secunda reached up to the shelf and fetched down three drinking bowls. 'Besides,' she went on, 'who do you suppose accompanied Paulinus to the lodging-house before we others got there?'

'That was Muta? But she doesn't speak! And she walks so badly!'

'That was an advantage, citizen. Paulinus had bought her a stola and a russet travelling-cloak, and of course she travelled in a hood and veil – as any matron with old-fashioned sensibilities might do. Anyone who saw her would remember just the cloak – it was an unusually fine colour dye of course – and the fact that the wearer was walking with a limp.'

'But Trullius and Priscilla must have seen her face,' I protested, and broke off. 'But of course, I remember. She retired to rest and did not come again until you had arrived. To greet you with affection, as I understand.'

'With affection,' she allowed, 'but not with words, at all. Paulinus did the talking, and Lavinia later on. No one expects a woman who is frail and tired to say very much.' She picked up the water-pitcher as she spoke.

'And then when you were dining she went back upstairs?'

She was pouring water into the little bowls and swilling them around to clean the dust from them. 'Of course the poor thing could not eat with us. She would not have known the proper rituals. So Paulinus took her to the room, and later on she managed to share something with the nurse when they sent up a plate of bread and meat.' She set the drinking-vessels upside down to dry. 'And then next day she came to see me off, and that is when it happened.'

I remembered that Priscilla had remarked that Secunda had seemed to move more easily in the morning after she had slept and that up to then she had hardly said a word. 'But how did you effect the substitution then? There were a lot of people in the court. You must have been observed.'

She shook her head. 'I got into the raeda as myself, of course, and Paulinus and the nurse came crowding round as well. Muta was in her travelling cape again, but this time she did not have the stola underneath. I was wearing that under my mantle, tucked up in my belt. I got into the seat in front of everyone, ostensibly settling while they brought down the box. I made quite a fuss – sending for extra cushions for my back, and ordering the maidservant to sit up at the front and while everyone was occupied I put the shutters up. Of course the box was already largely shielding me from sight. Muta leaned right in the other side, as if to give me an embrace, and while Paulinus crowded round the back, slipped her cloak and veil off and handed them to me.'

'Together with her wig?' I said. 'Priscilla said she had one.'

She nodded. 'It assisted the disguise. And it was necessary for me afterwards, of course. My Vestal hairdo might have drawn remark, even underneath a cloak and veil. That left Muta in her tunic, looking like a slave, and that was the most dangerous moment of the whole affair. She does not move quickly and there were people in the court though she tried to choose a moment when they were occupied. The nursemaid tried to draw attention away from her as well, by waving at the window of Lavinia's room – and it worked to an extent. The inn-slaves and the driver all looked up that way, but in fact Muta did not manage to get out unobserved. Priscilla glimpsed her from another room upstairs. Fortunately she took her for a goggling bystander.'

I nodded. 'She even told me so. Shouted at her to go away and get outside the gate. That was fortunate!'

That earned a little smile. 'Muta went, as fast as her poor legs would carry her, hurried into the forum and waited there for us. Meanwhile I slipped her cloak and veil on over mine and – now pretending that there was still someone in the coach – stepped out backwards and loudly said goodbye.'

'Taking your jewel-case with you?' I enquired.

'I had already packed it in a leather bag which Muta gave me as I got into the coach. I stuffed the wig in too, and simply brought it out. It looked like an exchange of gifts if anyone observed. Then I joined Paulinus – remembering to limp – and together with the nurse we waved the raeda off. I've never been more thankful to see anything depart. We hurried to an alleyway where I put on the wig and buried my own white cloak inside Paulinus's sack, then on to the slave-market where we arranged to hire the boy and met up with Muta. That was still a risk, since she had been spotted earlier, but we bought her a new tunic from the old-clothes stall and Priscilla never really looked at her again.'

'And then Paulinus went and fetched the cart?' I said.

She nodded. 'He drove it to the lodging-house and paid the bill, then I waited in the cart with Muta while he went back upstairs for the famous travelling box. The nursemaid had packed it and he carried it downstairs. He did it on his own – it was heavy but he didn't want the servants looking in, though I'd bought a rug to loosely cover up the child. I think you know the rest . . . But here he is! And not alone, I see.'

Paulinus indeed was entering the room, carrying a huge pail of something in both hands, while Modesta followed him uncertainly. Her thin face brightened at the sight of me.

'Citizen, the shadow is long past the paving stone. Fiscus sent to ask if you were coming soon. We are already waiting, but we can't get past the dog.'

We three citizens exchanged a glance at this, and I said quickly, 'I will not be long. Paulinus has a message that he hopes to send, expressing his condolences to the Glevum house. When it is written I will join you in the barn.'

'I'll tell him, citizen.' She bobbed her little curtsy and disappeared again.

Paulinus put down his heavy pail and stared at me. 'You really do not mean to tell Lavinius all this?'

'I will delay as long as possible,' I said, 'to give you a chance to get away to Gaul. But I really think that's all that I can do for you. After all, Audelia is legally at fault. She broke a contractual vow. That is a serious criminal offence for anyone at all. For a Vestal Virgin, it's unforgivable.'

Audelia herself was scooping apple-beer into the bowls. She set one in front of me, another one she gave to Paulinus, while the third one she took over to the shrine, and made a small oblation there with practised ease. If I had not known she was a Vestal up to then, that single skilful action would have alerted me.

She turned and signalled me to drink. 'I broke no vow. Or not deliberately. In fact I kept the only one I made. I promised Paulinus months and months ago, when he and Paulina came to see me at the shrine, that when I retired I would marry him and provide my dowry to help him with the child. Of course I had known the family for many years – I remember him from when I was a child myself, and he and his wife made many sacrifices with me after that, asking for Vesta's blessing on the home.'

Paulinus nodded. 'She lent me money once. I had applied to Lavinius for help but had been turned away.'

Audelia sighed. 'After that my uncle came to see me at the shrine. He was my agent, as I think you know and managed

my affairs in Glevum, so I trusted him. I taxed him with his
lack of charity, saying that the goddess requires us to be kind
to relatives, and telling him what I proposed to do. He deceived
me, citizen. He came again and brought a document, which
seemed to be agreeing to the match, and persuaded me to sign.
It would save me from a hundred importunate suitors, so he
said, and he would undertake to fund the wedding feast himself
the very day that I returned to Glevum from the shrine. I did
it willingly. The trap was in the name.'

I frowned. 'I do not follow you.'

'I undertook to marry one P. Atronius Marinus, my widowed
kinsman – you know how these things are phrased in legal
documents. I believed it was a promise to marry Paulinus – but
it was a trick. My uncle had arranged a deal with Publius – a
handsome sum if he could secure my hand – and he had no
scruples about deceiving me. A single iron-nib stroke was all
that it required to change the name to P. Atronius Martinus,
which is what he did.'

I gulped. 'If that could be produced in evidence Lavinius
could be arraigned in court – fined or even exiled.' I remembered my moment of disquiet at the gate when Paulinus came
over and introduced himself. I must have registered the simi-
larity of the names – though these things are not surprising
within a Roman *gens*. 'Tampering with a legal document is a
serious offence.'

'And how could I prove it, citizen? I would not have known
till I arrived in Glevum and met Publius at the games. Of
course the written contract was signed and sealed by me, and
is – by that fact – a legal document. A refusal to honour it
could be challenged in the court. With my uncle's word against
me, it would be exile for me, as well as losing everything I
owned. Lavinius knew he could oblige me to submit. If I had
protested they'd have fed me poppy-juice or even forced me
into intercourse. After that my word would be no more than
any other female's and my uncle could have forced me to wed
anyone he chose. Cyra heard them plotting.'

I gulped my apple-beer. 'So that's how you discovered
that you'd promised the wrong man? Cyra wrote and told
you?'

Paulinus nodded. 'It was her gift to us, in return for asking us to help Lavinia. Her husband, of course, had no idea she was in touch with us and he was gloating – so she told me – about his cleverness.'

Audelia sipped her drink with all the elegance with which she did everything. 'Publius had also promised to return a proportion of my dowry if I died and that, I think, was what alarmed her most. Publius had been married several times before, in Rome, and all of his other wives had died quite young, apparently of illness, but it made her think. It certainly made up my mind for me.' She reached out and squeezed her husband's hand. 'One way or another I was bound to break my word. I chose to honour the contract that I meant to make. Do you really blame me for that, citizen?'

Of course I didn't, and I told her so. 'In fact,' I said, 'I think it would be wiser to take Publius's advice, and forget everything I've learned about this whole affair. As far as he's concerned his bride-to-be is dead and decently cremated. Lavinius may try to seek the so-called murderer, but since there's no such person, he won't have much success. Better to report Priscilla's view of things – that it was either sorcery or the revenge of Druids. Or both.'

Paulinus looked at me as though he dared not trust his ears. 'You mean that, citizen?'

'I do.' I'd drained the drinking bowl by now and I replaced it on the board. 'Though there are two questions which remain unanswered in my mind. What happened to the contents of Audelia's travelling box? You cannot simply have exchanged them with your own, because you had to put Lavinia into that.'

Paulinus laughed. 'That was very simple, citizen. We put most of it into the sack that I took to town with me. It was mostly jewels and gold in any case, of course, and later it had the Vestal cloak in it. When we picked the cart up, we put the sack on it. The lighter items of the dowry – such as lengths of silk – I rolled up in the rug and put on top of Lavinia in the box before we left.'

'Oh, and of course I had my jewel-box with me from the coach, having loudly announced that I was giving Secunda several rings,' his wife put in.

I nodded. Priscilla had already hinted this. 'And when you

arrived here you dyed the Vestal clothes – I presume that is what is hanging on the bushes now?'

'Exactly, citizen.' That was Audelia. 'We are not so wealthy that we can afford to waste good clothing of that quality. And the other question?'

'Was it not against your vows to tell the other lie – that you were going into the forum to buy a pair of slaves. Yet, Priscilla tells me that is what you said.'

Secunda's lovely lips curled in a gentle smile. 'Citizen, I took a vow that I would never lie. I did not swear that I would not choose words which might disguise the truth. We worked out very carefully what we were going to say – that we were going to the forum to collect two slaves. And that, of course, is exactly what we did.'

I put my bowl down. 'Then I think that's all. If you would care to write that letter.' I fished into my belt. 'I actually have a writing-tablet here that you can use. It's a letter from Publius under seal promising to pay my expenses in the town.'

'Then you must certainly keep that, citizen.' Secunda put her own bowl on the board as well. 'Otherwise you might find it hard to hold him to his word. We have bark-paper here, and lamp-black ink, as I think you are aware. Paulinus will write something and you can take it back – saying that he's saddened to have heard the news and that he's about to leave for Gaul and take Paulina to the healing shrine.' She smiled. 'And there's no lie in that, either, citizen. When we heard the news about the nursemaid we were very sad indeed.'

Her husband nodded and went out towards the porch. I heard him moving in another room.

'Lavinius will not guess that you have married Paulinus instead?' I ventured.

'He could hardly say so, citizen, even if he did. Especially when there is supposed to be a corpse. That would be admitting to his own perfidy. And he can scarcely follow us to Gaul. Besides, he'll hear from the lodging-house that Paulinus had a wife before I disappeared. I think we're safe enough.'

I fought down an unexpected wave of jealousy. 'Then I hope you will be happy. I am glad to be of use.'

She gave me the most brilliant smile that I have ever seen. 'And there is another thing that you can do for me. I promised the horseman that he should have a ring, in recompense for all his extra work on my behalf. If I go and get it, will you see it reaches him? I was there – you can tell him – and I heard the promise made and I wished it honoured. Will you do that for me?'

'I would be delighted,' I said, truthfully, and she went away to get it. That left me quite alone, and that was how Modesta found me a moment afterwards.

'I didn't know if I should come in the house or not. Nobody seemed to answer when I tapped the door? Are you coming, citizen? Fiscus is alarmed. He thinks that we are going to get to Glevum very late.'

I was about to answer when the householders appeared and thrust a bark-letter and a small parcel in my hands. 'That concludes our business, I believe. The citizen is ready to accompany you now.' Paulinus gave the smile that transformed his face. 'I myself will come and see you past the dog.' He led the way outside.

As he tethered the still snarling animal I glanced back at the house. I could not restrain a tiny sense of loss. As I watched I saw a figure scuttle from the byre and make towards the side-window of the house. I looked the other way. Everyone else was still looking at the hound, making certain they were out of range of teeth.

I permitted Fiscus to help me on the gig and sat down on the seat. He sat down beside me, leaving Modesta to kneel in what little space remained. The gig-driver, who was scowling at me as though I were the cause of all his many woes, raised his whip and we were ready to depart.

'Wait a moment, citizen. I have a gift for you.' Secunda herself had come running down the path. She came across and handed me a piece of slate. 'A present from Paulina. I'm sure that's what she wants.'

I looked back at the door. The deaf-mute girl was standing there, grasping Muta's skirts and as I watched she smiled and raised a hand as if to wave.

The driver brought the whip down and we were on our way.

EPILOGUE

Marcus was sympathetic, but amused. That was a mild relief. I had half-expected that he'd be furious.

'Well, Libertus, it's not like you to fail. But you brought it on yourself. No one asked you to go rushing off, asking questions in Corinium like that. I'm not surprised that Publius was quibbling at the bill. You're lucky that he paid it.'

I muttered something to the effect that I was glad he had.

'He's fallen out severely with Lavinius, of course – says that the fellow struck a deal with him and has failed to deliver what he promised. He's threatening to sue. I think he finally agreed to meet your costs mostly because Lavinius did not approve of you.'

It was after dinner in his villa, and Marcus was drinking wine, reclining on his dining couch and eating little pastry-cakes left over from the meal. He had dismissed the other diners and the slaves, so we were all alone, but he hadn't asked me to partake of anything. It was part of my penance. He had sent for me as soon as he knew that I was home, and I had not had time to eat, but he hadn't finished with his diatribe.

'Once it was obvious that Audelia was dead, I don't know why you didn't let the matter rest. Even you can hardly expect to solve a case of Druid sorcery – I suppose I should be glad that you escaped unscathed. So I forgive you. I can't answer for your wife.'

It was true that she was angry, but I knew she would relent. It was mostly worry because I'd not been home for days. And she sensed that I was hiding something that I wouldn't share. Not yet. I would confide in Gwellia as I always did, and tell her everything – even show her the poison-phial which had duly turned up in Priscilla's midden-pile – but not until that little family were far away in Gaul.

In the meantime, I would have to live with her rebukes. I had not even earned a quadrans for my time. My toga was crumpled and in need of laundering and couldn't I have let her know a little sooner where I was?

But I knew for certain that when I got home again there would be my favourite hot stew awaiting me, and that oatcakes for my breakfast were standing by to bake. Like Paulinus, I was a lucky man.

Marcus scooped up the remaining pastry-cakes, put them on a serving plate and handed them to me. 'Take these home to her. It might win you a smile.' He gave his languid grin. 'In the meantime, I've had enough tonight. I'll see you in the morning. I've got a job for you. A little mystery I'd like you to sort out. If you haven't entirely lost the gift, that is.' He chuckled and waved me out of the triclinium.

I walked home in the darkness, clutching the plate of cakes and trying not to spill them on the uneven lane. It was cold and drizzling and the wind was getting up, but I was thankful for my lot. I had a cheerful home and a wife who cared for me, a healthy grandson by my adopted son, good slaves to serve me and enough to eat. Who could ask for more? I thought of a gentle couple who had been forced to dreadful lengths by family treachery, of terrible diseases that carried off male heirs, and of a child, not many miles away, whose whole world was silence.

I fingered the piece of slate that I carried in my pouch and went in to see my wife. She was no ethereal goddess, she was short and stoutish and her face was lined, but I loved her dearly and I always had.

When she had finished chiding me and I'd enjoyed the stew, I would show her the chalk portrait and tell her it was me – not a tree with fingers. I knew that she would laugh.